FINDING STARDUST

A HOLLYWOOD BY THE SEA NOVEL

JULIE CAROBINI

DOLPHIN GATE BOOKS

To my maternal grandparents,
Albert & Cecilia Miele,
whose legacy of love lives on

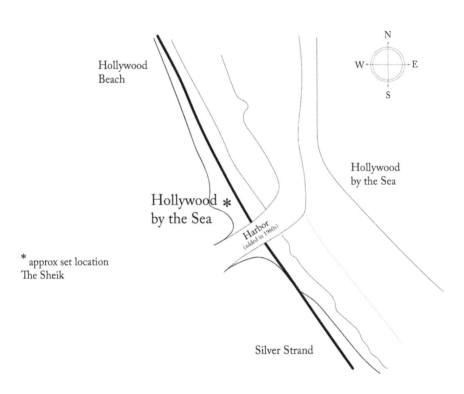

Hollywood
Beach

Hollywood
by the Sea

Hollywood *
by the Sea

Harbor
(added in 1960s)

* approx set location
The Sheik

Silver Strand

N
W — E
S

CHAPTER ONE

CLARA

MY HERO WALKED toward me carrying a yellow surfboard under one arm and my heart under his other. No, that wasn't right. My heart was in his *hand*. Better. Okay, let's try again. My hero walked toward me carrying a yellow surfboard under one arm and holding my heart in his hand. Hmm, did that work? I strained forward, holding my breath as my hero dropped his board onto the pavement—and his wetsuit, too.

Wait. Was he mooning the girl across the street?

Gross.

I groaned. I'd been standing out here on this second-floor, west-facing deck, looking out over the narrow street that abutted the beach and waiting for inspiration and thought I'd spotted him. Duped again. I rubbed my eyes with the back of my hand and cinched my robe tighter around my waist. I'd written dozens of romance novels. But now? I was flummoxed, baffled, bewildered, even. My creativity had taken a nosedive and, honestly, I was beginning to wonder if true heroes really existed anymore.

Another resigned sigh escaped me. Maybe if my favorite muse wasn't getting married today, just maybe I'd be able to come up with something amazing to propose to my publisher. I'd written the last book in record time, a secret baby novel with a beautiful, tenderhearted ending, if I do say so myself. It helped that I had written that trope three times before.

But with my sister officially getting married to Zac today, I'd found myself without a story to be told. Well, other than the one I'm not yet willing to face.

Anyway, some writers proclaimed that their significant other—husband, boyfriend, father, even—was the hero in every story they wrote. But I'd never had any of those in my life. So I'd settled on my sister, Greta. Turned out that she made a great muse, and for some reason, I never had trouble finding the right male counterpart.

Until now.

How long had I been standing here on this deck at the home next to Greta's, searching for the characters of my next story? No idea. But one thing I did know—I was late. Or I was going to be.

What kind of sister would arrive late to her own sister's wedding?

Reluctantly, I stepped away from the railing, padded across the deck in my bare feet, and pushed on the front door to the short-term rental where I'd been staying. My hand met resistance. That's odd. I pushed the door again, but it wouldn't budge. I jiggled the handle, softly at first, and then with a little more oomph. Nothing.

It has been said that our minds are capable of processing

two thousand thoughts per hour. As I stood there in my robe, the dawn of realization racing through my head, I'm pretty sure I processed an hour's worth of worry in a minute's time.

I tried the door again, just in case I had somehow done it wrong the last time. Locked. I swallowed. My face flushed and sweat made a sudden, heated appearance.

After a late night of making tulle bags filled with sea glass for the wedding guests—Greta's thoughtful idea of a personal touch—my sister had suggested I ride down to the chapel early with her. But unlike Greta, I had not inherited the morning-person gene. She and I both knew that I could be rather unpleasant before, say, ten a.m.

When I hadn't responded right away, she'd laughed and said, "I knew you'd say that, so I hired you a driver."

That's what happens when you live with a person your entire life. They know you well enough to anticipate your answer to every little thing.

"By the way, I'll need you to bring the cupcakes that Helen insisted on baking. It will be difficult enough for them to get ready and come to the wedding without having to remember to bring dessert."

Again, signature Greta. Always thinking of others.

I pushed away the thought that the life I had always known would never be again and cranked the door handle with the determination of the heroine in one of my books, a jilted bride. In one scene, Cassandra had gone from a docile flower to a force to be reckoned with. I groaned under the pressure, and when my efforts failed, I checked the kitchen window on the other side of the door. It, too, was locked tight. The only other window on this side of the apartment looked too high for me to reach, though trying might be my only option.

I glanced again at that kitchen window. So much to do before I left, starting with getting dressed. Oh, and those sparkly heels I'd found on a secondhand site! And I needed my purse, and that cute wrap Greta had ordered special to go with my dress.

A breeze lifted the corner of my robe, wrapping a chill around my ankles. My phone was inside the apartment, too. I heaved a sigh. I had written this type of scenario before in some of my novels, a scene in which my heroine gets herself into a tight spot, but I had never been in one quite like it myself.

If I had, maybe I would have written it differently. Or perhaps, not at all.

I let out an unladylike grunt and spied the lantern on the bistro table by the edge of the balcony. The light would have been helpful in the dark, maybe some kind of SOS signal. I stuck it on the floor. That left the table and the chair. The chair wasn't tall enough, but the table was slightly higher. After dragging it over, I scrambled on top of it, choosing to ignore its distinct wobble, as if it were telling me I was pushing its strength to its limit.

My hand grazed the center of the window, and I pushed my fingers against the glass, testing to see if it had been left open. Never mind how I would launch myself up there should I discover that the window had, indeed, been left ajar.

Dead end.

Below me, the street was deserted, the sun tempered by wisps of fog, the kind that kept people indoors to linger in the morning. I knew no one else here except for the elderly couple who lived next door in Greta and her groom's rental unit. They were likely getting ready for the wedding them-selves. I knew better than to throw a kink in their routine, which I pictured as measured and planned out—with a little bit of old-married-couple chaos thrown in.

While carefully hiking up my robe, I jogged down the stairs of Mermaid Manor—that's the kitschy name of the house I'm staying in—hopeful that Carter, the home's eccentric but pleasant landlord, had left a lower floor door unlocked. I'd been suspicious of Carter when my sister had moved into his upstairs apartment last summer, worried that she might get herself into some nefarious situation. As it turned out, he's a character of sorts—we'd spoken briefly more than once—but seemed as safe as a marsh bunny. And rather cute, too.

Truth was, I hadn't wanted Greta to leave Indiana for an extended vacation in California. I'd encouraged it—that's what sisters do—but, in the end, fearing she would fall in love with sunshine and sea air, I hoped she would change her mind.

She didn't. She rented the upstairs apartment in Carter Blue's home and fell in love with the guy next door: Dr. Zac Holt. And they're about to live happily ever after. The End.

I spied the front door. If I could get inside the main part of the house, perhaps I could let myself into my rental unit that way. But it was locked, as was every window and door that I could reach by tiptoeing along the weed-filled side yard.

This wasn't happening. I was not about to be late for my sister's wedding! I pictured myself at home in Indiana, curled up in my recliner chair, my aching lower back soothed by a cushion, as I typed away on my laptop. How would I have written my heroine out of this corner? Surely, all was not lost.

My writing career might have been dying a slow and

withering death lately, but I was determined not to take my sister's best day ever with it. I had to find a way inside that apartment.

My thoughts landed on the metal lantern I'd moved to the ground when I'd dragged that bistro table across the deck. My lips twisted, thinking about using it as a weapon. A broken window would be worth it if I could get inside, retrieve my things, and dash back out in time to meet the driver who would be here at any minute.

He would never even have to know of the adventure that had just occurred.

The lantern felt heavy in my grip. I swung it once, wincing in anticipation, but it bounced back as if the window was made of Tupperware. The beads of sweat that had appeared on my skin earlier had, apparently, made a call to friends, announcing a party. Perspiration began to dampen the thick robe beneath my arms.

With lips pressed together, I inhaled through my nose and swung hard, cracking the window. I exhaled, relief and adrenaline pouring out of me all at once. Shards of glass began to crumble and fall away with each strike until the length of my arm could fit safely through the hole. I unlatched the window, slid it up, then using that bistro table, hoisted myself inside.

I tried not to think about the picture I was creating—a woman with an abundance of curly hair wearing a robe and tumbling across the kitchen sink—oh, why didn't I bother to drain the dirty dishwater from it this morning?—and oozing onto the tile floor, hands first, then arms and elbows, followed by a thunk from the balls of my feet hitting the floor. A twinge in my lower back reminded me to get up slowly.

On my feet now, I scurried into the bedroom in search of my heels and found them still in their box. My new cute bag sat at the foot of the bed. Disheveled and heart racing, I caught a glimpse of my reflection in the mirror, not surprised one iota that my curly brown hair looked the same as it did when I'd scrunched it earlier today.

"Sure you don't want me to do some crazy updo with my hair?" I'd asked Greta again last evening.

She'd shaken her head. "I want you to look like you."

"But I never wear dresses."

Greta crooked an arm around my neck then and said, "I want you to look like you ... in a dress."

We'd laughed again. A little ache tugged on my heart just thinking about the banter we had both grown accustomed to and how it had already begun to fade from our daily lives. Not to be maudlin or anything, but how much laughter would be in my life in the future?

Never mind with the musings, Clara. If I didn't hurry, I would miss my ride. I would not only have to pay for my landlord's broken window but also bear the burden of holding up the event, small as it may be.

Heavy-sounding footsteps clamored up the outdoor staircase. My driver had arrived. I slipped my feet fully into the heels, spied my phone, and quickly tucked it into my bag.

I was just reaching for the door handle when a loud bang on the door, followed by a shout, caused me to freeze.

"Police! We're coming in!"

I clutched my bag close to my body, aware of the hitch in my chest. I was all for law and order, but someone pretending to be law enforcement? Color me suspicious! Or was this a joke? I glanced around, searching for a place to hide.

Another harsh pounding on the door, followed by the sound of keys jingling and the turn of the door handle.

I hopped one foot out of a stiletto and held it above my head, the spiky side out, grounded yet ready to pounce, my breath suspended in my lungs.

The door crashed open, and a meaty man dressed in a dark uniform with a badge on his chest barreled in. Behind him, another man in uniform held someone back with a baton.

Carter?

The officer who rushed in towered over me, a scowl further marring his slightly bloated yet remarkably suave face. "Ma'am?"

I gasped for air now, letting out a small, "Yes?"

"Put down the shoe."

Slowly, I complied.

"Are you authorized to be here, ma'am?"

The oxygen hadn't quite reached the part of my brain that formed sentences. So I nodded.

Carter's voice careened into the room. "The perpetrator is my tenant, officers."

Perpetrator? That's offensive.

The beefy cop held out his arm, rendering Carter Blue nearly invisible. "Not so fast." He eyed me. "Name?"

I lifted my chin. "Clara."

Carter ducked beneath the officer's outstretched arm. My landlord was dressed for the wedding. Or maybe a funeral. He wore a black suit with a blood red shirt and tie, and the chain of his pocket watch hung from a button on his vest. "She's the famous author, Vivian Blackstone."

I narrowed my eyes at him. So much for keeping my identity incognito. I swung my gaze back up to meet the officer's confused expression. "It's a pen name, Officer. I would appreciate it if you would keep it, uh, on the down low."

His lips twitched, though his black eyes refused to show any emotion. He broke eye contact with me and surveyed the small apartment, his gaze slowing at the kitchen window.

Carter followed his gaze, then swiftly quirked a look in my direction.

"That can be explained." I held up my bag. "I was locked out and needed to retrieve my purse."

Carter dipped his head, a comical expression in his eyes. "So you ... broke a window?"

"I needed my shoes, too."

"You could have called."

"Except that my phone was locked up. Besides," I said, "when I knocked on your door and you didn't answer, I thought you'd already left for the wedding. Aren't you supposed to be on parking duty or something?"

He grinned. "You're cute when you're annoyed. An usher. I'm to be an usher."

"Then why aren't you down there ... ushering?"

He gave me a sheepish smile. "Slipped in a showing early this a.m."

Right. A Realtor. I knew that.

I cleared my throat and turned toward law enforcement. "So you see, officers, there's nothing to be concerned about here. I was just leaving for my sister's wedding—"

"Dressed like that?" The officer raised two bushy brows.

Slowly, I lowered my gaze to my high-heeled shod feet sticking out below the hem of my robe. Several pithy comments came to mind, but I held them back. "After I, uh, finish getting dressed, that is."

The officer let out a heavy sigh, nodded his head once, and simply said, "Ma'am."

Carter and I watched in silence as he gestured with a flick of his head for the other officer to follow him down the stairs.

When he had gone, I hopped one-footed into the bedroom without saying a word to Carter. I shut the door, threw off the robe, and shimmied into my maid of honor dress. I forced my foot into the errant heel again and flung the door back open.

"I'd better go," I said. "My driver must be wondering what happened to me."

"That might be true, if he were still here."

No. "What?"

"A limo pulled up at the same time as the police presence."

"Oh no."

Carter smirked. "The guy took one look at the squad car, made a U-turn, and squealed out of here." He paused. "Wonder what he was wanted for?"

I thought about this. "So, in other words, you probably saved my life."

Carter lifted both of his eyebrows in surprise. "That's me, a life saver."

I laughed lightly at the absurdity of it all.

He reached for the bag that held the boxes of cupcakes. "On the way, I'll call my handyman and ask him to come by and board up that window." He offered me his arm. "Shall we?"

I took his arm, grateful that Carter had shown up just when I needed him most.

WE SCURRIED up the hill to the chapel. Carter carried the bags of tulle and cupcake boxes, and I struggled to keep my gown from dragging against the pavement. A man I'd only seen in photos, yet recognized instantly, stood in front of the chapel door wearing a deep charcoal suit and a scowl incongruous for such a happy occasion.

As we approached, he stopped pacing and snapped at me. "You're late."

He was even better looking in person, and regrettably, the frown he wore did nothing but enhance those rugged looks. I lifted my chin and stared into those obnoxiously gorgeous eyes. "And you are?"

He kept a poker face. "Your date."

A tiny gasp escaped me, drawing a tickle of a smile out of him. My face heated, and I set my jaw. Greta had said her brother-in-law-to-be was mysterious, and she may have mentioned that he had the face of a movie star, but ornery? I didn't recall that detail. Calling this a date was a stretch. Braxton Holt was the best man and I the maid of honor. We were obligated to stand next to each other. I guess.

He teetered close to me, his assessing, sky-blue gaze sweeping over every inch of my face. I blinked. What was I annoyed about again?

Carter cleared his throat. He tucked both packages under one arm and reached out to shake Braxton's hand. "Sorry for the delay, but she's here now. No harm done. Plenty of time for photos."

I groaned. "Right. The photos." For a second, I'd forgotten we would be meeting with the photographer first.

Some people were born photogenic, but my unruly locks and I did not fall into that category.

"Would you like me to stay, Clara?" Carter glanced at Braxton as he asked this.

I shook my head. Poor Carter. He'd already saved my life once today. Surely I could handle an alpha male just fine without him. "No, thanks. I'm good."

Carter gave me a closed-mouthed smile. "Well, then, you go and have your photos taken." He glanced at the boxes under his arm. "I'll take these to the kitchen or else Helen will have my head."

After Carter left, I turned to Braxton, who was eyeing me with way too much intensity for someone I had met only two minutes ago. Or was I imagining that? The search for my next hero and heroine had reached such a critical stage that, last weekend, I'd made the ultimate move in my search for inspiration—I watched *Pride and Prejudice* (for the sixth time).

I peeled another look up at Braxton. Yeah, grumpy Mr. Darcy vibes for sure.

Well, if we were going to be family, we'd have to get along—starting with the wedding photos that would forever capture our moods. I managed a smile. "Guess we should get going," I said.

"I suppose so."

I gestured to the chapel door. "Should we, uh ...?" When Braxton didn't move, I rolled my eyes—I know, real mature—and attempted to push past him. He gave me a smile that was either flirtatious or confused. Maybe both? Either way, he didn't seem to want to let me pass.

I buried a sigh, catching eyes with him. "May I pass by, please?"

He stared at me for a couple of beats, then stepped back. "Suit yourself."

"Thank you." I bit my lip and stepped inside the chapel. Fortunately, I had visited this stunning spot with Greta earlier in the week and knew what to expect and where to go. My footsteps resounded as I moved farther inside. "Greta?" I called out. "Zac?"

My voice echoed in the empty chapel. I frowned. "They're not here." I glanced over my shoulder to catch that weird smile on Braxton's face again. "Care to tell me where they are?"

"Out on the lawn."

I shook my head, stress heat rising in me. Time was getting away from us and he wanted to play games? "Seriously? You can't tell me in here?"

He chuckled. "I just did. The happy couple is"—he flicked his head toward the exit— "out on the lawn."

I stared at him a good long time. At least two seconds ... oh, he was going to be a hit at family dinners all right. I released a puff of a sigh. "Well, come on then."

Braxton offered me his elbow, but I declined. I lifted my skirt slightly and walked ahead of him, hoping, of course, that I was moving in the right direction. When I'd asked Greta about her brother-in-law, she hadn't had much to offer other than that vague comment about his enigmatic self. Zac hadn't even been sure that his brother would show. From what I gathered, he was a bit of a drifter, far different from his hardworking sibling. Zac had referred to him as "very private," which, fair or not, I interpreted as uncommunicative.

His hand landed on my forearm sending a current through me. I spun around. "Look, Braxton. It's been a terrible morning"—I wagged my forefinger at him— "don't tell my sister I said that! But I really don't need—"

"You're about to step into a pothole."

I looked down. Oh.

He let go of my arm, yet the awareness of his hand touching my skin had not diminished. I hadn't expected him to affect me this way, for a simple touch from a gruff loner to provide sizzle beneath the surface.

Or maybe the crazy morning had caught up with me. I thought back to the drive up here. Carter had filled me in about the various real estate markets we encountered along the way from Camarillo to Malibu, and because of that, I had not had the opportunity to replay my brush with the law from earlier. It still hovered somewhere in my mind, threatening to land.

Carter probably had planned it that way, to keep me distracted from the tumultuous morning. I took a deep breath, expelling it with the tension I'd brought with me. It wasn't right to bring stress into the best day of my sister's life. I would have to thank Carter for his diversionary tactics because they worked. Or they had—until Braxton's less-than-friendly welcome brought reality back.

Braxton and I walked up the hill together in silence. Suddenly, he said, "I'm surprised they didn't elope."

I slowed, peering over at him. "And not include us?"

He appeared to mull my question, a sternness to his brow in the quiet. "Zac's a stoic guy," he finally said. "I thought he would be more inclined to whisk his bride away to some exclusive resort, just the two of them."

"So you've thought about this?"

"Not for more than a minute."

It was my turn to be quiet for a moment. None of my

novels ever had an elopement. Why not? The thought intrigued me. "So ... you're saying that eloping is more romantic."

He stopped. "I don't recall saying that."

"But it's what you meant."

He furrowed his brow and concentrated those dark eyes on me. "I say what I mean."

"Okay. So ... you mean that you don't want me to read between the lines then?"

He sputtered. "Do you always parse a person's words for hidden meaning?"

"Of course. Doesn't everybody?"

He narrowed his eyes. "No."

I sensed he had more to add, that his intentions were hovering on the tip of his tongue. What made Braxton Holt tick? He seemed angry—not all that mysterious—and yet, did he have a soft side when it came to romance?

"You're staring."

"Not staring. Thinking."

He dipped his head. "About?"

"You."

One brow arched. Oh my. He could be a romance cover model. Yes, yes, he could ...

"Would you like to explain?"

I inhaled, clearing my head. "Well, for an enigma, you surprise me."

"An enigma? Who called me that?"

It was my turn to shrug. "Everybody. Your brother ... my sister ..." Uncomfortable heat began its way through my middle and up my neck, a sure sign that this conversation may have crossed a divide that it was never meant to cross. "Maybe I've said too much."

"You think?"

"All I meant ... well, the fact that you've thought more than a few seconds about your brother's wedding tells me that you've got the makings of a ... a ..."

"A what?"

"A romantic."

He rolled his eyes, an odd juxtaposition against his smoldering good looks. I suddenly wished I'd brought a notepad to write all this down, but taking a mental snapshot would have to do. I'd often written alpha males, stiff upper lips and all that. But Braxton challenged me and I wanted to know more about him. He very well could be my ticket out of this wicked creativity block.

Silence passed. I wasn't sure how long we stood there, staring at each other, a variety of emotions passing across his face.

"Did you have more to add?" There was a slight bit of acidity in his tone.

"No, I think I'm good."

He gave me a doubtful frown, and suddenly he was Mr. Darcy again and I that silly girl, Elizabeth. Well, silly to his mind, anyway. He turned away from me and said, "Let's continue on then."

I laughed at how easily he slipped into the part of one of Austen's most beloved, yet undoubtedly gruff, heroes. I continued to follow Braxton, his back an engaging canvas for my creative process, until the toe of my heels hit a rock and I nearly careened into him.

He turned suddenly.

"Sorry." I caught myself before knocking him over, thankfully. My skirt had hitched at my hip, so I smoothed it down nervously with my hand.

Braxton's gaze lowered to my hand. He must have realized he was staring because he jolted a look back to my face and cleared his throat. "I think they're around the corner, near the bluff."

"Well, then, carry on."

I shaded my eyes with my hands, until we reached a clearing with an overwhelming view of rolling green hills and the never-ending sea. Braxton had been right—at least about my sister. Up ahead, Greta was all smiles and beauty as her makeup artist practiced her craft. But the groom was nowhere to be seen.

Braxton scanned the view. "Looks like my brother chose to follow my advice."

"And what sort of advice did you offer the groom?"

He wicked a look at me, this one softer than the others. "To stick with tradition and not see the bride before the wedding."

I laughed at this. "Look at you! Braxton, I believe you're an old softie."

He rolled his eyes for the second time, making me laugh harder. He was a character—a hero—in the making with a few sharp edges, but I could feel my creativity stir.

"Call me Brax. And I don't know what's so funny, but I'll leave you here so I can find my brother."

I was memorizing the inflections in his speech and the stoic posture he held. Michelangelo said that every block of stone had a statue inside of it, and that it was up to him to discover it. Maybe that was my problem. I'd been looking for the statue when I really should have been searching for the stone. Brax was my stone, and my gut told me that somewhere inside of him, he had the makings of a hero.

He was watching me, waiting for my response, so I nodded. "Yes, okay. You do that."

Confusion washed over him, but he turned away from me without another word.

I didn't watch Brax walk away, focusing instead on the gorgeous creature who sat in a makeup chair outside on this sunny day high on a bluff above the Pacific Ocean. My sister didn't really need much help to be beautiful. She was the girl who woke up in the morning and didn't need to do more than brush her hair and teeth.

I, on the other hand, was more gifted—with curly hair prone to tangling, that is. Our mother, God rest her sweet soul, had spent many mornings trying to tame the tears that managed to surface each morning as I wrangled my locks into submission the best way I could.

Sometimes I would look at Greta with envy, and maybe a little exasperation. But then she'd do something kind, like sneak a second slice of cake into the bedroom late at night and share it with me in the dark or listen to me read a favorite passage from one of the dog-eared books on my shelf when she probably preferred to be sleeping.

She was difficult to stay angry at for long.

"You're here!" Greta squealed and lunged for me, as if we hadn't seen each other just this morning. The makeup artist stepped away, allowing us our privacy.

I looked her up and down. "You look gorgeous, dah-ling."

She curtsied a little. "Why, thank you."

Her dog, Sport, had been laying at her feet, nibbling on grass as if this was just an ordinary day and not the best day of Greta's life. She wore a jeweled collar with a few flowers tucked in it, and one happily bored expression.

"Brax picked her up this morning and brought her here."

"Really? You know, I could have done that for you." Well, theoretically I could have. No need to mention the boarded-up window that still needed dealing with back at the apartment.

She took my arm, reminding me of when we were little girls and she had a big secret to tell me. "Come and get your makeup done."

I teared up suddenly, a rarity for me.

"What's wrong, hon?"

"I-I don't really know."

Greta's expression fell. "You're missing our Gran."

Our Grandmother Violet had gently slipped out of this world and into the next more than two months ago. Greta came home to Indiana and together we said our goodbyes to Gran, then boxed up her things to bring back to the house that my sister and I had, until recently, shared. The home had been handed down to us from our mother.

Maybe Greta was right. I was missing Gran, the woman who had helped our mother raise us, who had regaled us with stories right up until the end. She would have loved today. When Greta brought Zac to meet her last summer, despite her frail health, she swooned. Saw it with my own eyes.

Witnessing that moment gave me hope that maybe someday I ... well, whatever will be will be. I had to admit, though, that Greta had outdone herself in the man department. I conjured up all kinds of heroes in my books, and her fiancé Zac had come awfully close.

If only true heroes existed ...

I brushed a tear away from my eyes with the backs of my fingers. "Don't mind me. You're looking positively scrumptious. I just hope our Zac can keep his hands off you long enough to say your vows."

"Stop it."

I smiled in defense. "What? I call it like I see it, and you are glowing."

Greta reached over and stroked my face. I blinked away the hitch in my throat and glanced out to the Pacific Ocean. Even from up here, I could see the whitecaps forming on the surface.

"And you are stunning," my sister said.

I laughed at this. "Liar."

She grabbed my hand, pulling me into the seat next to hers. "Come on. Let Emiline touch you up."

The makeup artist approached, an easy smile on her face, her dark hair pulled into a ponytail. She worked quickly, and I could tell she was spending extra time on the bags under my eyes. I would have to remember to thank her later.

When she was done, I kicked off my heels and released a breath. It really was gorgeous up here. I turned to Greta. "How'd you do it?"

"Oh, it wasn't difficult. I just called a few months ago and booked the chapel."

I shook my head, my voice suddenly small. "I meant, how'd you manage to change your life?"

She leaned her head against mine briefly. "You know I can't take credit for that. Not when our grandmother was praying all those prayers for me. I finally surrendered all my angst to God, and he was waiting there to patch me up." She paused. "She prayed them for you too, Clara."

I nodded, but added nothing. I could use some of my Gran's prayers right about now. I didn't want Greta to know how quickly and disastrously my little world was crumbling around me. My creativity had flatlined for months, and for the first time, I was struggling to come up with the next book.

All I knew was that I needed inspiration—soon.

The breeze hit my bare feet, sending an unpleasant chill up my legs. Two blisters had begun to form on my toes. I bit back a sigh. That's what I got for not breaking in my new shoes before the big day.

A woman with a camera strapped around her neck and comfortable shoes on her own feet approached. "Greta, I'm here to take some shots of you and your sister, when you're ready."

My sister gave us both a dazzling smile. "Wonderful." She looked at me. "Are you ready?"

I nodded and tucked away my truths, including a recent unspoken discovery that was slowly rocking my world. And not in a good way. My faith was fading fast, but I whispered a prayer and trusted that, somehow, Greta's photographer would not be able to capture the fissures forming behind my smile.

CHAPTER TWO

BRAX

I CHECKED my watch and glanced at the happy couple. Unease knotted my gut.

Earlier, the ceremony had a serious, almost spiritual element that I hadn't anticipated. Then again, I should not have been surprised by the soberness of it all. My big brother had always been the serious one, the guy who carried books home from school on Fridays when the rest of us tumbled out of the hallowed halls with our hands gleefully empty.

I loosened my tie, the room warm, the music standard fare for a wedding reception. No matter. An hour from now I planned to be back on the road, once I figured out who to hand the dog off to. Greta had asked me to keep an eye on her after the ceremony so I had looped the leash around my chair and the animal—Sport—had been laying at my feet ever since. Apparently, Clara would be dog sitting for the next few weeks, but I'd been given the reception shift.

Clara's voice cut through the din of the miniature ball-room. "You're humming."

I glanced at the petite brunette with the inquisitive eyes and bold tongue. We'd only met today, and yet an odd sensation crept up my back, as if I'd known her much longer. It was ... unsettling.

"You carry a tune quite well," she continued. When I didn't answer her, she stared at me with a kind of *did you hear me?* look in her eyes.

I searched my head for what I had been thinking about before answering.

"Are you shy about it?"

I scoffed. "What? Humming?"

She narrowed her eyes at me, not in a challenging way, but as if she were analyzing me. Her head was tilted, showing off her graceful neck. I'd noticed her point a similar look my way several times today—including one rather off-putting moment when the groom was saying his vows.

"Yes," she said. "Most people who hum do so because they can't sing. Can you?"

"Can I what?"

Her smile deepened. "Sing."

Did she really expect an answer to that?

The up-tempo of the music changed and a slower song was introduced. She swiped the air with her hand at my non-answer and grabbed me by the hand. "Come on. Let's dance."

I gripped her hand, not because I wanted to hang on, but to stop her. No way would I be joining my sort-of-new sister-in-law on the dance floor. Those days were over.

Instead of pulling away, she took my hand in both of hers and yanked harder. "Don't be a spoilsport. Let's see what's behind that poker face you've been wearing since the music started."

She was a stubborn one, but I was even more so. I held my ground, unwilling to bow to the pressure of a beautiful woman who aimed to have me do something I didn't want to do, like when our mom wanted me to skip playing baseball on that old empty field to attend a great-aunt's birthday party.

Not that I was comparing Clara to my great-aunt Margie …

Anyway, tact was in order. If my father had taught me anything, it was to treat women with respect. Always.

If only I'd adhered to that advice five years ago, before I lost the woman I loved—

I felt a hard jab to my side and jerked a look over my shoulder. Gus was poking me with his cane. "Don't make me sic my wife on you, young man."

Helen was carrying two plates of cake this way, the woman's expression pointed. In some ways, my brother's renter reminded me of our mother. Soft like butter on the inside, yet tough on the outside, unyielding in her opinions. By the way she charged toward us, no doubt one of those plates would end up in my lap if I didn't comply.

I nearly laughed. Then thought better of it and followed Clara onto the dance floor stopping when she spun around, still talking.

"You know what I think?" she said.

"I'm sure you'll tell me, regardless."

"I think we should try to get along for our siblings' sake." She wagged her forefinger in the air between us. "We're family now, you and me."

She was right, but what she didn't understand was that I

lived on the move. Preferred it that way. I might have wanted things to work out differently than they had, but that did not change anything now. I was no longer the guy with a plan to shoot for the stars.

Far from it.

Though I hid my reluctance, I took Clara in my arms, willing myself not to notice her softness. Or the way her eyes sparkled with her smile. It was just a dance. One dance.

A few beats passed before she spoke again. "Don't you have anything to add to what I said?"

I considered her. "What makes you think that a truce between us is necessary?"

"Because of the way you barked at me when we first met. Plus, you're brooding, a mystery, and frankly, a little difficult to figure out."

"Really." I knew I should ask her why she thought that, but then she might tell me. I switched course. "I agree that, technically, we are family now. But don't expect us to see each other very often."

"Well, sure. I live in Indiana and won't be here all the time—"

"Neither will I."

"Because you live where?"

I slid a hard look at her now. No filter. Next she was going to ask what I did for a living, how I spent my time, what kind of coffee I preferred—espresso or dark roast?

Finally, I said, "I live where the road takes me."

She frowned.

"Do you find something wrong with that?"

She shrugged and gave her head a small shake. "It's just such a cliché to say that. And evasive, if you ask me."

I didn't.

"So what is it that you do that gives you the freedom to live on the road?"

I didn't have an answer that sounded respectable. Not that hard work wasn't respectable. But I had been raised by hard-working parents who expected their sons to go to college, find great jobs, and retire with a beautiful wife, two kids, and a fully funded 401K. I swallowed, trying not to think about how disappointed they would be.

My silence seemed to spur her on. "You know what? Don't tell me. Let me guess." Clara slowed some, eyeing me. "You're a brain surgeon."

I grinned at the audacity. "Let's go with that, then. May I ask what gave you that impression?"

"Your bedside manner." She taunted me with her laughter. "Or lack thereof."

I raised a brow. She'd rendered me speechless.

It didn't take long for a pink tinge to reach her cheeks, though. "It's just an expression, you know. Bedside manner? Has nothing to do with an actual, you know, bed."

She was beautiful and awkward all rolled up into one woman, and for the first time all evening, I got the feeling she wasn't as comfortable making small talk as she appeared. Her questions almost seemed forced.

"So anyway ..." Her voice trailed off and she looked away. I should rescue her, but to my surprise, I was enjoying myself. At the same time, I knew better than to allow this banter to continue. Zac had made that clear earlier today.

"I want to talk to you about Clara," he'd said. We were putting the final touches on our monkey suits, both of us tripped up by the elaborate tie knot.

"Clara ... your sister-in-law. Got it."

"I'm serious, Brax. Don't take this the wrong way, bro,

but you're a big flirt and I'm asking you to steer clear of Clara tonight. She's a sweet girl and you're—"

"A big ... flirt." I wasn't questioning him so much as trying to figure out what he was trying to say to me.

"Remember all those girls who'd show up with cookies and whatever for you when we were in high school?" He chuckled. "Man, I ate more dessert in those days than I have in all the years since. Mom would get all fake angry when you'd leave all that stuff around, remember that?"

"She was always on a diet."

"And all your girlfriends were getting in the way of that."

"I never asked them to come over. You know that, don't you?"

"Didn't stop them."

I clinched my jaw, debating my response. I cut a look at Zac in the mirror, my voice low. "I think it's stupid of you to think I would make a play for your sister-in-law at your wedding."

He slowed his progress on that tie knot. "When you say it like that, I sound like a jerk."

You did sound like a jerk. It was Zac's wedding, though, and he only knew me as the rolling stone who'd tried—and failed—at marriage, and who had plenty of girlfriends before and after. I decided to give him a pass. But just this once.

Zac slapped me on the back, then pulled me into a bro hug. "Appreciate you being here, Brax."

The memory faded, and I pulled my gaze away from Clara and turned toward the ocean below. I'd thought about taking up sailing, and perhaps I still might. A man could get lost for a long time out on that sea ...

"So are you going to tell me what you do to put food on your table? Or—"

I found Clara's gaze unwavering, as if she missed the fact that I had been avoiding her questioning. "Or what?"

"Or do I continue playing twenty questions?"

"If that's what you'd like to do."

Her eyes did that scrutinizing thing again—they searched my face. I hardened my jaw against the inquisition. If it weren't for this wedding, I would be nowhere near here. I had come for my brother and his new bride, and then the only plan I had was to leave. I hadn't expected to be answering to anyone about where I'd come from and where I would be going next.

Then walk away.

I ignored the warning sign in my head and peeled a look at Clara's warm-colored eyes again. Trouble—that's all I saw. "What about you?" I said, sidestepping her questions. "What do you do for a living?"

She tilted her head again, her gaze brushing down my face. "I write."

"You … write? Are you a reporter?"

"Something like that."

"And what do you report on?"

"People. Relationships."

"You write features then."

She laughed lightly. "You could say that. Fifty-thousand-word features."

My vision narrowed, trying to figure her out. But she laughed again and said, "I write novels. Romances, to be exact."

Ding, ding, ding … we have a winner.

"It's all making sense to me now."

"How so?"

"Why you're such an … extrovert."

She smiled first, then her eyes grew wide. I forced myself not to marvel at their expressiveness, especially as she followed that smile with gregarious laughter.

"Was it something I said?"

She shook her head. "It's just that, well, I'm the biggest introvert you'll ever meet. I spend hours and hours each day in my writing chair, pouring words onto pages. By the end of the day, I'm so twisted into a pretzel that all I want to do is unfold and go to bed."

"Sounds painful."

She smiled ruefully this time. "It is, my friend. It is. But, you see, your impression of me is all wrong."

"With all due respect, I hardly think I'm wrong. You've been talking nonstop since we met."

Clara raised a brow, suspending it upward for longer than a beat. "You want me to shut up?"

"What? No. I never said that."

She shrugged.

Great. I've managed to insult my sister-in-law's sister. I should have jammed out of here before that 80s DJ spun the first record.

"Getting back to you, Brax," Clara said, her eyes duller than when we'd started this dance. "I wonder why my sister doesn't know what you do. She said Zac wasn't even sure if you would come."

I stiffened. "Is that right?"

"Yes. They were both so relieved and happy to see you."

Enough. Any illusions I had about showing up, honoring my duty, and slipping out just as the groom tossed the bride's garter to some unsuspecting chump were dashed. I suspected that Clara spilled something Zac hadn't intended her to.

The song ended, and without so much as two seconds of

fade, another song began. A much faster one. I let go of Clara's hand, gently of course, and stepped back, offering her a decisive, "Thank you."

Her hazel-brown eyes widened again, and the brows that framed them knit downward, as if she were about to protest. I couldn't allow that.

Zac caught up with me as I was striding off the dance floor in a hurry. So much for making my exit.

"Bro," he said. "I need a favor."

Something cold trickled its way through my chest. I had a construction gig waiting for me in Texas—or at least a potential one—and it would pay me enough and give me time to see if summers in the South were to my liking. I put on a smile. "Shoot."

"What're you doing for the next month?"

Was this a trick question?

When I didn't answer right away, he said, "Look, I know we haven't seen each other in a long time. If I had thought things through better, I would have talked to Greta about staying around here for a few days before leaving on our honeymoon, so you and I could ... catch up."

"But you didn't think I'd show."

Zac's expression froze. He stared at me for a long moment, then nodded slowly. His eyes flickered, like he was swallowing back a million replies. "Hoped you would, Brax. But, I don't know, you've been gone for a long while."

"I told you I would come."

"True. You did."

My eyes wandered back to the dance floor briefly. "Or maybe you thought you'd scared me away with your private school rules."

Zac laughed in a measured way. "About that—I shouldn't have said anything."

"You mean about staying away from Clara?"

Zac lowered his voice. "I know I can trust you around Clara, and I'm sorry that I indicated otherwise."

Why did I get the feeling he was still wielding a warning in his words? I shrugged it off. "Would it have mattered if I'd stuck around anyway?"

"I don't understand."

"You're a workaholic, man." I took a brief look over my shoulder where Greta was smiling and laughing with friends. "I hope your bride understands your penchant for long hours and cold ramen."

"I'm a changed man."

"Doubt that."

"You'll see."

I shrugged. "If I planned to stay, then perhaps I would." At that moment, I caught sight of Clara dancing with that dolt, Carter. Why did that annoy me? I pulled my gaze away. Wasn't any of my business.

"Speaking of staying," Zac said, "I was hoping I could convince you to stay at the house for a while."

I waited. Surely a punchline was coming.

Zac smiled. "I'm serious. Greta and I will be gone for almost a month. Stay. Relax." He paused. "Fix the projects I screwed up."

I pointed at him. "There it is."

Zac chuckled. "I may be the older brother, but you taught me all your remodeling hacks."

"You never listened."

"Hey, now. I've held my own."

I nodded. It was true. My older brother was born with

the responsibility gene. Our parents trusted him implicitly, and though I'd like to give him grief for it, I know in my head that he earned it. I, on the other hand, caused both of them to go gray at a young age. So they said.

"Seriously, how about it?"

"Thank you for the offer, but I'll be leaving after sunrise."

Zac's smile dimmed, and he watched me for a moment. "You know, we've never really talked about what happened with Kate."

"And we won't."

"One of these days, I hope we will. I know I wasn't there for you back then and I'm, I'm, well, I'm sorry."

I sucked in my top lip, wishing away this conversation and the baggage that came along with it. Then I flashed him a smile. "It's your wedding day. Not the right time to bring up the past."

He nodded once. "Right. Yes." A beat passed between us. "I'd really like you to stay. Hey, you used to sing. There's a place down on Harbor where you could—"

"I don't do that anymore."

"I see." He paused. "I'm not as altruistic as you think I am."

"I didn't really think you were."

My brother grinned. "Could I change your mind if I told you that it would help me out tremendously if you considered staying at the house and looking after things while we're gone? Apparently, Clara had an incident with a broken window today and a visit from law enforcement."

This news was ... unexpected. "Did she now?"

Zac chuckled. "Carter spilled her secret. I think Greta

and I are feeling a little guilty that we're jetting off and leaving her here."

"Sure you are."

Zac laughed, nodding. "Okay, all right. Fine. We can't wait to get out of here. Still, it would be nice to have you stay and watch over the place. Who knows? Maybe you'll end up making it a permanent move—"

"What happened to *Stay away from the maid of honor*?"

My brother shot me a confident smile. "I apologized for that, bro. I know you wouldn't cross any boundaries. I trust you."

I cut a quick glance at Greta and Carter on the dance floor again.

"There's more," Zac said, pulling me back. "Gus and Helen, well, Greta's concerned about them. More than once they've set off the smoke alarms, and—"

Ah, bingo. The real reason for this inquiry. "So you're asking me to stay and babysit ... to make sure they don't burn down the place."

"If you wouldn't mind."

I locked eyes with my brother, considering his request for me to stick around. I wasn't used to him being so touchy feely and guess I had Greta to thank for that. I was the one who'd been described as a pile of mush, the guy who could make girls cry with his lyrics and swing a hammer on his days off. In other words, I was a running joke.

Zac looked happier than I'd seen him in years, and an unanticipated swell of pride came over me.

Still, I put my hand on his shoulder and shook my head. Maybe it would be better if I hit the road sooner rather than later. "Sorry, bro. I wish I could help."

Clara

CARTER WORE ME OUT. Or maybe it's the heels. Whatever. I was tired and pain radiated down my leg. My lower back hadn't had this much exercise on one day in I-don't-know-when. I fished inside my clutch purse and pulled out a tab of ibuprofen, swilling it down with a swig of water.

"You cut quite a rug out there, Sister Clara." Gus had rolled up in his wheelchair and was smiling appraisingly at me.

"Why thank you, Father Gus."

"Father Gus?"

"You called me Sister, as if I were a nun."

Gus slapped his thigh and let out a guffaw. "I'm no priest!"

Helen cut in. "Well, that's for sure!"

Greta pirouetted into our circle, the skirt of her wedding gown fanning out wide. "What's this about my sister joining a cloister?"

Helen laughed uproariously.

"No one said anything about joining a cloister or convent or anything." I winced and pressed a fisted hand into my lower back.

Greta's laughter died away. "What's wrong? Your back giving you trouble again?"

I waved her off. "No. I'm good. Just had an itch." I'd done a pretty good job of hiding my worsening back issues from my sister and I wasn't about to start whining about them now as she's about to head out on her honeymoon.

She flashed a tentative smile at me. "If you say so."

Brax appeared next to Greta. He touched her elbow. "I have to leave now, Greta."

"So soon?" Greta's expression fell. "We've hardly had a chance to chat."

His smile looked sincere, but admittedly, I was parsing it for subtext. Why was he dashing away already? As my Grandmother Violet used to say, "It's just the shank of the evening!"

"Afraid so," he was saying. "I'd like to get a few hours on the road before pulling off for the night."

Greta hugged him and then pulled back. "Thank you so very much for making the trip. It meant the world to Zac. And to me."

If I weren't mistaken, his stony expression faltered. He raised that wall back up in a hurry, though.

"Thank you. Congratulations on a beautiful wedding. My brother is a lucky man. I hope he knows that."

Greta flashed him the gentlest of smiles, the kind that could melt even the grumpiest heart. Have I mentioned how adrift I was now that my muse had gone and gotten herself married off to her prince? I glanced around at the slim pickings. Not a whole lot of inspiration left.

Or was there? Another slow song began, "Thinking Out Loud," by Ed Sheeran, and my strength began to rally. Just as Brax started to walk away, without saying goodbye to me I might add, I reached for his arm. "One more dance?"

Greta goaded him on. "Yes, please stay for one more, Brax. This is such a great song."

Brax cast me a look of resignation mixed with a kind of suspicion. I laughed and pulled him onto the dance floor. "C'mon, you."

He took me into his arms again, though admittedly more stiffly than the last time. I searched my brain for something to say that would stir up conversation. An image of a hero had begun to emerge during our last dance, but I hadn't fully formed the idea and hoped to find more inspiration in this dance. I liked the enigmatic part of Brax, but where was his humanity? So far, he'd griped at me and was about to leave his brother's wedding in a hurry. He was hotter than Mr. July in a calendar of firemen, but surely there had to be something more likable about him.

"What kind of dancing is that?" Helen showed up next to us like a chaperone at the prom. Only instead of sticking a ruler between us, she was trying to corral us closer using her short, pudgy arms that belied their strength. "You two look stiffer than one of those sticks holding up the Ventura pier."

Gus rolled his wheelchair onto the dance floor. He smiled warmly at his bride. "Let's show these youngsters how it's done, Helen."

Really, was there anything cuter than these two?

Brax grunted, but it came out sounding more like a sexy growl. My inspiration was growing by the minute, despite the man's lingering sour attitude. I buried the truth that my body felt a little too tired for this right now because I was more than willing to keep going if it meant I'd have another chance to brainstorm a new hero. Earlier, Carter had me twirling and dipping, his confidence making up for my lack of it. But the pain pill was kicking in, and with a much slower tempo, I found myself relaxing against Brax's super-hero chest. Seriously, I could feel the hard mountains and valleys beneath his shirt, and I had to say: impressed.

Helen sat on Gus's lap and spun his chair around like an anemic version of the teacup ride at Disneyland. My face shook and Brax let go a woosh of a laugh at the spectacle. They kept twirling, and at one point, Helen splayed her arms out like Rose in *Titanic*, shouting, "I'm flying!" Laughter spilled out of me until I cried dribbly tears right onto Brax's lapel.

"They're too much," he said, his voice all garbly, sexy.

I tipped up my chin to find Brax looking down at me beneath heavily lidded eyes. He smelled good, like a musky man in uniform. Or a tux. Either way, I wanted more of it ... I mean, my heroine would want more of it. The one I was writing. I'd have to add that scent to my files for future reference.

We were swaying now to the music, he and I, and for a whisper of a second, a contentment I'd never known began to settle over me. I was beginning to think that everything would be all right. I would be fine living on my own in Indiana, without being my sister's sidekick all the time. The lingering question about my past, and what I'd recently learned, would be safely tucked away. And most importantly, my next novel, written without my usual muse and her dating antics for inspiration, would end up being my best one yet.

A ripple of a sigh escaped me. Then a jolt of pain against my leg. My knee buckled and you know that falling thing that happens as if in slow motion but in actuality is really quite fast? As we tumbled backward, Brax groaned for real—it didn't sound like a sexy growl this time. And I landed on top of him with an *oof*.

Voices surrounded us.

The music died down.

Apologies came first from Helen. Then Gus. We'd been run over by an out-of-control wheelchair.

I was sprawled across Braxton Holt on the dance floor, but instead of the kind of elation I might expect from the hero of my dreams over this turn of events, his face registered ... pain.

I pushed myself up, aware of the unladylike contortion of my maid of honor gown twisted around my torso. Carter appeared, a look of hilarious concern in his expression, and reached out a hand to me. I took it and stood, straightening and brushing my skirt down with my free hand.

Helen was still fussing about me, brushing away bits of dust from my dress. "I'm so sorry, honey. Gus and I got a little out of hand."

Gus cut in. "Yes, sirree, we did. We were dancing and spinning and the next thing I knew, Helen's orthopedic shoes were flying in a circle!"

"With my legs attached!" she said.

"It's fine. I'm fine." The sudden attention around me made me feel like a giant among Victoria's Secret models. My introverted nature, which had been hiding itself all day, had gone on high alert. I had an urge to find my blankie and a bucket of ice cream and curl up on my recliner chair back home.

As that fantasy was making its way through my head, I looked down at Brax. He had hardly moved. He grimaced, and I searched for a sign that he was being dramatic.

Gingerly, I knelt down beside him. "Did I hurt you?"

"I'm fine." One eye popped open and he pulled himself up, his curvaceous lips now in a straight line. I looked away. Was just giving him some privacy. That's all.

The music had started again, and Zac appeared. He reached his hand down to his brother. "You okay, buddy?"

Brax turned an evil eye on him. The likes of which I

hadn't seen since I was a child and my mother found me using her makeup brushes as characters in a story about two kids who go to the local swimming hole, aka the toilet.

I scrambled up and gave Brax some space. That's when I noticed his ankle had swelled up as big as a baseball. "Oh, no, Brax, your ankle ..."

He shot me a look that told me he was well aware of his injury.

I averted my gaze, my stomach roiling. Guilt trickled through me. Brax hadn't wanted to dance—I had seen it in his eyes. But contrary to my usual mouse-like self, I pushed him into it, desperation driving me to see what the guy was made of. Now he was hurt. And as unhappy as a cow who'd overslept during milking time.

Zac whistled and took my place squatting next to his brother. "I haven't seen it look like that since we were kids."

"Yeah, well." Brax rubbed his face with his palm, his voice sober. "It's like an old friend who shows up without bothering to call first."

Zac slapped a hand onto Brax's shoulder. "Don't get up yet."

Greta reached out to the caterer. "Would you find us some ice? My brother-in-law is going to need it for his ankle."

The woman assured her she would and dashed off in the direction of the kitchen.

But Brax wasn't listening. He turned onto his good knee and pushed himself up, as if he was going to openly defy that swollen ankle and the pain that wasn't going anywhere. The grunt he let out wasn't fooling me. Nor Zac, apparently, who ducked into place beneath his brother's arm, allowing Brax to lean on him.

Carter spoke up. "I'll drive you back to the house, if you want."

"That won't be nec—"

"Actually," Zac said, "if you wouldn't mind, that would be great."

Brax began to protest again, but Zac shut him down once more. "It's probably a sprain."

"It's definitely a sprain," Brax said through clenched teeth.

"But I'll want you to go by the hospital for an x-ray just to make sure. You can do that on Monday. Until then, there are clean sheets and towels in the guest room."

"Stop babying me, big brother. I've got this. Help me to a chair and I'll wait there till this blows over."

Now see, if Greta had barked at me like that, I would've straightened my shoulders and growled right back at her. Of course, she probably would have laughed in my face and told me I was cute or something, but nevertheless, I would not have smiled at her the way Zac was smiling at Brax.

"Let Carter take you home so you can put that leg up."

"Can't. My car's here. I'll be fine. Let me—"

"I'll drive your butt home in your car!" I hadn't expected the music to end right as I shouted my offer to Brax. In the quiet, my declaration swiveled a few heads, many wearing bewildered smiles.

Zac gave me a grateful smile, then swung a look at Brax. "It's settled then. The party is winding down, anyway. Carter and I'll get you to the car, and Clara will chauffeur you back up the coast. Done."

Brax cast a look at me that was anything but grateful, but I shrugged it off. Poor guy was in pain. The least I could do was drive him home so he could rest. Was it my fault if I might want to distract him on the journey home with a few more questions about what made him tick? What better way for him to keep his mind off the pain, right?

Our small entourage made it to Brax's Jeep. I had been holding Sport's leash, and before I realized what was happening, she scurried into the back seat. Zac whistled for her to jump back out, but I stopped him. "I'll be taking care of her, anyway. Might as well take her back with me now."

Zac cut a look at Carter, then back to me. "If you're sure."

"I am."

I slid behind the wheel, fished out the last pain med from my purse, and handed it to Brax. "You have any water in here?"

"Yeah." He reached under his seat and retrieved a bottle of water, then swallowed back the pill.

My new brother-in-law slapped the hood of the Jeep, you know, the way guys do. I turned the ignition and let it whir for a few seconds, wondering if I even remembered how to drive.

CHAPTER THREE

BRAX

I PEELED a glance at the woman in the driver's seat. No one had ever sat there. Even Kate preferred to drive her own car. "Yours is too loud and fast," she'd said. Like those were bad things.

The road curved and dipped, but I tamped down the unease that rose in my gut. It had been a long time since I was a teen driving this route but was cocky enough back then to think I could do it with my eyes closed.

I glanced more fully at Clara now, looking for any sign of cockiness and grateful to find none. She hadn't taken either hand off the wheel, nor her eyes off the road, since we'd left the reception.

I cleared my throat. "You know your way?"

Her brows dipped, but she kept her focus ahead of her. "I think so." She tapped the GPS, but didn't look at me. "Zac put the directions in here after they loaded you in. You might not have noticed."

"You make me sound like a piece of meat."

"I'm sure it's not the first time."

I coughed a laugh, then winced. She was quick with the retorts, that's for sure.

"I'm not buying the false modesty," she said.

I pulled back, squinting at her. "Is that so?"

She didn't answer right away, her attention hyper-focused on the road. I could appreciate that. Finally, she said, "You do know you're a good looking guy, right?"

"Are you flirting with me?"

She wrinkled her nose. "Okay. He's shy about his rugged good looks. Noted."

Despite the wretched pain radiating from my ankle, this drew a smile out of me. A rueful one, anyway. What an absurd conversation. "Rugged good looks? What am I, a hero in one of your romance novels?"

For the first time since she'd taken a seat behind that steering wheel, Clara turned her face to me. Both of her brows were raised, as if silently transmitting, *duh.*

"You ... you're kidding."

"Why would I be?"

I paused, turning that over. Sordid. Twisted. I shifted in my seat to make sure she wasn't messing with me, but her eyes were squarely back on the road again. Dawning came over me. "No wonder the twenty questions today. You were looking for the next character in your book, weren't you?"

"Oh please. We're family now. I was just being friendly." She tightened her grip on the steering wheel. I could tell by the whites of her fingers.

"You were being more than—"

She held up a hand in front of me like a stop sign. "Could you... shhh?!"

I followed her gaze. We were approaching the winding-most part of the coast highway—two lanes sandwiched between temperamental mountains on the right and unforgiving cliffs on our left. As a teenager trying to get out of the Valley, I had driven this road more times than I could count but never, until now, given it much thought. Three cars lurched by us, one after the other, right before a passing lane ended. Clara braked so hard I had to catch myself from careening forward and losing the paltry dinner I'd consumed.

I peeled a look at her. "You all right?"

"I'm fine." Her fingers appeared to grasp that steering wheel even tighter now. "Fine. Uh-huh."

I ignored the throb in my ankle and focused instead on Clara, whose unsettling expression made me wonder if it would have been safer to hitch a ride from a stranger in a windowless van. She took the next turn with all the confidence of a kid with a lighted Student Driver sign on his roof.

"I just remembered that you're not from here." I eyed her, a pause hanging between us. "I suppose there aren't a lot of winding roads like this where you're from in ... Indiana, is it?"

"Mm-mm. Not true."

"Let me give you some advice anyway."

She narrowed her eyes but kept them on the road.

"It might help not to brake so hard, especially when you're going through the turns. It's best to just allow the car to take them gently."

She exhaled. "Look who's suddenly turned chatty."

And look who's suddenly lost her chipper glow. I shut my

mouth, caught between giving her a forced, yet good-natured, smile, and fearing for my very life. I instinctively hung onto the armrest on my door.

But keeping my thoughts to myself only seemed to annoy her. "Stop stressing me out!"

A guttural sound escaped me. "How am *I* stressing *you* out?"

"You're giving off stress vibes!"

I bit the inside of my cheek before saying, "Hey there, no need to go so fast."

"Stop backseat driving already. I know what I'm doing!"

"Do you? Because the way you're taking these turns, I'm not so sure."

"Lovely."

"You do have a driver's license, I hope."

"Yeah, somewhere."

A warning bell sounded, though I was the only one to hear it, apparently. "You're not carrying it."

She flipped her hand in the air like a wave, then must've thought better of it and slapped it back onto the steering wheel. "I said, it's somewhere."

"I get it. You changed bags and left it in the other one."

She smirked.

"What's that look for? I have an ex. I'm not completely oblivious to female rituals."

"Oh, you did not just say that ... female rituals? Really?"

I shrugged. "Got my point across."

"For a caveman."

I scoffed. "As a romance novelist, I'm sure you are aware of the differences between the sexes."

"Oh right. Important differences, for example, girls wear purses and boys have pockets."

"Among other things."

"Such as?"

I paused, collecting my thoughts here. She was setting me up, and if I wasn't careful, I would fall headfirst into her carefully woven trap. Like mesh over a drain.

"All I'm saying is that it's easier for men to carry important things like their driver's license because most of us only have one wallet."

She hummed some kind of response that I couldn't decipher.

"So ... this license. It's current?"

She turned her chin, melting me with a stare full of heat. And not the good kind, though I couldn't deny how cute she looked when fully peeved. Thankfully, we were on a straightaway. "I see."

She laughed, though it sounded strangled.

"What's so funny?"

"You. Thinking I should name a character after you."

Oh, we were going back there now. "It's not that ridiculous," I said, "and I didn't think you should—I just figured out your MO."

"Well, I have been thinking of moving into writing suspense novels, and I suppose I could make you the villain. Always looking for a good antagonist."

"Kind of an oxymoron, you know, good antagonist and all, but if that's what you think."

The car swayed then and I darted my gaze to the windshield. "Hey, Clara, you should slow down before the last curve coming up."

"Uh-huh."

I was much too old to be rolling my eyes, but I wanted to. When she came out of the turn, I couldn't help myself. "I'm guessing you don't drive very much in Indiana."

"I almost never drive. I mean, only if I have to."

"Never? As in ... you don't drive? Wait. You don't actually have a driver's license, do you?"

"I have one, but I've no idea where it is. I used my passport to get here."

"So you travel?"

"No." She paused. "But I'd like to."

She said that in a wistful way, and if I weren't so intrigued by her driving admission, aka she rarely did it, I would ask her more about that.

She navigated the last turn without killing us. From here on out, the road would be relatively straight. I slid a look at her, her jaw still taut. *She's* angry? What about her precious cargo? That's what my mother used to call Zac and me whenever she'd drive us around as kids, and though I never appreciated it much back then, I did now.

Neither of us said anything much on the rest of the ride home. When we arrived at Zac's place at the beach, I tried to make nice. "Thank you for getting me home, Clara. I appreciate the effort."

She narrowed her eyes at me. "Gee, you're welcome." She slammed the car door shut after exiting. I swung open my own door and Sport bounded out, leaving me to fend for myself. Carefully, I climbed down to the ground, leaning on my good leg.

I limped toward the house, then stopped. Zac lived upstairs. I'd completely forgotten that he rented out the bottom-floor apartment to Helen and Gus. Sport waited at the top, whimpering, her tongue hanging out of her mouth.

Clara's voice, somewhat softened, interrupted the

battery of questions running through my mind. "Come on. I'll help you." She offered me her arm, and though I doubted she could bear much of my weight, I gave it a good show, leaning on her with one side while using the handrail to pull myself up each step.

By the time we reached Zac—and Greta's—front door, my palms and face were sweating. She took the keys from me, and I didn't protest. The door swung open, Sport rushed inside, and I turned to her to offer my thanks.

"Well, get in there already." She waited for me to move. I wasn't used to being ordered around. If anything, I was the one doing the ordering. I found myself wanting to stare long at Clara's face, her expression a mixture of frustration and curiosity. If only I could decipher how much of each, I might have a better idea of how to respond. She reminded me of a small dog ... with a really big bark.

I bit back a burgeoning smile.

She rolled her eyes. "Looks like the meds are kicking in. Time for bed."

Again, I curtailed both a smile and a response. She was mad, and though we hardly knew each other, and probably would never spend all that much time together, I was already learning that Clara could not be easily figured out. Hot one minute, cold the next.

No matter what I might have thought about that. The fact remained that Clara had driven me home on that crowded and danger-prone highway, though she had, apparently, been avoiding the driver's seat for a long, long time. Had to admire that.

I limped into the house and she fussed about for two-point-five minutes. And then she took the pup—and left.

Clara

EXHAUSTED. My mind searched for a stronger word, one that would convey how deeply tired I felt this morning, right down to my bones. I hadn't had any wine last night, but my head ached just the same. Probably just being spiteful. My face felt bloaty and I was stiff all over. Pretty surly, too. Though, come to think of it, that wasn't all that out of the ordinary.

Then I remembered the dancing. Me. Dancing! Didn't everybody know that, *hello*, introverts don't dance? At least, they didn't dance and then talk about it EVER AGAIN.

"Ugh!" I rolled over, groaning into my pillow. Sport barked once and began tap dancing those little nails of hers all over the wood floors, trying to convince me to go out in public before I'd had the chance to drink coffee or replay every last second of my brazenness last night—including the white-knuckle drive along a treacherous highway.

Did I mention I hadn't had coffee yet?

Sport yelped again, something that sounded awfully like, "I don't care, darling."

I twisted my mouth, then threw off the covers. "Fine!"

Out of bed, my back tweaked a little more than usual, as if it were throwing out accusations with every step.

Boy, that mouth of yours was on fire last night!

Did you think you were a contestant on Dancing with the Stars or something?

Heels? Really?

I rubbed my lower back with my fist and mouthed my

feelings for my newlywed sister. Walk the dog first thing in the morning? Did Greta not remember my aversion to mornings?

The dog yelped again.

I glanced at her. "Stop or I'll suggest a nice feline as a sibling for you."

This caused her to pause, apparently, because she halted and twisted a look up at me that said, "Would you really?"

I pulled myself together, aka rolled myself into sweats and a beanie, then traipsed outside where the dew and mist greeted me like a tepid sauna. A passerby waved, but I could only manage a shy smile.

My social anxiety, which had miraculously hidden its face at Greta's wedding, unfurled to life this morning. How much did I really talk yesterday? What did I say? And … how much dancing had I done?

I resisted the urge to pull my beanie down as far as it could stretch, as if that would provide camouflage from the world around me. Then again, nobody knew me here. If only I could pull together a decent story for my editor, then this place, far away from my home, could provide me with the quiet and solace to write the next book.

Whatever that might look like.

I shook my head and slowed until Sport tugged on the leash. Her persistence caused me to scowl and to keep walking when what I really should have been doing was, well, writing. For years, writing had been my constant companion, the one who wasn't a fair-weather friend. Other than my sister, of course. She was great, but didn't count. Blood relative and all.

Still, there was something I hadn't told even her. Greta's revelation last year about my father had come as a shock, but after a brief stint of talking through what she recalled, we both dropped the subject. After all, no one else in our circle seemed to know anything about that time in our past. I, myself, had no memory of the man only known in my sister's memories as Dalton.

A ripple of a sigh overtook me. Why hadn't I let that nugget of history go? So many other pieces of our family history had long been buried, why not plow this one under too?

Maybe it was because searching one's DNA past was not only easy these days, but expected. Want to know if you're Italian? Or Brazilian? Or French? You could find out. Better yet, for less than a hundred dollars you could spit in a tube and—voila!—find yourself a new family.

In a way, that's what I had done. Received the smart little box in the mail, slid open the lid, collected my spit in a plastic pouch, and sent it off to strangers to see if anyone, anywhere, would claim me as their own.

Problem was, I had kept my findings from Greta and now I felt ... rotten. It wasn't as if she had kept the truth from me on purpose all these years. Once she figured out what had been buried in her subconscious, she spilled it out like an overflowing fountain.

I kicked a pebble with the toe of my flip-flops, effectively refiling this confusing topic in the recesses of my brain. I hadn't come here to ruminate on my past or my findings, few as they were. This trip was all about Greta and Zac and the new life they'd created. I was only here as an observer.

Sport paused at the base of a spray of sea grass and relieved herself. I looked off toward the west, as if she cared a thing about privacy. The ocean stretched and yawned its way toward me, not quite as blue as the day before.

The wedding had been beautiful, my sister gorgeous. A tiny needle of discomfort poked at my windpipe, and I swallowed it away. I was reminded again of our grandmother and how she would have loved every minute of those seaside nuptials.

On a personal note, Gran would have also been my secret partner in crime, so to speak. She would have done some serious people watching, and in a few short hours, presented me with an array of characters and plots for them to carry out. I should have done that myself, but let's be honest here—I had been much too busy pumping Brax for information to come up with a story with an actual hook in it.

Sport and I continued our walk, my mind waking more with each step, the achiness dissipating. Guilt crept into my thoughts. I'd pushed myself beyond my introverted limits, had showed Brax the part of me that usually only found a voice on paper. He hadn't wanted that last dance—I could tell by the look in his eyes. But I had goaded him into it, my well of research still needing to be filled. I was fresh out of heroes and when I saw that man's chiseled mug in the flesh, I knew I'd found a potential fit.

Only he wasn't cooperating as I'd hoped and kept shutting down, as if my questions were somehow prying into his life. Whatever. I still felt stuffed with guilt that he'd gotten hurt. I exhaled, trying to erase the memory of his—our—fall. Not to mention my sour attitude on the way home.

The man had annoyed me with his backseat driving and directions, carefully and cautiously phrased as if I were a teenager behind the wheel for the first time in my life. Then again, I was tired. Even I knew how snippy I could be when my socializing meter had been filled for the day. Or in this case, overfilled.

"Hello there, Clara."

"Wha ...!"

Carter had appeared on foot, out of nowhere. "I scared you."

"What was your first clue?"

He chuckled. "Water?" He handed me a bottle from the bag in his arms, icy cold droplets running down the side.

"Thanks."

"Restocking for an open house later today."

"The Realtor who never sleeps."

"I actually do, but don't mention that to my clients. To them, I'm working tirelessly twenty-four-seven." He winked at me before taking a swig, then recapping his bottle. "You're up early—it's only a little after nine. I would have pegged you as a ten-o'clock-or-later kind of gal."

I held up the leash in my hand.

"Right. The mutt."

"Now, now." But he was right. It was early and I wasn't a fan.

"I meant that in the most charming way possible."

"Does your bitterness toward this adorable creature here have anything to do with your deep and abiding love for Zac?"

A cool smile came over Carter. "Zac and I have buried the hatchet. It's all water under the bridge now, Clara."

"Any other clichés you can think of?"

"That's right." He wagged his pointer finger toward me. "A writer. You know stuff."

I laughed. "I ... know stuff."

"Writing stuff."

"You're so weird."

"I'll take that to mean you like me."

I laughed. Oddly, yes, I did like him. He was cool and weird and a little rebellious, so what's not to like?

"Speaking of your new relatives, any sign of the interloper who's staying in Zac and Greta's place?"

I laughed harder. "You're ridiculous. And no, I haven't checked in on Brax today. Frankly, you were right, if I'd been the one making decisions this morning, I'd still be in bed."

Carter nodded. "That's why you'll never see me with a pet. I like my independence too much."

Sport tugged on the leash, but in the direction of home. I sighed. "So much for mine. Guess we're heading back."

"See you later this afternoon then."

I smiled. "Sounds good. Oh, before I forget, I never got the Wi-Fi password from you and I'm ready to do some research. May I have it?"

"Ah, working on a new book."

"Um, yes. Well, I will be." That wasn't a lie. "Can you text it to me, so I don't forget by the time I get back?"

"You won't forget. First, you'll want to look for the Wi-Fi name Carter Blue Real Estate Professional."

"Naturally."

"The password is blueiscool. All run together."

I nodded. Of course, that would be his password. Why had I not guessed? "You're right. I won't forget that." I thanked Carter and sent him a wave as Sport dragged me back to the house. So I guess I knew at least a couple of people in this small beach town, after all.

Coffee called to me, and a shower, but at the base of the stairs to my rental, I paused long enough to cast a long look at Greta's front door. I'd said I would look in on Brax, but was

that supposed to mean first thing in the morning? Sometime
during the week? He was a grown man, for crying out loud.
He could leave whenever he wanted. I peeked at his Jeep,
still in the drive from last night.

Then why hadn't he?

"C'mon, girl. Let's check on the brother-in-law." She
spun around like I'd told her we were headed to a squirrel
farm and charged up the stairs. At the top, I knock softly.

Nothing.

I knocked again. "Brax? I'm here to check on you." That
sounded so lame, and I felt silly saying it, yet a muffled male
voice answered. The door clicked and opened slowly.

I wasn't prepared for the impact of seeing Brax first thing
in the morning. His expression was drawn, and his blue eyes
still tired from sleep, yet I drank in his firm-set jaw patterned
with golden brown scruff, and his brown hair, ruggedly
tousled, rather than smashed flat like mine (hence my
beanie). Honestly, how unfair was this to wake up looking
like ... a hero?

My heartbeat began to race. Had I somehow missed
something yesterday?

His deep voice broke my musings. "It's barely after nine.
You want something?"

Not a morning person either. Check. "You know, you
could make a girl swoon with all the sweet talk."

His brows rose.

"Why yes, Sport and I would love to come in." I pushed
against the door as he hobbled toward an oversized chair.

Greta had explained that this was not the official entry
point of the house, but the most convenient to the main
living area. Gus and Helen had once owned this house, fell
on hard times, and had to sell, but Zac made sure they could

stay here by renting the downstairs apartment out to them. A more formal entry to the main house was located on the side of the house.

Sport took off, skidding down the hall, and my guess, to the kitchen. She'd find a water dish, but joke's on her—I'd taken her food bowl with me to Mermaid Manor.

"How are you ...?" I frowned. Hot or not, Brax's expression looked decidedly pained, the lines next to his eyes long and pronounced. I moved closer and gasped. "Oh no. Your ankle's so swollen!"

Brax ran a hand through his hair and leaned his head against the wall. "'Fraid so."

"Let me take you to the hospital."

He looked at me like I'd lost my mind. "That won't be necessary."

"But it could be broken. You should get an x-ray, and maybe some stronger pain meds."

"Thanks, Dr. Clara, but I'll be fine. Grounded, but fine."

"If Zac was here, he'd make you go to the hospital."

"Well, he's not here, is he?"

Reflexively, I stepped back. "Okay, Mr. Grumpy Pants. No need to get snippy with me. When's the last time you iced your ankle?"

He stared at the ceiling like he was Beth in *The Queen's Gambit*, trying to figure out her next move. I shook my head. "Never mind already. I'll get you some ice and then root around in Zac's medicine cabinet for his hospital stash."

I didn't wait around for him to bark at me again, instead setting out on my quest for ice and meds. That didn't stop him from calling out to me from his sick chair. "Not so sure my brother would approve of you prescribing medicine without a license."

"No reason the good doc needs to know, is there now?" I shot back.

"Is 'rooting around' even legal?"

I ignored him and wandered into Greta's bathroom like I'd done a thousand or more times before. Only this time, she shared it with a man. A man! I shook my head. Would I ever get used to my sister being a married woman? We'd lived together for a long, long time ...

The cabinet was rather sparse, but this was to be expected with the happy couple away on their honeymoon. I slid a few bottles over and turned some around, but nothing. Not one prescription med in the bunch. It was like he locked up his meds the way a sheriff locked up his guns. Didn't even look like a doctor lived here!

I returned to Brax with a bag of ice and a bottle of ibuprofen. "Sorry. This is the only pain relief I could find. Such a disappointment. All the more reason to get you to the hospital, or urgent care at least."

"Thanks." Brax took the bottle from me and the ice and leaned it against his ankle. "Now my brother can keep his license."

Whatever.

He started to get up, looking mighty awkward, but I stopped him. "Whoa. Can I get something for you?"

Brax looked at the bottle. "Could use some water."

"Sit down. I'll get it."

"If you don't mind, ma'am, I think I'll sit in front of the TV for a while."

"I appreciate the politeness, but ma'am? Really?"

He offered me a crooked grin, though marked by pain lines. "Here." I offered him my arm, and surprising me, he took it. "Lean on me."

I helped him get comfortable on the overstuffed couch in the family room, then padded into the kitchen. My thoughts washed over this scenario as I filled a glass with water. Brax was still here as a result of my actions. At least I could help him with the basics—food, driving, laundry—until his ankle healed and he could resume doing whatever it was that he did.

I delivered the water and found him with his leg propped on the coffee table. I'd never really fantasized about my future, only my next book (which had been carelessly absent lately). But for a brief, ridiculous second, this moment felt awfully domestic. Of course, I could be the housekeeper in this scenario rather than someone with a ring on her finger ...

"Sit with me?" I nearly looked over my shoulder to see who Brax was talking to until he caught eyes with me and patted the couch next to him. "Take a load off."

Hmm. Definitely the housekeeper.

He fiddled with the remote, cycling through channel after channel, finally settling on reruns of *The Twilight Zone*, which made a ton of sense right now. After less than a minute of watching, he switched again, this time to an old musical, *Singing in the Rain*. Breaking out into song and dance was out of the question, obviously.

After a few seconds, he sighed, clicked the TV off, and dropped the remote onto the couch. Turning to me, he said, "You've done enough penance."

"Excuse me?"

"You drove me home last night, tucked me into bed—"

"I did *not* tuck you into bed!"

"Figuratively speaking, Clara. Now you show up here to

check on me, bring me meds and water. I appreciate it, kiddo, but it's not necessary."

Kiddo? I stood up.

"You don't have to go."

"Actually, I do."

"You're angry."

"Um, no. I'm ready for my coffee. Since you don't need me, I'll—"

The house phone split the tension in the room. Brax cast a scowl at it. "Zac says he keeps it for emergencies."

"Then you'd better answer it."

He raised his brows at my tone, but I didn't care. He was being snippy with me, and frankly, a little condescending. He could answer his own phone!

He picked up the receiver. "Hey."

Look at him, answering that phone with a sexy *hey*, that, let's be real, sounded more like a growl. Like that's the most normal way to greet a caller.

Brax avoided my eyes. "Yes, of course, Helen. I will handle it. No, no. My ankle is doing perfectly well right now." He listened for a few seconds more after that lie, nodding, and trying several times to end the conversation. It was mean, but I kind of enjoyed watching him struggle.

He hung up and attempted to stand, which I ignored until a clearly honest wince crossed his features. Was that sweat on his brow too? Fine. I put out my hand like a stop sign. "Wait. What does she need?"

"My car's blocking the path and she can't get Gus's wheelchair through."

Oops. I really should have thought of that last night. Sigh. He must have noticed my expression because Brax said, "Apparently, your landlord carried Gus in last night and then delivered the wheelchair to them."

"He did? Aw, Carter's so sweet."

Brax ran his hand through his hair, a sly smile dangling from his mouth, but said nothing.

"Don't you think so, Brax?"

"He's alright."

"Give me your keys and I'll move your Jeep."

Brax eyed me. He obviously wanted to tell me to get lost, but he also knew that putting more weight on that ankle was a very bad idea. He grabbed them from a side table where they sat next to his wallet, and handed them over.

As I backed Brax's car out and repositioned it in the driveway, it occurred to me that I had driven more in the past twenty-four hours than I had in the same number of months. It wasn't that I was afraid of driving—okay, a little—but the truth was, I really hadn't needed to go anywhere all that much. Especially after Grandma Violet had passed on, and even before that, I'd often hired car ride services to drive me.

As I exited the Jeep, something in the back caught my eye. A ... guitar? I pressed my face against the window. Well, would you look at that ... Quickly, I unlocked the tailgate, opened her up, and tugged the guitar from its case.

I had intended to return Brax's keys with a haughty sigh, a pointed acknowledgment of his earlier dismissal of me. The truth was, the man had met a different me, a writer so desperate to uncover her next story that she was willing to step out of her skin to make it appear. I exhaled. Poor guy probably didn't know what to think of all my questioning yesterday, well, until he figured out my motives on his own. Drat.

My mouth twisted at the sight of his battered guitar, cold

to the touch after a night of sleeping it off in the Jeep. The thing looked like it had a million stories of its own to tell, which meant that Brax probably did too. The guilt over his predicament came over me again. By the look of that ankle, he was grounded for the next few days, at least.

I glanced at my rental apartment next door. Still hadn't had any caffeine today. Or a shower. Brax probably had neither of those things either. I gripped the guitar and hurried back up the steps, guilt—and curiosity—overtaking my usually unshakable need for a morning cup of coffee.

CHAPTER FOUR

Brax

I refused to make eye contact with her. It wasn't necessary. The plan was simple. I would carefully skirt her questions, she'd get annoyed with me—I had already proven how easily she did that—and Clara would be on her way without any more false notions.

Every time she watched me with those large, glittering eyes, I found myself caving, wanting to know that much more about her. She had all but admitted that she'd been grooming me for a character in her next book—crazy talk, that was. So maybe I was off, that what I was conjuring in my head was the stuff of fairy tales.

Still, something didn't sit right in my gut. I'd seen a similar look in a woman's eyes before, the way she watched me for longer than a few beats, the way her gaze sometimes slipped downward to my mouth. Didn't matter how much I wanted to return Clara's gaze, or how many times I'd thought of brushing the curls from her cheeks, or of allowing my hand to touch hers. I would not allow them to grab a foothold.

I stifled a sigh. If it were not for this bum ankle of mine, I wouldn't even be here to have this mental conversation with myself.

"You're not going to show me how you play?" Clara stood in front of me, one graceful hand on her hip and the other wrapped around the neck of my guitar. I absolutely did not notice how her soft-looking sweats appeared to hug her curves.

I reached for the guitar. "Thanks for bringing that in. You didn't have to."

"It could've been stolen last night."

My stomach tightened at that thought. "Then I owe you."

This seemed to satisfy her, at least momentarily, because she smiled. "Great. Play something for me?"

"Maybe some other time."

She smiled. "How about now?"

"Weren't you about to go make yourself some coffee?"

She gave up. "Greta has amazing coffee in the kitchen. Want some? I'm going to make myself a cup—maybe a whole pot." She laughed, then waved a hand at me before walking down the hall. "What am I thinking? Of course, you want coffee."

I swallowed. Getting her to leave was going to be harder than I thought, at least without appearing rude. So was ignoring how my heart raced watching her saunter into that kitchen.

With Clara out of sight, I hauled in a rough breath and huffed it out again, hoping to clear my head. I should be on the road, heading for Texas. Instead, I'm trapped by a body that betrays me at the most inopportune times, like when a gorgeous woman has me captured in her crosshairs.

Well. My brother hadn't been able to resist a Barnes woman, but I wasn't Zac. He'd always been the serious one, the one that weighed and measured his every decision, so I had to believe that he had not made his commitment to Greta lightly.

But neither had I with Kate. And look where that got me.

When Clara appeared with two mugs of coffee in her hands and an impish expression on her face, I told my guard to stay put. I would not be letting this friendship with my sister-in-law's sister be anything more than family formalities. And I certainly wouldn't be playing a concert for her in the living room, no matter how hard or often she batted those eyelashes-for-days.

Clara settled into the loveseat, folding her legs under her. Sport trotted into the room and curled up at the base of her chair. My heart plummeted ten floors. She probably wrote cozy scenes like this in her books, which made me wonder if she had already written my lines and planned how it would end.

After a few sips, she said, "What is it you really do for a living, Brax?"

"You mean other than posing as villains?"

Clara stared at me wide-eyed over the top of her coffee mug. "You pose?"

She got me. My face split into a grin and I shook my head. "You win. I once owned a company that repaired machines, like cash registers, copiers, etcetera." I snagged her eyes with mine. "Real superhero stuff, right?"

"To those with a broken cash register, I bet you were."

I broke eye contact. That was about as deep as I was willing to go.

A few seconds passed, when she asked, "Why don't you want to play your guitar? Is it a new thing?"

I savored the coffee. Would it be that terrible to lie and say yes? "You could say that." Lying came easier than I thought.

She nodded. "I can respect that. I don't show anybody what I'm working on until it's finished, so I guess that's kind of the same thing."

"Hmm. Yes."

She sipped her coffee awhile longer, her gaze so intense it burned. My jaw clicked. My ankle throbbed. Suddenly, Clara crossed the room and scooted herself next to me on the couch, her eyes never wavering from my face.

"Can I tell you a secret?" she said.

Saying no would prolong things, so I said, "Of course."

She set her mug down on the end table and gave me a solemn look, which, basically, was eyes so large and expressive I could fall right into them if I didn't steel myself. But I was being very, very careful ...

She bit her bottom lip. "Have you ever kept a secret from Zac?"

I frowned. Was this a trick question?

She continued. "I haven't even told Greta what I'm about to tell you, and I feel so guilty about it."

My eyes tracked the dip in her brow, the conflict in her eyes. "May I ask why you haven't told her?"

"I'm not really sure." She needled that lip again, then yanked off the beanie and brushed her hair out with her fingers. A curl drifted over one eye. "For one thing, she's been so busy planning her wedding and new life."

"And you think she wouldn't have time for you."

She scowled. "You're making me sound like a child. I just didn't want to bother her. Maybe I should have told her, but —" She reached for her coffee, took a long, slow sip, and placed the mug back on the end table—"I also didn't want to hurt her."

The part of me that wanted to bolt the minute Clara had charged in here this morning with her tumble of curls and concern for my injury became intrigued. What could she tell me that she wouldn't tell her sister?

"I'm just gonna spit it out. I think I've discovered that I have a brother."

I shifted, still trying to take in what she was confessing. "And you don't think Greta would want to know she has a brother too?"

She shook her head. "If it's true, then he's only *my* brother because Greta and I have different fathers. I only found out about that last year." She paused. "Greta does know about that, in case you're wondering."

I stared at her for a good minute. She was being straight with me, and I wasn't used to that. Kate had never told me her secrets, not until it was too late for us ... how she'd felt abandoned when she was a kid, how my pursuit of a different life brought all that up again. It's why she could never accept me again after what happened ...

Clara breathed a heavy sigh and put on a brave smile. "Anyway, it felt good to say that out loud. Almost felt like this news had been strangling me. Now I can breathe again."

"What are you going to do about it?"

She turned up a palm, briefly, as if considering my question, then looked straight at me. "I'm not really sure. Before our grandmother died, when she had moments of lucidity, she said my father was dead."

"And you're sure that's the truth?"

"Well, she wouldn't lie to me. At least, not once I knew about him."

I must have confused her with my silence, because she added, "My sister figured it out last year and broke the news to me. She only had his first name, but our grandmother filled me in with what she could, which wasn't much."

The earnestness in her expression made me feel like a jerk. When Clara showed up this morning, ostensibly to check on me, I'd expected either more of the same intrusive questions from yesterday, or a repeat of her testiness from last night. Maybe both. I had *not* expected her to drop a major revelation over coffee, and the part of me wanted to keep her and her secret at arm's length made me officially look like an ogre. I felt like one too.

Finally, I said, "Now that the wedding of the year has passed, I suppose you have some decisions to make."

"I suppose I do, only, I'm not all that sure of where to start. According to the family tree I found online, we share such a high percentage of DNA that there's little doubt we're brother and sister, well, half-sister. But first I have to find him."

"Shouldn't be too hard, right?"

She shrugged. "I don't do Facebook, but I made a fake one to try to find him. I Googled once, too, but beyond that, I've done nothing else. To be honest, I spend so much time writing all day that I hate being online once I'm done, and that has made me rather shaky at it."

"It could be overwhelming. Not a big fan either."

"Yeah. Or maybe ..." She shook her head and reached for

her mug again, taking another sip. The only other sound in the room was the rise and fall of her sigh. "Maybe I just don't really want to know. How's that for armchair psychology?"

"Sounds plausible." I let a beat of silence pass. "I'd help," I said, "but I'm not sure how I could."

"I wouldn't ask that of you." She shook her head, then looked at me dead on. "Brax, promise me you won't mention this to Zac or Greta. I'll tell them after they're settled."

"Of course. I'll keep it to myself."

"You'll probably be long gone by then anyway."

"Right." I glanced at my ankle, knowing I could leave, but probably shouldn't. Not yet. Thing was as large as a boulder and would only get worse if I put my weight on it. Or drove hundreds of miles with it.

Silence, awkward and unwieldy, sat between us. I wondered if she was rethinking her decision to tell me her secret. Giving her assurance would be a good idea, but something held me back.

As if she'd had enough of the lack of conversation, Clara stood and collected our mugs. I listened to her feet traipsing down the hall toward the kitchen, followed by the unmistakable sounds of dishware being rinsed and added to the dishwasher.

"Sure you don't want me to drive you to Urgent Care?"

I jerked my head up at the sound of her voice. Her stealthy return surprised me.

"You okay?" she asked.

"Fine. Yes."

She winced, but didn't say a word.

"And you?"

"And me, what?"

"You have a pained expression on your face. Are you unwell?"

A twist of a small smile appeared on her face. "Um, no. Not *unwell*."

"Something wrong with my question?"

She smiled, but winced again as she shifted. "One of my heroes—Alistair—used to speak like that. Took me back to that story, is all."

"With a name like that, I bet he put caviar on his toast in the morning."

"He was quite regal, I'll have you know. Sophisticated ... noble—"

"And stuffy?"

She laughed. "All right, enough with you. If you're really okay, Sport and I will go now."

Sport's ears perked at the sound of his name. Without fuss, she trotted over to Clara's side, but when Clara bent to pick her up, she winced again.

"It's your back, isn't it?" I said.

She sighed like she'd been outed. "I think it's all the sitting I do. I'm really forcing myself to walk more while on this trip, to get the kinks out. Well, Sport is forcing me anyway."

I nodded, uneasiness further creeping into my gut. Tension could make those back issues worse and I knew it. Harboring secrets had a way of affecting more than the mind.

Part of me wanted to solve her problem, to sit in front of the computer and help her find her brother, confident that it would not be an impossible task. Then maybe she'd be freed from the tension that was surely twisting up her insides.

The other part of me wanted to keep my distance from

anything that would tether me here to family, to memories. And admittedly, to Clara.

"By the way," she said, "I promised Greta I'd water the planters in back while they're gone. Just wanted to give you a heads up so you didn't think I was a prowler or anything."

"Yes, we can't have your landlord bailing you out again."

She paused. "You heard about that, did you?"

"Maybe."

She rolled her eyes and stopped with her hand on the door. I denied the shaft of morning light that brought out the fiery highlights in her mess of curls. Nope. Wouldn't notice those at all. "If you need me," she said, totally ignoring my teasing grin, "I'll be doing some research on the internet. And maybe calling a glass guy. So just text if you need anything. Bye now, Brax."

After she'd gone, I stared at the back of the door, the hollowness of the room taunting me.

Clara

I BLURTED out my secret to Brax before thinking about it, giving me more to feel guilty about. He was a partner to my crime now, well, my crime of omission. Why didn't I just tell Greta when I had the chance? It's not like she would have kept me from pursuing a relationship with a blood relative now that I know, or believe, that one existed.

I mean, I don't think she'd do that.

Truth is, I'd been holding my secret in so long that it was beginning to make me feel really uncomfortable, like an itch scratched so often that it looked more like an ugly red rash. I should have felt better, but now all I felt was exposure—like I had just shared a major plot point before my next book was finished.

I sighed and dropped my chin to my chest. I really needed to stop being so hard on myself. Brax will be out of here soon anyway. And wasn't that the point? To spill my heart to someone who, as family, might actually care, but would also keep it to himself?

I settled into the couch in my place, wishing for my comfy old recliner chair at home, but knowing this would have to do. With my laptop open, I connected to the Wi-Fi and opened up my notes to the scant information I had been able to gather from the family tree on the DNA website:

Dalton Smith. Died eighteen years ago. One son named Justin, older than me by nearly ten years.

No mention of any other children (including me).

I stabbed my bottom lip with my teeth. No indication where they lived, either, though I assumed somewhere in Indiana. I couldn't even find Dalton's obituary. Basically, I'd hit a wall.

Not sure which was more disturbing, the fact that I had no idea where to turn next in my search or the fact that my real last name was even more boring than the one on my driver's license.

I poked around the internet for a while, surprised when an hour had passed and I hadn't noticed. This is why I rarely used the features of my smart phone, and also why I discon-nected my computer from Wi-Fi when I was writing. Too easy to waste time!

On the other hand, while idly scrolling around I'd landed on a blog that talked about the importance of not sitting all day (tell me something I don't already know ...) It also suggested that one way to relieve stress would be to lay on the floor with my legs on the wall.

Maybe the interwebs weren't so bad after all ...

I unfolded my legs from their pretzel pose, trying not to let the squeak in my joints set off warning horns in my mind. Stiff joints at thirty was totally normal (Right?). As if to test my flexibility, Sport showed up at my feet, jostling for me to pet her.

"Hang on a sec, cute one." After a few quick stretches, I was on the floor, inching my feet up until my thighs were flush with the wall. Sport sniffed around my face and promptly sneezed her doggy breath right on me. Gross. Once she realized my attention was far from her, she trotted to the back corner of the room, curled up, and fell asleep.

Oh, to be a dog.

I laid there awhile, my mind a whir, until I realized that what I really needed to do was relax. Breathe in slowly. Breathe out the same. I did this over and over again, my toes peeking down on me to make sure I was paying attention. And I was. The posture surprised me with its ability to remove some of the anxiety that had been floating beneath the surface. Until I sprang my secret on Brax, I don't think I even realized how close to the edge I'd been flying.

I'd never had writer's block before, and until now, didn't think it existed. I had figured out the beats of market romances by instinct. Pretty easy to do after reading literally hundreds of grocery store novels as a teen and well into my twenties. Mom used to say that reading was the best education a girl could have. I'm not sure if she meant this kind of reading exactly, but it worked. I had learned to write novels by reading them. And until now, that knowledge had served me well.

Sport appeared, her stinky breath in my face again, but this time, she barked. Okay, fine. I slid my legs off the wall to the side, then carefully got up, still marveling at how much more relaxed I felt. By now, Sport was doing the potty dance, her nails clacking across the floors in every woman's Morse code.

Quickly, I slipped my feet into flip-flops and let her outside. She bounded down the stairs and went right to the planter in front of Mermaid Manor. Thankfully, Carter wasn't around to witness that. I made a mental note to steer Sport to a light pole next time.

The fog had gone, and in its place, sunshine blanketed the beach. Cars and vans were wedged into every available spot, and more umbrellas than I could count dotted the sand —a far cry from the sleepy, hazy morning I'd encountered yesterday.

I leashed her up and Sport led me south toward the harbor mouth. We wandered past a wooden house named Windy Gables that looked like it had been built for dolls, and a couple of Spanish-style cottages right on the sand. One of them bore the name Casa Valentino. I laughed out loud. Greta was sure our great-grandmother, who lived here many years ago, had once had a torrid affair with the famous actor.

A bead of sweat ran down my neck, reminding me I hadn't worn sunscreen. Then again, my hair hid so much of me that the sun really didn't have a chance now, did it? We reached the end of the peninsula, where two beaches had been split in two by a wide channel that allowed boats to motor or sail out to sea and right back in again.

Greta had told me some of the stories she learned about

hooch runners and barrels of rum found buried in sand dunes in the part of the beach known as Hollywood by the Sea. Actually, they were Carter's stories, and as he told it, smugglers hid in sand dunes high as those in the Sahara Desert, long before the harbor, and other development, flattened them.

The phone in my pocket rang, and I got a little giddy when I saw the number on the screen. "What're you doing calling me on your honeymoon? Miss me already?"

"I'm checking on my favorite sister."

"You mean your only sister." That we knew of anyway ...

"How are you, Clara?" Greta said. "Are you getting along okay?"

"Are you asking if Sport is starving and if your flowers are dead?"

"Clara!"

"What?!"

My sister sighed. "Be serious for one minute."

"Proceed."

"I really am just checking in on you. We hardly had a chance to talk at the reception and then you so heroically drove Brax home." She paused. "Has he mended up and moved on?"

"Actually, he's still here. I checked in on him yesterday and his ankle looked awful. He didn't want to see a doctor about it, and I wasn't about to make a grown man do anything he doesn't want to do."

"Good move."

"Is your tropical honeymoon everything you dreamed it would be?"

Greta sighed one of those bubbly sighs that I've written about but never actually felt. I wondered if it was as nauseating on the page as it was over the phone ... "It's gorgeous here. My photos don't do it justice. The water is so clear and the sky looks like a painting."

"That's nice. Can you grab me some brochures? Maybe I'll send my next couple there at the end of the book."

Greta laughed in that light way of hers. "So the writing is going well?"

Sport was sniffing around a sculpture of a sea lion looking toward the water. I pulled on her leash and made her come with me to a bench. She jumped onto my lap and snuggled against my belly. "It's, uh, going fine." Why tell her how lost I am now? I'll get past this. I'm sure I will.

"That bad, huh?"

"Stop. You're not supposed to be thinking about your little sis right now when you've got that hunk of manhood with you on a stunning beach."

"I'm sure it's going to get better, hon. A change of pace should be good for your writing, right? Maybe visit that little church I told you about. Find some real stories to write about."

"Real stories? Oh, because my stories are what? Unrealistic?" I didn't mention the obvious, that I didn't have a man (like her).

"No, that's not what I meant!"

"Change of pace. Go to church. Talk to people. Check. Anything else?"

"Why are you so angry all of a sudden?"

"I'm not. I'm just"—I scanned the deep blue sea in front of me, sailboats and kayaks bobbing along in sync, yet felt a scowl coming on—"I don't know. It's pretty here. It's different, too. But I'm uninspired so far."

"Well, then, maybe you need this vacation, Clara. I-I

hope you can allow yourself some time to really relax. Not just talk about it." I could hear the tentative smile in her voice, like we were back on solid ground. "As long as you don't forget to water my flowers or feed Sport, that is."

"Can I ask you something?" I didn't wait. "What's Brax's story? He has a guitar, but won't play it for me. Won't tell me anything personal and seems to want to get out of here as soon as possible."

Greta sighed. "I'm not too sure, honey. Zac once told me his brother was a terrific singer and played the guitar well, but then suddenly stopped. He won't talk about it with Zac."

Aha. So he's not new to playing the guitar!

"Anyway," she said, "I think the two have some unfinished business, and all I can do at this point is pray about it and—"

"Knock their heads together?"

"Sure. That sounds like it would work well."

"Well, as long as you have a plan."

I heard a husky voice in the background, followed by some jostling of the phone. "Clara?" Greta said. "I have to run now. We'll see you in a few weeks, but please, darling, if anything comes up—"

"Call you and interrupt your bliss? No, thank you."

Greta laughed lightly, as if I hadn't really meant that. "I love you. Bye."

The road back to my rental took us past boat slips, a museum, cyclists dodging traffic, and a cute shell shop. I peeked in the window, spotting all kinds of eclectic items along with kitschy shell decor, and promised myself I'd pop in again when I wasn't so tired.

For some reason, the twinging I'd been feeling for days had started up again. "Slow down, doggy," I called out to the exceptionally peppy animal that dragged me down the street.

"Fancy meeting you here." Carter pulled up in his shiny black Mercedes, his blond hair flopped over one eye, a Realtor-bright smile on his mug.

"Oh, thank goodness," I said. "Give me a ride?"

His smile dropped. "You want to bring that mutt into my car?"

"Seriously, Carter, it's like five blocks."

He continued with that frown.

"Fine. I'll hold him out the window."

Carter appeared to be thinking about this. "Are you strong enough?"

"Oh, for goodness sake! I'm not holding Sport out the window. Forget it already." My version of the evil eye was getting me nowhere.

"Hold up. Wait." He exited the car, popped open the trunk, and retrieved a beach towel. "Wrap him—"

"Her. She's a she."

"Okay, wrap *her* in this. I can throw it out later." I burst out laughing while swaddling Sport in the beach towel. Brax hadn't blinked when Sport jostled her way into his Jeep.

I kept Sport on my lap while Carter drove us home. The house, with its weathered siding and tattered flag out front, didn't look like its owner was all that concerned with appearances. Unlike this car.

Carter turned off the engine. "Want to sit on the deck with some crudités and wine later, like I used to do with your sister?"

"Um, sure. Except the wine. Will put me to sleep and I really need to write tonight." Or try to, at least. "I'll meet you up there with sparkling water."

"Right-o. See you in a few."

Sport took the stairs two at a time, quite a feat considering how small her legs were. "I'm impressed," I told her.

She ignored me, and for a few seconds I wondered if she was hurt over not being welcomed in Carter's car. Animals sensed things, right? But when she went right for her water bowl and began to slobber down gulps of it, I realized she'd already forgiven Carter. And hopefully me too for not thinking to bring her a bottle of water to slurp on in the first place.

Twenty minutes later, Carter and I were on the deck, the rickety table between us. It was unspoken that we would not be mentioning anytime soon how I'd used it for a ladder the other day. For his part, Carter appeared to have forgotten about the, uh, incident, though the board hadn't been replaced with glass yet.

"Don't forget—I'm paying to replace the window. Sure you don't want me to call someone?"

He indicated no with a shake of his head. "A handyman owes me some favors, and he's working me in. I recommend him to new home buyers."

I cringed, hated being the reason he'd have to use up one of his credits.

"Enough about that. Your sister and I used to sit out here for wine and conversation," he told me.

"I'm aware."

"She was quite into me until Zac started getting moony over her."

I gasped and some of the bubbles from my sparkling water went up my nose, making me cough and sneeze in rapid succession. So embarrassing.

But Carter just smiled and sipped his drink. "Your sister

did the same thing, as I recall."

"I hate to break it to you, but Greta was never into you."

"Perhaps you're right, but I could have had a shot." He lowered his voice. "When he invited her on his yacht, I knew I was sunk. I apologize for the pun."

"Oh you do not." I laughed. "And an electric boat is not a yacht."

"Whatever."

"You're messing with me, right?"

He smiled those picket-fence teeth at me. "Maybe."

"I guess now would be a good time to tell you how worried I was about Greta staying here with you. I mean, not *with* you, but, you know, in the same house. Sort of." I cleared my throat. "I wanted to make up a safe word if she ever felt scared."

"Do I really look all that dangerous to you, Clara?" He wiggled his eyes at me. And honestly, what was I to make of that? Hopefully, he's not into me, although I did find him kind of ... interesting.

I forced myself to look at him the way I had since day one, as my landlord. Nothing else. "You do not," I said, not making eye contact. I wasn't into him, right? Just because I wrote romance novels didn't mean I had actually been in love myself. I'd never said that out loud or even allowed myself to think much about it. Instead, I'd read everything I ever could. And I'd watched my sister's dating escapades. A couple of times her relationship ended before I had finished the book. Shew. Those were difficult to finish.

Writers were often told to write what they know, but I used my imagination to fill in everything that I had never actually felt before. And I'd managed a decent living (most of the time). Pretty proud of myself for that.

"Then allow me to regale you with some of the same stories that I told Greta almost one year ago today ..."

Carter had this way about him that made every story seem richer than reality. For the next hour or so, I listened to him tell stories that I'd already heard from Greta, but the smugglers and the actors and the tourists of yesterday, as told by my landlord, appeared in my mind in vivid color this time.

He told stories the way I wished I could right now, and I was warming to his presence across from me.

Carter frowned. "What's he still doing here?"

I followed Carter's gaze to the house next door, where Brax was leaning on the railing outside of Greta and Zac's front door.

I stood to get a better view and called out to him. "You shouldn't be on your feet, Brax."

He didn't move. From across the divide, I could see the tickle of a grin on his face, a haughty one that said, *What're you gonna do about it?*

"I mean, unless you want to be stuck here in this one-horse beach town longer ..." Even as I said it, I wondered if psychology worked on guys the way it worked on children. Apparently so because he pushed away from the rail and offered me a salute before heading back inside.

Why did that make me feel weird? I muttered something about being over to help him soon.

When I looked up, Carter was watching me.

"What?" I said.

"I didn't peg you as the motherly type."

"I'm hurt."

His voice made a scraping sound, like he didn't believe me. He was right—I wasn't hurt. At all. I tipped my head to the side, explaining myself. "I feel guilty for making him dance the other night when he clearly didn't want to."

Carter's eyes met mine. "He wanted to."

"No, no. He didn't."

"He knows how you feel about all that frivolity and he's milking it. It's impressive, really."

"Oh please. If I hadn't talked him into it, the man would be on his way to Texas to do whatever it is he had planned."

"Trust me. When a beautiful woman encourages a man to dance with her, he's not upset about it. That guy was standing taller than he had all night."

I sat there, mouth open.

"Cost me a pretty penny to have Helen and Gus trip him up, though."

Ha! "You're ridiculous." I laughed.

Carter smiled that quirky smile of his and offered me a salute of his own, this one a glass of wine that had just been refilled.

We sat out in the waning afternoon, noshing on gluten-free crackers and chunks of cheese that fattened them up a bit, while Carter continued with his stories of Hollywood by the Sea as if I were a client looking to settle down in this quaint beach town. I didn't know if the tales were tall, such as Clark Gable once owning a house here and Charlie Chaplin making this area one of his go-tos for vacation, but like my sister before me, I was enthralled and wanted to know more.

When Carter had gone, I wiped down the bistro table so as not to leave behind goodies for the seagulls. Enchanted as Carter's take on everything around here was, I found my gaze drifting to the house next door, where a man with a swollen ankle might need some help.

CHAPTER FIVE

CLARA

I MANAGED to avoid going over to check on Brax last night. For one thing, I still wasn't sure how bright it was of me to share my secret with him. For another, see point number one.

Today, though, guilt weighed on my shoulders like a mink coat from the Roaring Twenties. I had to check in, had to keep making amends for the damage I caused him. Maybe even offer to drive him to Urgent Care to get that grapefruit-sized ankle looked at finally.

Gus greeted me at the bottom of the stairs. He was sitting in his wheelchair and watching the scant traffic go by.

"'Morning, Clara."

"Good morning to you, Gus. Where's your beautiful wife today?"

"Can't say that I know." He checked his wristwatch.

"The woman insisted on going to the drugstore before I could even pull my pants on. She's a stubborn one."

How sweet. Gus reminded me of a little boy out here, waiting for the neighbor girl to show up and make his day. I glanced out to the empty road. "Did she have to drive very far?"

He lifted his chin, his eyes squinting at me in the morning light. "She gave up driving a long time ago. Had trouble seein' over the top of the steering wheel. No ma'am. She took an Uber ride."

Ah. I should have guessed, given the fact that I, too, had often called various companies back home for a ride. I was just about to offer to walk down the street to see if I could spot Helen, when a small black car turned in to the driveway.

Helen emerged slowly from the passenger seat, hanging onto the door like it was a four-pronged cane. I rushed forward. "Let me hold that for you."

She looked up, like I was a giant towering over her. "Thanks, dearie. But you go on now and get my bags from the back. I can take it from here."

Gus cut in. "You almost gave this old man a heart attack."

I took two drugstore bags from the driver, offered him a thankful smile, and followed behind Helen who wobbled up the drive. "Hold your horses," she was calling out to Gus. "You did not almost have a heart attack."

"Well, it could have been a minor one!" He looked at me. "Those can be dangerous, too, you know."

I smiled. "Let me get the door for you two. I'll bring in your purchases."

Once inside, I deposited the bags on the kitchen counter.

Helen, who wasn't all that strong on her own, was already helping Gus to the couch like she had done it a hundred times before. I scraped my bottom lip with my teeth. Should I help out here? Or let them be?

"Can I move the wheelchair out of your way?" I asked.

"Thank you, Clara, but that thing is always in our way."

"Hey!" Gus said. "Be nice to my wheels."

Helen slapped him on the shoulder. "You haven't had nice wheels since that old Mustang you used to speed around in!"

Gus's eyes lit. "Those were the days, weren't they?"

An idea came over me, something I would never have asked in the past. Could I now? I slid a glance at Helen. Her lips were pursed, her eyes tiny. "Cat got your tongue, Clara?"

I bit my lip harder. "I ... well, I was just wondering if you, uh, might be willing to loan me your wheelchair for an hour, Gus?"

Gus's eyes widened. "You gonna pop some wheelies?"

Helen scoffed and gave him another slap. "Of course not! I bet she's going to give that handsome brother of Zac's a ride around the block in it."

I smiled at Helen then cast a look at Gus. "Would you mind? I thought it might be nice for him."

"What did I always tell you, Helen?" Gus said. "My ride is a chick-magnet all right!"

Helen clucked and I shook my head, laughing. "It's nothing like that, Gus, I assure you." I reached for the handles and wheeled the chair around. "I promise to get it back to you soon."

"Don't you worry, Clara. I promise, it won't turn into a pumpkin on you!" He was chortling and slapping his knee as I shut the door behind myself. I peered up the stairway to where Brax was staying and my heart sank. *Forgot all about how to get him down here.*

Maybe this wasn't such a good idea ... I peered upstairs again. Wait ... was that a face in the window? A tiny smile made its way to my mouth. The face disappeared, but no doubt about it—Brax had been spying.

I laughed a little, jogged up the stairs, and gave the front door a light knock. "Brax? I know you're in there."

He opened the door with a start. "I'm not hiding."

I slid a glance at the window then back to him, barely able to conceal my smile. "Okay."

"What can I do for you?"

I tilted my head, trying not to fixate on the charcoal-colored V-neck tee he wore and the way it artfully clung to his biceps. "Actually," I said, "there's something I want to do for you."

He frowned, though I could tell his eyes weren't having any of it. The man was curious.

"The thing is," I said, "you're gonna have to make it down those stairs so I can give you your surprise."

Indecision passed across his features. Was he not sure he could make it? Or not sure he wanted to have anything to do with me?

When he didn't say anything, I added, "I'll help you."

He slanted a look at me. "I can make it."

"Perfect."

Brax hobbled down the stairs, his muscled arms flexing as he gripped the bannister. Again, I second-guessed myself. Could I really push all that brawn around in Gus's wheelchair?

"So," he said, breaking into my thoughts, "you said something about a surprise?" His tone teased, like maybe I had made it up.

"Yes. I thought I could, well, that we could—"

"She wants to give you a tour of Hollywood by the Sea!" Gus pressed his face against the screen of an open window. "Go on now and sit in my chair, Brax."

Brax's mouth opened and froze there.

I grinned. "I promise I'll drive safely."

He raised his brows, his expression doubtful.

"Come on. Let me do this."

He crossed his arms and wagged his head. "I can't. You don't owe me anything, Clara."

Helen's voice burst through the window opening. "Oh go on, you big lug! The Holt men have the thickest heads, don't they, Gus?"

"That they do, my dear. That they do."

I laughed, feeling more confident now, and smacked the seat back a couple of times. "Time's a wastin'."

He quirked a grin that pulled up the corner of his mouth. Wavy lines crisscrossed his forehead and he heaved a heavy sigh, but he sat down anyway.

"Put your feet up on the footrests," Gus instructed.

Helen called out, "Let the boy alone. He knows how to sit in a wheelchair!"

I grabbed the handles and turned the chair to the south, trying not to grunt. My lack of upper body work in the fictional gym I belonged to was already showing.

"Clara," Gus said, "make sure to take him by Casa Valentino at the end of the peninsula—"

"And go see Errol Flynn's famous pagoda house with the sunken bar," Helen hollered. "He was a romantic guy!"

Gus cut in. "Can't miss it. It'll be on your way back if

you go around toward the harbor side. Rumor has it the place was a brothel in the late twenties."

Helen gasped. "She doesn't want to hear about that!"

I laughed lightly, gave them a wave, and pushed the chair down the street since no sidewalks existed there.

Brax turned a look over his shoulder. "Just stay away long enough to make Helen and Gus think we covered the loop."

"Not a chance. This is my workout today."

"You work out every day, then?"

"Yes ... starting with today."

He chuckled and dropped his face into his palm.

"Seriously, Brax," I said, "I feel guilty you're stuck here, so I thought I'd help you get some fresh air without hurting your ankle further."

He puffed up his cheeks, resigned, and shoved out a sigh. "Well, then I guess I should say thank you."

I peeked at him. "In other words, you're stuck."

He shrugged, offering me a hint of a smile.

The music of the waves landing on the shore served as the backdrop to an otherwise quiet walk. Ocean views were blocked by tall, narrow houses, but every once in a while, we'd reach a small cottage with low doorways, doll-like dormers, and an ample view of sky and water over the roof. In those moments, I was transported to the past, when my great-gran walked here in this coastal community. I knew little about her, but the more I traipsed along this road, the more I understood why my sister had been so drawn to this area.

Brax shifted, and I bit back a smile. Kind of railroaded him into this chair, but too bad. No one knew more than me what it was like to stay inside all day. I didn't want to be responsible for him not getting fresh air and a tour before he left again.

I broke the silence. "Brax, can I ask why you won't go to the doctor?"

He twisted a look up at me. "Because this has happened before and I know the drill."

"Huh."

"You don't have to believe me."

What an odd thing to say. I stepped up the pace. "It's not that I don't believe you. What happened?"

He flicked a look out to sea. "I slid into home when I was a kid right as the infielder's throw missed the plate. Hit me square on the ankle."

"Ouch. Were you out?"

"Nope."

"Okay, now that's a decent story."

His laugh held an incredulous tinge. "What does that mean?"

"It means your injury didn't happen by you doing something dumb, like falling off a curb or tripping over a hairdryer." Not that I knew what that was like ...

"Yeah, because I store my hairdryer on the floor."

"All right. Fine." I tsked. "Since you've been through this before, what's the prognosis?"

"You mean, when will I be out of your hair ... ?"

"Ha ha."

"I'll be grounded for a while. Couple of weeks, maybe. Then it'll snap back to its old self and I'll be on my way."

"So you'll be staying until the lovebirds return."

He didn't answer right away. Finally, "Zac's bookcase is unfinished. Might paint it for him, otherwise it'll probably be like that until their first child goes to college."

I laughed. "Sounds like you know your brother the way I know my sister."

He nodded but didn't add anything. I continued to push him along the street, both of us swiveling our gazes at the sights. At the end of the peninsula, the sandy beach disappeared from view as the harbormouth apperaed, splitting two communities.

Suddenly, I gasped.

Brax perked. "The pagoda house, I presume."

"It has to be, right?" The house was much larger than I had predicted, with a circular roof, two chimneys, and a large balcony. It also had a scaled-down quality that made me think it truly could have been there for a hundred years. "Look at those views!"

Brax nodded, turning his chin toward the waterway. "Unobscured."

I sighed, drinking it in. The yachts and fishermen, the kayakers, and even the silvery back of a dolphin broke the water's surface in the distance. No wonder actors from Los Angeles escaped the city for this place back then.

I glanced again at Brax, watching his masterfully chiseled face look upon the water. A niggle of something I couldn't exactly discern fluttered through me. When he swiveled his gaze to me, I looked away. Seconds passed, and I began to push him back up the peninsula.

Twenty minutes later we rolled up to Gus and Helen's front door. Brax carefully stood, limped over to the staircase leading to his own place, and leaned on the railing. "Thanks for the ride, Clara." A soft grin tilted his mouth, his gaze intriguing, undefinable. I wanted to study it, to know what he was thinking ... about me. If anything. "Rest assured," he said, "your penance has now been paid."

Whatever I might have been sensing evaporated. I waited for him to make his way slowly back up the stairs and disappear inside.

Brax

THE PAIN in my ankle was the least of my problems. As I fought my way down the exterior staircase in the early morning light, I also pushed off the music in my head and the irrational and impossible thoughts I'd had all night long about a certain woman named Clara. I blamed her. If she wouldn't have shown up last night carrying a homemade dinner and wearing a smile on those curvy lips of hers, I'm sure none of these invasive thoughts would have persisted.

She hadn't planned to stay long, especially since we'd already spent a couple of hours together in the morning. "Just wanted to bring you this Cobb salad and a glass of Cab so you won't starve," she'd said.

"You don't expect me to eat all that alone, do you?" In retrospect, I could have just accepted her generosity and seen her out. That would have been the safer call.

"Well, I was planning to watch a movie tonight. Want to watch It's a Wonderful Life with me?"

"Isn't that a Christmas flick?"

"Your point?"

"You're suggesting we watch a film outside of its window."

"What window is that again?"

"The cutoff for a Christmas movie is Thanksgiving until New Year's. No exceptions."

"Pffst. The civilized don't follow rules like that." She reached for the remote control.

"Fine." I hoisted my leg to the coffee table and settled my ankle on a pillow. "I've never seen it anyway."

Clara gasped and my core muscles tightened. I was certain she'd seen a spider and I was going to have to spring into action. She turned on me. "You have never seen the greatest Christmas movie of all time? How is that possible?"

She said that like it wasn't. I crossed my arms and chuckled. "Because I'm a monster, obviously."

"Well, you, my friend, are in for a treat." She flicked a glance at my uneaten dinner. "Eat your food."

I tipped my head. "Yes, ma'am."

Whatever frost I'd sensed from her had thawed.

"Ooh, I found it. And it's the black-and-white version too. Perfect. I'm going to stay quiet because I don't want you to miss a thing."

"I take it you've seen this movie more than once."

"I can recite the lines, Brax."

I chewed my salad, thinking about that. "It'll be hard for you not to fill me in, won't it?"

"Shush. It's starting."

I smiled into my bowl and tried to eat quietly so I could focus on the movie. Easy enough, because only a few minutes in and I could tell this would be a long one. I searched it out on my phone—more than two hours to be exact. Toward the end of the movie, when all seemed lost, I glanced over at Clara, who was hugging a pillow to her chest. I'd expected to find her dozing because, after all, by her own admission, she'd seen this movie countless times.

But she was watching it, rapt, her eyes wide and awestruck. Or was I describing myself at taking her in? At some point, she'd stretched her legs out to share the coffee table with me, occasionally adjusting her position until our toes touched. She jumped away whenever that happened, probably in deference to my sore ankle. But even the briefest touch sent my head into a spin.

What happened next felt like a sneak attack. George Bailey's running around town after being given another chance. He knows he doesn't have much hope against his debts, but he hollers out Merry Christmas greetings to everyone he sees—even the vile Mr. Potter. But then ... he arrives home. He's going to be arrested, but doesn't care because he sees his kids again. And his wife. He's smiling, ready for what comes, when the unthinkable happens—the entire town comes to save him, to bring him enough money to settle his debts. Even his war hero brother shows up to offer up a toast.

It was all too much.

"Are you crying?" Clara's attention was turned on me now, that spot of skin between her eyes rumpled together like she'd never seen a guy cry before and didn't know what to do about it.

I grabbed a napkin and blew my nose. To her credit, she didn't laugh. Instead, she leaned in close and put her head on my shoulder while we watched the credits roll. Zac would have gone nuts to see us cuddling on his couch. I'd be uninvited to all future family events, for sure. Not like I planned to stick around for them anyway.

Hours later, I woke up in the middle of the night. I blinked a couple of times in the dark, trying to remember what had pulled me out of an otherwise deep sleep. My late-night snack? The movie? It hit me like a fire bolt. It wasn't the movie that had pulled me out of a deep sleep, but something else entirely—the memory of spotting Clara sitting on that deck outside with Carter.

I pressed my eyes together, willing them to take me back to whatever adventure I'd been dreaming about before coming upon that scene. My eyes failed. Truth was, Carter's ease with Clara bugged me. Not that it should have. I'd be leaving California as soon as Zac and his bride returned. She could spend time with whomever she wanted.

Zac had called to check on me, and in a moment of weakness (read: throbbing pain), I agreed to stick around here on the coast. I rubbed my ankle with my good foot. Yeah, that wasn't going to be strong enough to climb any ladders for a while. Might as well stay and figure out where I wanted to go next.

I lay there for a time, shadows like waves across the walls, until the next thing I knew, gentle light filled the room. It was early morning, and a fragment of a melody played in my mind. I couldn't shut it off if I wanted to, though I longed to stick the notes in a box and bury the key. I'd left my guitar in the back of my Jeep for the same reason that I'd made a one-eighty turn from music in the first place: so I wouldn't be tempted to play it. But I should have sold the thing when I had the chance before a new song began to form inside of me, bringing with it more heartache.

I made my way to Zac's backyard, if you could call it that. The space on the side of the house was hardly as wide as me. It led to a tiny but neat area with wild, colorful flowers, a potting bench, and a couple of worn wicker chairs with newer cushions. I took it all in, Greta's influence throughout.

You did it again, Zac. Always the boy with the golden touch. Unlike me ...

Well. I'd come out here to get the music out of my mind, to take advantage of the morning sun in privacy. Not to wield my own gardening skills through a yard full of personal touches. I spotted two beach cruisers along the wall and limped over to take a closer look. I nudged one of the pedals forward with the toes on my bad foot, biting back a wince almost simultaneously. Salt air had done some damage, but otherwise, usable.

Clara might like to take one of these out for a ride ...

I jerked a rag from the potting bench, plunked myself on the ground, and began the work of cleaning away the grime. Was this a complete waste of time? I didn't know if Clara liked to ride a bicycle. Why would I know that? Then again, she seemed to have some back issues. And as she so roughly told me the other night, she hardly drove anyway.

So ... wouldn't the option of a bike to ride be something that would interest her? I scrubbed away dirt and some rust along with it, using muscle to assuage my muddled brain and gut.

Truth was, Zac had been right. I hadn't wanted to come back here, to watch him get married and ride off into the sunset, like he pretty much always had our entire life. But I heard my mother's voice chiding me, and though I wanted to argue with her—like *I* too often had—I knew she was right.

So I came. And the memories of my own failed marriage flooded in with the first note of "The Wedding March." I'd wanted to run, but that photographer had her lens pointed right at me. Well, not me, but Zac, and I was right next to him. If she were to catch me scowling, and that expression was pressed into the endlessness of digital memories, I'd hear about it for the rest of time.

If only ... if only I had been able to escape right after the vows had been said and the minister's proclamation sealed the deal, as I had planned. I would be in Texas now, swingin' a hammer, bartending on Friday nights, and putting my boots up on a scarred-up wooden table on Sunday afternoons. The only music I'd be playing was what could be streamed out on my porch.

I sat back, vaguely admiring the polish job I'd given the rusty old beach cruiser. Yeah, it would do. The burnt orange crud was gone, giving way to the sky's hue—the same soft color it had been the day I met Clara.

CHAPTER SIX

CLARA

LAST NIGHT, I had intended to leave Brax alone with his salad and wine. But then he'd invited me to stay with a kind of half-hearted invite, and, I don't know, I guess my curiosity outweighed my ego. I suggested a movie to give us something to talk about, not make him cry. A smile found me. For a guy who wore a gruff attitude as loyally as his denim, he sure was an old softie.

I hadn't slept much, so early this morning, I bounded out of bed, realizing that insomnia could be the gateway to my next novel. An hour later I had already written six pages about a woman named Sara who attended a costume party only to be mistaken for a serving wench before realizing I'd already written a similar mistaken-identity novel two years earlier. That heroine's name was also Sarah—with an "h" on the end—but she wore a black uniform to a party only to be mistaken as the housekeeper.

So much for the power of insomnia.

I closed my writing program and brought up a search engine. For the next half hour, I found myself following all kinds of rabbit trails again. I learned nothing at all about the ancestors on my father's side, but I did discover some weird trivia, such as, that dolphins slept with one eye open, and white cotton shirts were pretty much equivalent to SPF seven. Unless wet, I supposed.

Speaking of random facts, I read on one site that motion is lotion for the joints, which reminded me that my aching back might just need some time away from the computer. I logged off, closed the lid of my laptop, and wandered outside. Sport danced at my heels, and I was beginning to wonder if my sister had done this on purpose. She never liked coming home to find me still curled up on that recliner chair. Maybe talking me into staying here to dog sit, knowing full well the number of times Sport would need a walk, was Greta's way of "encouraging" me to get outside.

Score one for Greta.

And one for me as well, because I was enjoying the doggy more than I thought I would.

Yesterday, when I went next door to water, I had not been able to find any gardening tools. So this morning I wandered down the side yard of Mermaid Manor, past an old work bench covered in silt and webs. At the back corner, I spied a narrow plastic cabinet, opened it and—bingo!— found a bucket of gardening tools and even a beat-up cushion to kneel on.

Sport must have sensed my excitement because she leaped up and smacked me on the thighs with her paws, then led the way over to Greta's backyard like it was no big deal. As I made my way across the divide of houses, my thoughts tumbled about. If I were honest, the past year had been a blur of writing, visiting my feisty grandmother, and helping Greta plan her wedding, mostly from afar. Now I missed both of the people closest to me and was fresh out of great book ideas for the first time in my life.

So not only would moving around keep me from getting stiff—something I've known intuitively but pretty much ignored my entire life—it promised to help the brain with creativity, something I could use a whole lot of right now. I glanced around. Greta's backyard was the size of a postage stamp, but it would do.

"Okay," I said. Sport's head tilted, her look expectant. I'm not sure what she was asking with that expression, but I patted her furry little head, saying, "Go on now and do some discovering, why don't you?"

The animal wandered off to sniff and investigate, while I continued to inspect the garden. I set aside the watering can, satisfied that the fog from the night before had left behind enough moisture for Greta's lavender bushes to thrive. They were natives and could probably go without water for months. But the weeds! Just like at home in Indiana, they'd sprung up almost overnight.

After a few side stretches, I knelt down and began the work of pulling the unwanted growth, only the job proved much easier than it did back home (not that I weeded the garden all that much, mind you). The sandy, wet soil let the roots go without a fuss, unlike the dry cracked dirt back home. Despite the surprising ease of the work so far, there was a lot of it. I was surprised, though I knew the past few months had kept her busy. Greta had this thing against weeds springing up, almost as if they insulted her with their presence, whereas I tended to let them sprout up until they'd married and produced a bounty of little ones.

Okay, so maybe that's why it was so much harder to weed the flower beds back home.

I reached for a long stem that had flopped over and a ladybug leaped onto my hand. She was perfection in her shiny red coat, almost like she had dressed up for a day downtown, or in this case, at the beach. Carefully, I released her in a section that I'd already weeded and watched her take refuge in the succulent ground cover.

I paused, leaning back on my feet. Part of me felt like crawling under the shade of a vibrant succulent myself, but the other part—again, being honest here—felt good to do something other than the norm.

Like fuss over Brax yesterday.

He told me he didn't need anything, that he was getting along fine, but when I slid a bowl of freshly made Cobb salad with my homemade avocado dressing in front of him, he dug in. Even complimented me on it as I grabbed the remote to search for the movie.

My mouth quirked at the picture of big bad Brax all teary-eyed while watching the end of the film.

The light strum of a guitar replaced the silence around me. Someone nearby must have left their window open. The sound ended, then seconds later, repeated itself. I closed my eyes and leaned into it the third time it played, memorizing the melody and wishing for more. Suddenly, like a DJ's mixer, the music jerked to a halt.

My eyes popped open. I peered up toward the sky, trying to decipher where it had originated. Homes were placed so closely here, that sounds seemed to ricochet, making it tough to pin down their source. The quiet stretched into a minute, and after a few more seconds of waiting, the moment vanished. I breathed in the sea air and returned to weeding, taking pleasure with each pop of root from the soil.

My mind wandered back to Grandma Violet again. We'd spent a good bit of my time together over the past year until she, well, until she moved into her "mansion in the sky," as she liked to call it. She knew where she was headed when the lights went out—told me so many times, and I hung onto that.

Truth was, she didn't need me all that much. She lived her last days in a wonderful home with caregivers who handled all her needs.

Except, maybe, the familial ones.

A pang of emotion caught in my windpipe and wouldn't shake loose. I forced myself to breathe in and out. Gran was the one constant in our lives for so long, especially after our mother passed, and I missed her. Desperately sometimes. I shook my head, slowing, pressing my eyes shut to hold back an impending downfall. Funny, faithful—and mighty forgetful at the end. Our gran.

I stabbed the earth with the tip of the rusty trowel. As a writer, I'd learned to question everything. Why did he do that? What's her motivation? Will they or won't they? (Spoiler: They will.)

Admittedly, I had questions spurred by my sister's repressed memory about my father, the explosive tidbit that our grandmother was able to confirm before she passed. Greta and I had different fathers, though we'd been raised to believe only one man held that title—the one who'd left us when we were young.

So I'd had not one, but two fathers bail on me. Lucky me. That had to be some kind of record, right?

Out of respect for our little family of three—Gran, Greta, and me—and all the memories we had created over the years, I hadn't asked most of my questions out loud. The biggest one being, where was the rest of my father's family now?

I froze, thinking of the implications. I felt the rhythm of my breath and heard the confusion in my heart. In the end, did it matter anyway? I'd been loved and cared for, had a great (usually) career, and good health, well, except for back pain that vexed me at times.

Still, I wondered ... had my father ever thought about me? Before he died, did he have remorse over the past? Like my own mother, had my father found faith in his old age? I froze, my mind rocking questions that somehow felt as if they were moving to the forefront of my thoughts.

I made a mental note to find the church Greta mentioned. Gran would like that, and frankly, it had been too long since I'd voluntarily stepped inside one.

A worm slithered out of a hole I'd created in the loamy soil. "You are one fortunate little bugger, aren't you? One inch closer and I might've sliced you in half."

"Hadn't pegged you to be a girl who took pleasure in dicing up varmints."

I jerked a look up. Brax leaned against the wall of the house, a self-satisfied grin on his impossibly handsome face. I reached into the soil, picked up the wiggling worm, and dangled its long body in front of him. "Hungry?"

He didn't flinch. "You are one strange girl."

I put the worm back onto his home of dirt and watched him slither away. "Tell me something I don't already know." Silence drifted between us for a beat and I allowed my gaze to drop to his ankle, which was wrapped. "Looks less swollen today."

"It is."

"Might as well walk on it some more, maybe even go for a run, you know, to test it out."

He groaned. "You're being sarcastic."

"A little."

"Well, *Mom*, thank you for your concern. I heard a bunch of ruckus down here and thought it my duty to check it out, being that I'm the house sitter for the next few weeks."

I ignored the very decided sinking of my heart. Did I really think that Brax had come out here solely to see me? Of course, he was doing his duty. I mean, there could've been an escapee from the county prison back here, someone waiting in the shadows to pounce on an unsuspecting ... gardener. I made a mental note to consider writing cozy mysteries in the future.

He continued, "Do you usually spend your vacations gardening?"

"You think I'm on vacation?"

He glanced around like he really didn't care, his arms crossed, his body leaning against the wall. "I think you should be."

This teased a small smile out of me.

He pushed off the wall, only a small wobble in his gait as he crossed the tiny backyard. He rolled a bicycle with a cock-eyed front basket toward me.

"You going somewhere?" I quipped.

He grinned and my stomach dropped. Hard. He was all kinds of yummy, and it was becoming more and more difficult to deny it, though I still planned to. I broke eye contact with him and pulled another weed from the soil. That's right —deflect, girl. Deflect!

"Thought you might like to ride it."

I turned a look over my shoulder. "Maybe I will."

He cleared his throat. "Was sorely neglected out here."

I paused. Neglected? I took another peek at the shiny bicycle. It was pretty enough to be added to a beachfront hotel's travel brochure. "Mr. Holt, are you telling me that you hobbled down here and dusted off that bicycle?" For me? Did he do this for me?

"I might have."

I turned more fully now and stood up, his hopeful smile an unexpected draw. Instead of the self-satisfied expression I had expected, his eyes held a hint of timidity, like he was holding his breath, waiting for my response. It was ... charming. And maybe a little suspicious. I was going to hang onto the charming part, though. A simple act that I could use in my next book. If only I could jot it down without him noticing.

I glanced again at the bike, seeing it in a better light. It was light blue and the seat soft-looking and shiny. I snapped a look into his eyes and a shudder ran through me, but I swallowed it back. "May I?" I asked, reaching for the bike's handlebars.

Carefully, he stepped away from the bike. He had to be in pain, so I searched his face for some sign of discomfort. Instead, vulnerability stared back at me. I had an antenna for these types of emotions when putting them on paper, but in real life, that piece of wire was twisting in the wind, looking for a connection. Maybe what I saw staring back at me was good old-fashioned pain, the kind that happened when a guy stood on a bum ankle for far too long.

I rolled the bike back and the pedal stopped.

"It has a foot brake," he said. "Some might call that old-fashioned—"

"It's perfect."

He looked up.

"I mean, I like old-fashioned. It reminds me of the bike I had as a kid." I pushed off the memories, but they rushed forth anyway.

"You okay?"

My eyes fluttered uncontrollably. I would not cry. No way, no way. "I, yes, I am. It's just ... I'm not sure I remember how to ride anymore."

He smiled. "I'd say it's like riding a bike, but that would be—"

"Obvious?"

"I was going to say it's a cliché, and figured you wouldn't like that."

Oh brother. Why did everyone in my life assume that about me? "Not at all. Although clichés are ... not for the faint of heart."

He laughed hard now, his face registering unabashed happiness. He'd found a way to forget about his ankle for a while, and I couldn't let him down. I took a deep breath and tried to forget that I hadn't ridden a bicycle in probably fifteen years.

I hopped on the wide seat and found it surprisingly comfortable and stable as I rode down the narrow side yard, which took all of three seconds. I dragged the bike, turning it around, and rode right up to him.

"Guess I remember after all."

"Think you'll use it to get around while you're here? The basket could carry things, like groceries."

I stared at him.

He squinted, a smirk on his face. "What did I say?"

"I just figured out what this is about—you don't want me driving your car anymore!"

"That is not true."

He looked all flustered now, his arms uncrossed and a pouty growl on his face. The urge to kiss that pout away overwhelmed me and I was ... appalled. So I hopped off and leaned the bike away from me, handing it back to him.

His expression fell. He turned into a little boy who'd just had his skateboard kicked out from under him by the neighborhood bully. Reflexively, I laid my hand on his forearm. "It was very sweet of you, Brax. I promise to ride it. Thank you."

He reached for the handlebars, his gaze brushing over mine. "What was the look for?"

"The look?"

"When you saw the bike, I thought you might, well, cry —and don't you dare bring up Jimmy Stewart!" A small grin flashed across his face before he sobered. "You have me wondering if the bicycle brought back bad memories of something."

Now for some reason, his observation delivered a knot to my throat. This was starting to become a habit and I wasn't sure what to make of it. All I knew was that old emotions I never thought would surface had recently begun to do so with annoying regularity.

"The Thompsons lived across the street from us. Six kids all spaced out by exactly two years. Greta and I always thought that was hilarious."

"You actually talked about that?"

I batted a hand in the air in front of us. "Anyway, their dad taught each one of those kids to ride a bike. I was the youngest in the neighborhood and used to watch him do it from our front porch. He would literally run behind them holding onto the back of the banana seat—"

Brax chuckled.

"Then he'd let go and run beside them with his arms open wide shouting, "You did it!" like some kind of maniac. If I close my eyes, I can hear his shout and the kids' squeals, and even the way I would fold my hands together and jump up and down a little when it happened." I took a breath, remembering. "Is that kinda what you meant by memories?"

His mouth hung open a little, and correct me if I'm wrong here, but was that fear in his eyes? "Not really. I thought maybe you fell off and skinned your knee or something."

"Oh." I laughed lightly. "Maybe I should ask my book editor to follow me around some days. Just think of how little I'd say out loud if I had someone weeding out extraneous words before I said them."

Brax laughed at this. "Clever."

I tilted my head, a sudden question in my mind. "Were you playing your guitar earlier?"

One of his brows shot up, but he didn't reply. I could see him searching for the right words.

"It *was* you."

He shook his head. "Only tuning it."

"Baloney."

He pushed away from the wall and rolled the bike toward the back of the yard. "Carry on with your weeding."

"Brax?"

He returned my gaze.

"Whatever you were playing was beautiful. I kept hoping for more."

He nodded now, his lips still pressed together, his body

language telling me he had no intention of sticking around any longer. It also told me how hot he was, but I supposed we weren't going to discuss that either.

"You like musicals?" I asked suddenly, attempting to change the mood.

"You mean like *Dumbo*?"

"I'm more of a *Lady and the Tramp* type."

"Of course, you are."

"I was asking because I'm thinking of watching *La La Land* sometime this week. I figured we're not that far from Los Angeles, so I really should."

"Naturally."

"Want to watch with me?"

He returned from putting away the bike. "You're a movie buff, aren't you?"

"It's what I do in my downtime. After writing all day, the last thing I want to do is read anymore. Which is really sad, if you think about it."

"But understandable. About the movie, I would if they hadn't ruined the ending for me."

"Aw, look at you, all opinionated and softhearted."

"There it is. I knew you couldn't leave it alone."

I laughed at the little boy face he wore. "What are you talking about?"

"I can assure you that the kind of emotion you may have seen last night is not an everyday occurrence for me."

"You mean you don't rave over everyone's Cobb salad?"

He grinned. His shoulders dropped as if relieved that I didn't bring up the blubbery tears, but why would I when they were so warranted for a first timer?

"Anyway," he said, "as a romance writer, I'm sure you agree that the ending of that film was a miss."

"Not really. I thought it was ... bittersweet, realistic."

His eyes did that narrowing thing again, his mouth open. "More like plain old bitter. She made the wrong choice, obviously."

"How do you mean? She got a man, a family ... a career. How was that wrong?"

"How very clinical."

I laughed at this. "Even romance writers understand that happily-ever-after is the exception rather than the rule."

One dark brow rose. "Is that what you think?"

I paused, the air suddenly electric. My arms prickled as our eyes met, his stare down nearly palpable. "What I mean," I said, quietly, "is that love isn't frivolous. It may start off with music and dancing, but the stuff that lasts the ages— the romance I write about—will stick it out through life's messy bits."

"Well, when you put it like that, I sort of see your point. But ... that movie still bugged me."

He made me laugh. "Okay, then, rewrite it. How would you have ended it?"

Brax's eyes flickered, and he glanced away, toward gulls who had gathered on the balcony of the house behind my sister's. I barely heard him say, "It should have ended with the dream sequence."

I thought about that for a moment. Yeah, that would have worked. Get viewers all worked up that the heroine had run off with someone else then *pow*, hit them with a one-eighty turn.

Brax shook his head like he'd just come to after being smacked in the skull with a baseball or something. "I can't believe you have me talking about chick-flicks."

"You started it."

"Uh, unless I've suddenly become forgetful, you're the one who invited me to watch another movie with you."

For once, I didn't have an answer. My mouth opened but the words wouldn't come. My cheeks felt the heat of a blush. *What in the world?*

He broke eye contact, as if sensing my discomfort. "I'll leave you to your gardening."

I swallowed, still unsure of what to say but pushing myself through it anyway. "It's just, I saw her new man as her hero. The expression on his face every time he looked at her melted me. I mean, it obviously melted *her*."

"You don't think the other guy looked at her that way?"

I shrugged. "Maybe. But she wasn't his first choice—he made that clear."

"So he wasn't hero enough."

"Every romance has to have a hero and a heroine. Them's the rules."

He smiled, though it seemed forced, almost as if lights were set off in his mind. I wanted to pivot back to the weedy garden, but he looked a little lost all of a sudden.

"Am I still the villain in your next story?"

Now the lights went off in my head. He was remembering the ride home in his Jeep when I blurted out the truth behind all my questioning. Drat. He hadn't forgotten about that.

"Well, you *could* have been my villain with that grumpy attitude you were displaying when we met." I lowered myself back to the garden bed. "But you fixed up a bicycle for me, so I'd say you are moving swiftly into the protagonist category."

He scoffed and ran a rugged hand through his mess of hair, then darted a look toward the gate. Planning his escape, maybe? "In all seriousness, Clara, you need to know that I'm nobody's hero—and never will be."

Without another word, he turned around and hobbled out the gate.

Brax

I MANAGED to avoid Clara for the rest of the day. Nighttime had shown up again, the sun out there fully set, and I sat idly by Zac's computer avoiding all thoughts of ... her. Except, it's not working. When I shut my eyes, her smile appears. When I turn on a random TV show, her wide eyes stare back at me. When I glance out to the street, it's her curvy body walking away from me.

Everything about these thoughts were ridiculous. I had become wholly and completely ridiculous, like a sixteen-year-old noticing a bubbly girl with perfect skin meeting his gaze head on for the first time ever.

Right. It's nothing like that at all. It's richer, meaningful, something that—if I were so inclined—I could write a song about. And this is exactly what makes my thoughts, my actions so ... dangerous.

Problem was, I'm not the guy Clara thinks I am ... not that she's actually thinking of me. She could be out with Carter right now, for all I knew. Maybe they're downstairs in his lair, curled up on the couch sipping wine and watching *La La Land*.

My stomach heaved. I stood up and stalked into the kitchen, added ice to a glass and filled it up with filtered water until the excess splashed onto the floor. The gulps went down hard in my throat but did little to wash away the images of Clara and Carter playing like a reel in my brain. Clara and Carter. Great. People would call them "CC" for short. My gag reflex triggered again.

I convinced myself that she and her landlord actually were watching *that movie*. No big deal. Not at all. We couldn't agree on the outcome of *La La Land*. Shoot, we couldn't even decide who the hero was.

But we both knew there had to be one.

She wasn't his first choice.

In Clara's mind, the guy in the movie had chosen music over the woman he loved. I didn't agree. The guy wanted them to pursue their futures, their passions, their lives— together. But if my past was any indicator, I was in a poor position to prove my theory.

It all started with a girl named Kate and ended when she left me after one too many nights out gigging. Kate had wanted me to make different choices. Get a real job. Be home for dinner. "Take care of *us*, Brax!" she would say.

I tried things her way, but she knew my heart was other-wise engaged. To her, my efforts were too little, and far too late. Forgiveness was fragile. When it came to my mistakes, Kate could never let go of what happened to her that night. To us.

I hung my head, my mind mired in the past. Sometimes I wished that my mistakes could be rewritten in a way that, *shocker*, I was the hero. I winced. This was all Clara's fault. She had me thinking in story, and everyone knew that fiction was popular for a reason: it's fake. Unattainable. Impossibili-ties mixed with fairy tales.

Mercifully, a text broke into my thoughts.

ZAC: How're things going out there?

ME: Fine. Only one fire so far.

ZAC: Pretty sure you're kidding.

ME: Pretty sure you're right. Okay, here goes: ankle's better. House is clean. Neighbors are quiet.

ZAC: Good.

Several seconds pass.

ZAC: Greta's wondering how Clara is doing. Have you seen her around?

I ROLLED a look up at the ceiling. So much for avoiding all thoughts of the brunette beauty who had me randomly cleaning up bicycles in the backyard. I try to think of some quip to shoot back, but felt lost. I puffed out my cheeks, releasing a sigh, then typed out another text.

ME: Yes. She seems fine.

ZAC: Thanks, bro. I'll assure Greta that you'll text if anything comes up.

ME: You bet.

MY THUMBS HOVERED over the screen. Did my brother really need any more than that? Nope. He did not. Would he read something else into it? Possibly. He'd apologized for insinuating I might make a play for his wife's sister, but was he fishing right now?

I groaned. Realistically, he was my nerdy older brother who, in my opinion, lucked out with Greta. The guy's too book smart to read any more into my text than its face value.

I hit send and tossed my phone onto the couch. It bounced against the neck of my guitar and I scowled at the instrument. Of course, Clara heard me testing it out today. Didn't mean anything, but I also wasn't wild about someone hearing me. Was a one-time thing. *A one-time thing that I'd missed more than I knew.*

A thought torpedoed me. Did those old YouTube videos still exist? The ones of me singing on stage? Surely they were old enough to be long buried.

Zac had left me his login underneath the computer keyboard. I punched it in, watching the screen fire up. A few keystrokes and I'd know. I punched my name into the app's search engine and—bam—found my ugly mug, clean shaven and a good six years younger. This one was filmed the night my single released. More people there that night than had probably bought the song, but man, I'd been heady from the adrenaline. Stoked to sit up on that stool, lights blinding me, and sing my heart out.

Kate had shown up that night, too, watching me from the floor. I'd taken that as confirmation that I was on the right track, when really, she hoped it was a one-time thing. Memories of the arguments that followed, the tears, the slamming of doors and late night silent treatmetns filled my head.

I glanced again at the screen. The next two videos were of other singer songwriters, but after that, another one of me. Then another. I frowned. There had to be a way to wipe the channel free of all videos from those years of my life.

Right?

I grunted aloud and clicked out of YouTube, wondering fleetingly what Clara would think of the old me. Hopefully, she'd never have a chance to find out. That was the plan.

I opened a search engine and let my thoughts hover there. What had she said her father's name was? Her brother's?

I typed in their names, one at a time, finding the same info Clara had mentioned—or lack of it. And yet ...

Pages and pages of results turned up. I jumped forward a few pages, digging deeper, all the while my mind fixated on the conversation Clara and I had outside. There had been a wistfulness in her voice as she relayed her memories of the Thompson family and their bike riding sessions. It was almost as if ... oh. Regret twisted like a scalpel to my heart. Clara and Greta had grown up fatherless. She'd acted like the memories were happy ones, but her face had betrayed her.

That must have been hard for her to sit by that window and watch Mr. Thompson teach his children, one by one, to ride their bicycles. I tried to look away from my thoughts, but they ran on a loop showing me a little girl, her face overrun with curls, her eyes intent on all the fun going on outside. The coldness of the blinking curser against a white background stilled my thoughts.

You'll always be ... my hero.

The words came without effort, a lyric to a song I had no intention of ever writing. I rubbed a hand across my bristled face and turned back to the computer screen. Making music again might be out of the question, but solving a mystery for a ... friend, wasn't.

Gonna be here all night, Justin Smith. Gonna be here all night.

CHAPTER SEVEN

Clara

"Want to be my tour guide?" Brax was straddling a second bike he'd found at Zac and Greta's place. "Or we could ride aimlessly, if you want."

"Are you sure your ankle's up for it?" I gave his bum foot a doubtful look.

"We'll see now, won't we? I wrapped it in so many layers I could barely get my shoe on."

"Brax ..."

He laughed. "No pain, no gain."

I smiled but also wondered about his change in demeanor from yesterday. He must have noticed because his expression turned remorseful. Brax reminded me of a little boy, except for the whiskers and overall hotness, that is. "First, I'm sorry I was so short with you yesterday. I know it was rude."

"I didn't consider it rude. Although I will say, you did ruin a perfectly good conversation about *La La Land.*"

"I was right about that."

I flashed him a smile. "If you say so."

That's not what I'm talking about though." He paused and raked his wavy hair, then plunked his hand onto the handlebars. "Clara, there are some things from my past that I don't like thinking about anymore, and yesterday I came close. But that's not your fault—it's mine. I'm sorry."

He'd been honest with me, and I didn't want to spoil it by probing for more information. I'd already made a pest of myself with my questions, so I simply said, "Apology accepted."

"So you'll go on a bike ride with me?"

I glanced upstairs toward the upper deck. The handyman who owed Carter a favor would be showing up soon to fix the window, and did I need a reminder of the incident before Greta's wedding?

I swung my gaze back to Brax. "Sure. Why not?" I wasn't sure how long I'd last, since I hadn't ridden a bike in years. But I put Sport safely in the backyard and we took off.

We rode next to each other down the narrow street, often having to skirt sand drifts that had blown as far as the middle of Ocean Drive. I learned about dodging them the hard way after my tires got stuck in several inches of sand and I had to slide and skid my way out or fall right over on the street.

We cycled past that same eclectic hodgepodge of houses we'd seen before, some small and quaint, hearkening from way before our time, and others that soared three stories tall. We slowed at the harbor mouth, and I followed Brax to a couple of sea lion statues gazing toward the west. I slid off my bike and onto one of the lions.

"Pretty sure those are for kids," Brax said, watching me with a side eye.

I shrugged. "Why do they get to have all the fun?"

He relented and sat on the sea lion next to mine, then exhaled as he looked upon the water. A boat left the harbor with its sails up. Where was it headed? Who was on it? I snuck a quick peek at Brax. A look of relief softened his expression, and I wasn't immune to that. The undulating water mere feet from us had a way of carrying away stresses with each loft.

"How's your back?" he asked.

"My back?"

He turned. "You mentioned it was a struggle to sit all day. Was hoping the bike riding would loosen it up some."

He remembered that? I rubbed my spine. "It's actually pretty good right now."

"I'm glad to hear it."

His arms were crossed, and he didn't seem in any hurry to leave. The breeze coming off the ocean plastered his T-shirt against rippled abs, and I needed to come up with something else to talk about. Shoot, if I could speak at all without drooling, that would be advisable. Greta had said she hardly knew Brax, so I wondered if he knew the story of how she came out here in the first place.

"My great-grandmother once walked that beach over there," I said, pointing to the sand that abutted a jetty leading out to sea. Looking off into the distance made it easier to avoid gawking at his form-fitting shirt.

"That's a long way from Indiana."

"It is." I swallowed, remembering. "Did Greta or Zac tell you her story?"

He glanced at me, one brow raised. He was really listening. "I'd love to hear it."

Our great-gran traveled here in the 1920s. She was a starlet—an up-and-coming actress—and had a small part in a Rudolph Valentino movie that was filmed right there. It was called *The Sheik.*"

"Wow."

"They filmed here because all the sand could pass for the Sahara Desert."

"Did she become famous, your great-grandmother?"

"No." I allowed myself to look at him again. "But it's crazy to think of the far-reaching impact her coming out here has had. I mean, if she hadn't come, Greta wouldn't have flown out here to walk in her shoes, and she wouldn't have met Zac."

Brax tossed me a look. "And you and I wouldn't be sitting here on these lions having this conversation."

"Hmm. Yes."

"I've been meaning to ask you, Clara, about your travels."

"Sorry?"

"You have a passport, so it sounds like you come from a traveling family. Your great-grandmother traveled all the way out here a hundred years ago. It wouldn't be a stretch to guess how unusual that was for the time. And then your sister came out here to see where your great-grandmother once lived. So...?"

"So?"

"How about you?"

"Me? I just came here to be in the wedding and dog sit."

He spilled a laugh. "I mean, where have your adventures taken you?"

I licked my lips and abruptly looked back out to the

harbor water that flowed toward the sea. Sudden tears lodged at the base of my throat, and I wasn't sure why.

"Did I say something offensive?"

I snapped a look at him, and his earnestness really made me want to cry. I shrugged. "No, you didn't. I-I, well, the truth is, I haven't been anywhere." I let the words flow out like a sigh. "My readers probably think I've traveled the world. I've written books set in all corners of this country, and three in Europe—so why wouldn't they?"

"I get that, Clara. That's where your imagination steps in." He pursed his lips and sent his gaze back out to the water. A moment passed before he quietly said, "You told me your secret, so I guess I can tell you one of mine."

I looked at him expectantly.

"I wrote some music in the past."

"You did?"

"I don't do that anymore. Not saying that I have any idea what it's like to write a ..."He bit his lip, like he was holding back a smile.

I leaned over and gave him a shove. "A romance novel?"

He cleared his throat, his laughter garbled. "I meant any type of novel. But I understand that you try to put yourself in another role, and when it works, the music—or words, in your case—can really flow. No matter if you're sitting in Indiana or some island in the Caribbean."

A sort of relief covered me. I thought he was going to skewer me for having a passport without any stamps in it. I mean, I'd seen *While You Were Sleeping*—I remember the spat Lucy and Jack had over that tiny little fact. Though, let's be real, in the end, she got her trip to Florence. All was not lost.

"Thank you for not giving me a hard time about the passport," I said quietly.

"You're welcome. But may I ask why you think I would?"

He really did look sincere. Brax didn't seem at all like the guy I'd met at the wedding, the stranger I'd linked arms with who, though smiling, seemed to seethe with some underlying regret. This Brax was open to my world, small as it was.

"The truth is that"—I sighed—"I've been stuck for a long time, afraid to get up off my recliner chair and go out and experience all I'd written about. There. I said it."

"And now?"

Now I was ... sitting on a sea lion and talking to a guy who looked exactly like the ones in high school who were always staring at the girl next to me. He could be back at the house with his bad ankle elevated, but for now, the guy with chiseled movie star looks was here, lending me an empathetic ear.

Still, I couldn't shake the feeling that I was out of my league. Way, way out.

I shrugged, and slid off the sea lion's back. "I don't know, Brax. I'd love to travel, to see what inspiration is out there." I wiggled my hand through the air. "But what if I couldn't pull off a change to my daily structure, to my process? What if changing my well-planned life produced something I hadn't planned at all?"

Brax slid off his lion statue, too, and onto his good foot, his smile revealing white teeth and a dimple I could let myself fall right into. He reached out and brushed a curl from my cheek. "You won't know until you try."

My hair was a hot mess. It's mid-morning, and after a night of sitting out on the deck, followed by the windows being left open all night, my hair had become an explosion of curls goaded on by excessive moisture in the air. Back in Indiana, we had plenty of humidity, but the beach added an ingredient of salt to the breeze that I'd never had to deal with at home.

Other than sneaking out this morning to let Sport pee, I stayed inside to hide my curls from the world and forced myself to outline. It was an emergency measure, one I rarely succumbed to, but my current situation—desperation—called for it.

On our ride home yesterday, Brax suggested I try writing outside sometime, said that he often found inspiration that way. That conversation did a number on my creativity, inspiring me in new ways, a good thing considering that today I was facing bad hair *and* an ultimatum.

My editor, Joanie, had called yesterday asking for a synopsis. A synopsis! Didn't she know that was like asking a homegrown chef to write down her recipes? Or a musical savant to pencil out some sheet music?

Okay. Maybe a little dramatic. But I had not written a synopsis for years. How could I write something if I didn't know how it would end? For me, that was the thrill of writing my romances. Yes, I knew what my readers wanted. Boy gets girl. Or the other way around. But part of the fun was getting there. Sometimes, I didn't know how my hero and heroine would push through all the "stuff" of life, so much that, by the end, I was as surprised as my readers.

I re-read Joanie's email, the one she wrote as a follow-up to our recent coversation, and sighed. It's not like I didn't usually provide some sort of work up. In the past, I put together a summary based on our back-and-forth emails. Hmm. This sudden request for details *before* our volley of emails might not be so sudden after all.

Maybe the past requests for short summaries, a one liner, a paragraph, a page were small steps toward this much larger request. Trite as this might sound, I'm the frog in the kettle, unaware that the heat had slowly and deliberately been turned up.

And I didn't like it one bit. Between the wily curls and the blank page, I'd had enough. This was a main difference between Greta and me. Really, she should have been the writer. She was the organized one, more deliberate in her thought processes, while I was always more of the wild child. Well, the wild child who preferred to curl up at home and write whatever came to mind.

"You're just as unruly as your hair, child," Mom would say to me with a laugh. Then she'd pull me close, smack a kiss on my forehead, and spray something shiny and smooth through my hair.

That's kind of how writing had always been for me. A little wild, a little unruly, but in the end, with the help of my editors to smooth things out, my stories shined. Readers wrote to me. Editors still acquired my books. I'd been so lucky.

Well, there was always tomorrow, right?

I pulled up YouTube on my phone and found the video I had been staring at lazily last night, the one with a girl named Tara who knew all kinds of tricks to keep her curly hair "luscious" even in times of humidity. Maybe I wasn't in the mood to pull a synopsis out of nowhere, but I could certainly give one of Tara's hair tricks a try.

I watched as she poufed and pulled and flipped hair

under and through so fast that I had to start and stop the video multiple times until I got the hang of one of her designs. I was sweating by the time I copied what she'd done and had to fan myself with a nearby magazine. Carter had left copies of *Real Estate Times* in the rental, of course. I examined myself in the mirror—shocked. My hair looked that good. *Where have you been all my life, Tara!*

Satisfied that I had accomplished something worthwhile this morning, I allowed myself some passive scrolling through YouTube. I was offered a mishmash of videos with no clear agenda. How to invest, yoga poses for lazy people (I should probably bookmark that one), and an ad for electric bikes. That one made me smile. If I hadn't just spent an amazing day with Brax touring Hollywood by the Sea by bicycle—a bike he had cleaned up for me—I might have taken a second look at that ad.

Idly, I scrolled through video thumbnails, nothing catching my interest, probably because I was also chewing my lip and daydreaming of Brax. A regular montage slid through my head: Brax's strong hands gripping the handle-bars, his willingness to ride bareback on a sea lion sculpture, and those abs that played peek-a-boo through his clingy cotton tee.

I laughed aloud, waking up Sport. Poor doggy jumped up, snorting a bark or two and ready to fight. My fingers poised over the mouse to click out of the app, when curiosity nicked me. I'd never started a channel of my own, but wondered ...

I searched for my pen name.

Oh. My. Word.

The page filled with videos. I smiled. Some of them my publishers had put out, trailers for my books, mostly. Had completely forgotten about those. They would always send me a copy by email, and I'd watch it, maybe once.

Another video stood out to me, this one presented by a reader group called Tropes that Make Us Swoon. I laughed and clicked play. Three readers on a video chat were talking non-stop, interrupting each other at times, about romance tropes. I listened to their banter awhile, still unsure of why my pen name had brought up this video.

After about four minutes, I heard it.

"Vivian Blackstone. We've probably all read some of her books."

Giggles all around.

"Yeah, well, if you've read one you've pretty much read them all."

All out cackling now.

"I think she just changes the characters' names and occupations, doesn't she?"

A lot of hums of agreement.

A sigh. "Yeah, but we love them anyway."

Nodding heads. "Yes, yes we do."

I shut the video down. Joanie had always told me never to read reviews, but hearing them live took them to another level of destruction. If I hadn't been churning out story after story, month after month, for the past few years, I probably would have ignored her warning and gobbled up everything I could find.

To be honest, I didn't have a lot of head space left over for reviews or the internet or social media. "Your absence is part of your mystique," Joanie always said. I took that as a compliment. Now I'm wondering if my head had been buried in the proverbial sand (which was kind of poetic considering my proximity to the beach).

Well. If what those women said was true, that what I did was as easy as swapping heads, changing names, why hadn't I been able to write a new story these past few months? What was blocking me? And why? All I knew was that every time I moved forward, some sort of force field held me back.

I snapped another look at the screen. Should probably shut down the computer and go for a walk. Sport sent me the stink eye earlier when I told him to use the doggy door next time. My fingers scrolled idly again, my self-loathing growing, when another idea popped into my head.

I glanced over my shoulder, as if I was about to do something sneaky. In the search box, I typed Braxton's name. I'm not sure what I expected to find. Maybe Brax wearing a tool belt while shirtless? (Could happen.) Or possibly clad in a smoky gray pinstripe suit, explaining to listeners the difference between index and growth funds? (Personally, I'd follow his advice...)

I squinted at the screen. What? Video after video of someone on stage who looked a lot like Brax without scruff. I turned up the sound. My heart rose in my chest. You know that feeling when a melody can grab your windpipe and give it a little squeeze? The sound coming from this video gave me all the feels. Every last one of them.

I knew it ... Brax could sing. I'd told him that at Greta's wedding, but he'd written me off. Scoffed in my face. Why deny that? He was even cagier when I mentioned the music surrounding me out there in the garden recently. I'd taken to it immediately, the melody staying with me.

But ... wait. Yesterday ... yesterday he mentioned something about writing music some time ago. I thought he said it only to make me feel better about my own writing process (or current writer's block). Oh, I believed him, of course, but I didn't get the sense that writing music had been as central to his life as all *this*.

I played the video again. Well. Would you look at that. The sound quality lacked, probably made on an audience member's phone, oh, but it didn't matter. He sounded so good and should be proud of his performance.

I licked my top lip nervously, thinking, wondering. Did he know these videos existed? I scrolled around. None of the channels had his name on them. When we'd talked, he said he didn't spend all that much time online. He and I were probably the last two holdouts in existence. Under the age of seventy, that is.

The world needed to hear him. I felt it down deep. Without a channel of my own, and frankly no interest in starting one, I switched over to Facebook. My publisher had created a page for Vivian. Someone at the company ran that page, but I had access to it myself.

Did I dare share a video or two there?

I dug around in my email and retrieved the long-forgotten password, then logged in. Or tried to. Apparently, if you don't login for a while, Facebook thinks you're a criminal or something. First, confirm my email. Done. Drum my fingers on the desk and then, yup, get a code on my phone. Punch it in. Done.

Oh wow. So much activity. I scrolled up and down, frowning. Guilt crept in. So many comments from readers ... how did I not know about these? I groaned a little. I'd been wrapped up in my own mind for so long that I guess I'd not realized readers had been having a little party on my page. For months.

I sat up, empowered. My muddled mind had little to add to the conversation, but I could share Brax's videos, right?

Start a conversation? Give readers some insight into my family life, starting with my sister's new brother-in-law and the videos I had unearthed from the archives?

Quickly, I set about sharing links and adding captions so readers would know why I was sharing Brax's videos with them. Other than the obvious reason, i.e. he was *hot*. I laughed aloud. Greta would snicker and tell me to knock it off if she heard what I was thinking. Satisfied, I clicked *post* and sat back, happy with myself. Who says I couldn't conquer social media? Okay, so Vivian conquered it. Whatever.

My phone rang, startling me. Joanie. I considered letting it go to voicemail. *I'm on vacation, remember?!* Then again, maybe she saw my Facebook post and knew I was available. Sigh. I let another ring go unanswered, still wavering.

Didn't feel right, though. Joanie had been my cheer-leader for years, poking me with her magic red pen whenever my word count took a dive. Wasn't all that often—surely not like these days when it's practically non-existent. Still, she didn't deserve to be ignored.

"Hey, Joanie."

"Clara! You picked up."

"For you, always."

She laughed darkly. "Well, you haven't answered my emails."

Silence.

"Right," she said. "You're on vacation."

Was she reading my mind?

"How was the wedding?" she asked.

"Beautiful, of course. Breezy, sunny, lots of smooches."

"Sounds like fodder for you. I hope you took notes."

I swallowed. Her transition to the real reason for her call

was a boulder, rolling down the hill toward me, picking up speed. I had two choices: jump out of the way or let it flatten me on impact.

Or I could trap it with my super powers, which is what I chose to do. "Speaking of notes," I said, "I have plenty of them on the new story." So what if most of said notes had been scratched out?

"Great. That's what I want to hear. How's the synopsis coming?"

That word again!

I skirted the question. I grabbed a pen and paper—the old school way. "What would you like it to say?"

Joanie made a sound that reminded me of ... surprise. "You haven't started it?"

"I thought we could brainstorm instead. Or if right now is not a good time, I can send you some thoughts and you could email yours back. Like we've done in the past."

"I know what we've done in the past, Vivian, I mean, Clara." She sighed. "But that's not going to cut it anymore. The team upstairs is putting our titles under the microscope. Not just those currently on the market, but the ones coming up in line."

"What are you saying?" I wasn't sure I wanted to know. My titles weren't always the hottest ticket, but they were solid sellers with fans who wrote in regularly, asking for more. Although ... come to think of it, I couldn't recall the last time the PR department forwarded fan mail. Hmm. Maybe someone new was in charge. I'd have to follow up on that.

"I'm saying that you have to craft something amazing and spell it out for the top dogs to fully understand every twist and starburst. By the way, you'll have to include comps and market data."

"Wait. Comps, as in books comparable to mine?"

"You always say that you're old school, well, the new team is too. They want all the deets from you, Clara."

"You're not asking for a synopsis, but a … proposal? I've written dozens of titles for you and now I'm suddenly in the slush pile?"

She tsked. "Take some of that outrage and funnel it into your synopsis, Clara. Oh, and add some chapters, too. And an outline. For this next one, you're going to need some fire."

"You didn't answer my question."

Joanie sighed. "I'll be straight with you. You're definitely not in the slush pile, but, well, the team is considering a new direction." She paused. "Unless your next idea knocks it out of the park, so to speak, I'm not sure there'll be a place for you here."

I shut my eyes, unwilling to parse out all that could mean. My fingers curled into a ball, trying to grip a metal cleat as the boat tried to pull away from the dock, the water churning, unforgiving against my need to hang on.

When I didn't reply, Joanie added, "Though you know how much I want you and your books to stay in our lineup. You do know that, Clara, right?"

I didn't know that. Not really. After all, we weren't really friends, just co-workers, only she depended on me to help provide her paycheck. So maybe our relationship was a little lopsided, though I had never noticed before.

Probably wasn't fair of me to think this way, but it hit me that if I didn't come up with something soon, Joanie would drop me like newsprint in the twenty-first century. The last piece of my life that had yet to change was suddenly rolling down that hill, ready to free fall off a cliff.

A knock on my door woke me from the dark musings. Sport leaped up and barked once, then ran over to get me, all kinds of squealing flowing out of her. "Sorry, Joanie, I have to go. Someone's at the door."

"You okay?"

"Mm-hmm. Yeah, I'm fine. Thanks." I hung up and padded across the room, my mind still on the contents of that call. I opened the door without thinking.

"Good morning."

Brax stood on the threshold of my apartment, the day's light a halo around his head. Yet why did that devilish smile on his face keep me from thinking he was an angel? "Hey."

"You gonna invite me in or do I have to stand out here on a sore ankle."

I raised my brows and stepped away from the door so Brax could follow me inside. I couldn't shake my conversation with Joanie, how it had burst the idea that I could continue to play hooky for the next few weeks.

In the kitchen now, I puttered around, wiping the counter while he took a seat on a stool. He was watching me.

"What?"

"Your hair looks nice." He paused. "That's all."

This teased a smile out of me, and if I weren't mistaken, a bit of a blush. "Thanks. I learned it on YouTube." Saying the words out loud suddenly reminded me of what I'd done. "I have something—"

Brax put his hand up, stopping me. "Sorry to interrupt you, darlin', but I have some news for you."

I leaned my head to one side. "For me?"

"You might want to sit." He stared at me with eyes as

clear as the sky. A skywriter was doing loop-da-loops in the air, writing me little love notes in puffy white cloud ink ...

"Clara?"

I startled. "Did you say something?"

He gave me a sideways grin then turned very, very sober. "What is it?"

"I believe I've found your brother."

CHAPTER EIGHT

Brax

"I don't get it. How did you ...?" Her voice trailed off, her expression bewildered at best.

Seeing Clara's reaction made me want to scoop her into my arms and carry her around. She's that adorable. Those owl-like eyes of hers, round and inquisitive, grew larger still, pulling me in. One look and I was lost. Suddenly I couldn't swim, though I was reaching, frantically, for the side of the pool.

Finally, I found my voice. "You were right. Justin S., aka Justin Smith, was tough to locate. For one thing, there are thousands of them."

"Obviously didn't get my creativity from that side of the family."

"I suspect not. But it was really kind of a simple thing. Turns out his last name isn't spelled with an 'i' but with a 'y'. No 'e' on the end, in case that's what you're thinking."

"Like Smyth?"

"Yes, it's another version of Smith."

"A more creative version." Her voice was a whisper, like she was taking this in slowly. She darted a glance up. "How'd you figure it out?"

"I called a kid who used to work for me. Heard he designs websites now so I figured he might think of looking in places I hadn't considered." I set a fist on the counter. "I tried calling him the other night, after seeing you in the garden, but he didn't pick up. So I called him again last night."

"This is unbelievable! Thank you so much for doing this, Brax. I-I don't know what to say."

Just don't call me your hero.

She came around the counter and put her arms around my neck, giving me a quick squeeze. As she pulled away, my hand reflexively covered hers, stopping her. I turned my head at my own risk, and oh, was it ever well worth taking. Our eyes collided, her gaze sizzling, like I was the frying pan she'd just tossed water on. Before I could stop myself, I licked my lips. Her eyes dropped to my mouth, lingering there.

Finally, she said, "Braxton Holt I will remember your kindness forever." Her eyelashes glistened, her blinking rapid. "Such welcome news after a hard morning."

Slowly, I unwrapped her arms from my neck. "What happened?"

"Work stuff. Nothing I can't deal with, but just, well, hard. You know?" She smiled then. "Since we're sharing information, I have something to tell you as well."

She pulled fully away from me now, and immediately I missed her touch. She brought her laptop and put it on the counter between us, then fired it up. She bit her bottom lip and stole glances at me as she typed. Whatever happened, she was pretty happy about it. Or maybe the unabashed smile on her face was from the news I had just delivered to her.

"Don't think I'm a stalker or anything, but I found these videos of you on YouTube." She tilted the laptop toward me. "They were pretty buried. Did you know they existed?"

I'd been sucker punched. By the look on Clara's face, though, she had no idea she'd been the one to deliver it.

It was one thing to find those old videos and relive them alone. Quite another to see her discovering the old me for the first (or second) time. I was on the precipice of a cliff, the earth crumbling beneath my feet, sending pebbles into the abyss. My pulse quickened at her response to my voice. I had let that past go and now I needed to figure out how to make sure it stayed good and buried.

She reached to turn up the sound control on the laptop but I stopped her. She stilled, sending me a curious glance. Man. She was so ... beautiful. I swallowed, reaching for the words to tell her that I'd rather not visit yesterday, that just last night I'd wondered how I could get those videos taken down.

But those thoughts were caught in a cyclone of other more dangerous ones. What would it be like to kiss those pink lips? Were they as soft as they looked?

She curled her fingers around mine, the power she had over me unexpected, alarming. I wanted to pull away, to extricate myself from her touch. I was leaving soon, wasn't I? My brother was married to her sister and that made this ... complicated.

I'd made my decision. I had to break free of her hold on

me, to put a divide between us and ask her to forget everything she had seen online. That was my old life. Gone. Done.
Finit! I was still trying to find the new one, though I had yet
to nail down what it should look like.

All I knew was I couldn't go back.

"Why can't you be like your brother?" Kate had
screamed at me the night of her accident. I'd heard versions
of that line so many times growing up, though never quite so
dramatically as that night. It was laughable, boring even.

"What's wrong?" Clara's voice cut through my memories, which I blinked away. My eyes lingered on her mouth,
every muscle in my body aware of her closeness. I blinked
again. *Really need to shut this down, Braxton.*

What happened next I couldn't explain, even if I were
sitting under the stark, sweltering heat of an interrogation
lamp.

Officer: Did she or did she not kiss you?

Me : I ... I .... I ...

Officer: Answer the question!

Me: I ....

Clara's mouth landed on mine so suddenly and so
sweetly, answering every question I'd ever had about what
kissing her would feel like. Actually, not true. She leaned
into me, a small high-pitched sigh escaping her, delicate
hands cupping my face. She was answering questions I never
knew I had.

Clara gasped again, although this time she added a
sudden jump backwards. In retrospect, her kiss had left me
too paralyzed to react. Her leg caught on the laptop cord,
and as she fell backwards, the computer came careening
forward. I caught it mid-air. Unfortunately, I couldn't say the
same for Clara.

She lay sprawled on the floor now. I slid the laptop onto the counter and dropped to my knees next to her, forgetting all about that ache in my ankle. Her hands covered her face. I was asking her if she was hurt when she started to ... laugh. She giggled into her hands, and her shoulders shook.

"Clara?"

"I'm such a klutz!"

"Let me help you up."

She was still laughing when I pulled her up into a sitting position. She couldn't stop laughing so I surreptitiously checked her head for bumps.

"I don't have a concussion, if that's what you're checking for." Once again, she dissolved into a fit of embarrassed laughter. As I smoothed away some of her flyaway curls, she tucked one behind her ear, her hand briefly grazing mine.

Our eyes met.

"I'm so sorry," she said, her lips upturned, her smile still vaguely embarrassed. "I don't know why I did that."

I smiled but didn't reply. I'd turned mute. I wanted to tell her I was glad she kissed me, that she had read my mind, and with that kiss, had simultaneously satisfied my curiosity while also leaving me wanting for more. Much more.

Maybe it would be better if I helped her up and then ran —or limped—right out that front door. I stood and reached my hand down to her. She allowed me to help her up. Never mind the tweak I felt in my sore ankle. Totally worth it.

Once again, we were dangerously close. I found my voice again. "You okay?"

Her lips turned up into a smile. "Yeah." She didn't make eye contact this time.

Gently, I lifted her chin with my fingers. "Hey."

Her eyes sparkled.

"It was an amazing kiss."

She wrinkled her nose and pressed those pink lips of hers together. I wondered if she used some kind of lipstick to make them look like bubble gum ... *Snap out of it, Braxton.* Doubt clouded her eyes. "Something wrong?"

"No, nothing. Well, other than the fact that I practically attacked you."

I grinned. Couldn't stop myself. "Yeah, I feel so used."

She laughed at me. "Stop. It's just"—she sighed and flipped some loose tendrils of hair over her shoulder—"that song you were singing in the video. Your voice, Brax. It was ... you are ... well, I was overwhelmed."

My smile dimmed. She might have well said she was *under*-whelmed.

"You're frowning. Oh no. I'm sorry I made you uncomfortable."

"You didn't. Believe me, Clara. Being kissed by you is the highlight of my day."

She laughed nervously. "But?"

"About those videos you found." I stepped back, putting some serious distance between us, and ran a hand through my hair. It landed on the back of my neck and I worked to massage away the knot that had formed there. I peered at her. "I'd rather you not mention those to anyone."

"But why? Was it because of the video quality? Because if it was, I guarantee nobody cares."

"No, no, it isn't." I reached for both of her hands, knowing how stupid that was. Didn't I just put distance between us? Somehow, though, her touch helped me find the words I needed. "Those songs and the guy you saw singing them are in the past. They represent a time I would rather forget. I alluded to all that yesterday, but the bottom line is, I've moved on."

Her expression was anything but blank. She wrinkled her nose while she formed her thoughts. Both cute and annoying—because I knew that what followed would be her opinion. Her very bold two cents. "That's why you told me you couldn't sing ... at the wedding."

I nodded.

"And why you didn't want to talk about the melody I heard yesterday, in the garden."

She understood. Wow. My mood buoyed. Maybe shutting down this interest of hers wouldn't be as tough as I'd thought. That kiss, though, might take longer to put aside. If we ever could.

"Brax," Clara said, "it might be too late."

"Too late for what?"

She bit her lip. I'd seen her do that before and thought it was cute. Right now, it sent prickles up my spine and not in a good way. "I already posted them."

"Posted what ... the videos?"

She opened the laptop and typed furiously. "I'm hardly ever online." She looked over her shoulder briefly. "I think I mentioned that. But I found my reader page, the one set up by my publisher, and posted them there. If you really don't want them up—I think you're crazy, but whatever—let's just take them down."

Vivian Blackstone's Facebook author page appeared, and Clara gasped.

I squinted over her shoulder. "What?"

I heard her suck in a tiny breath. "It appears that your video has already been shared more than two hundred times."

"That can't be."

She stepped to the side so that I could see it for myself. She was right. Two hundred shares. Wait, make that two hundred and one.

Her quiet voice drew me to look at her. "You already have a legion of fans, Brax. Are you sure you want me to stop the momentum?"

I'd had fans before, the kind that would show up at the bar the minute the doors opened so they could camp out in front of the stage. They were steady and loyal, but not many. Kate liked to point out that I had sacrificed our marriage for a few "straggly" fans. I hated when she'd said it, but eventually, when the contracts didn't come and the crowds didn't swell, even I had begun to question. I often wondered, if the accident hadn't happened, where my singer-songwriter career might have taken me. If anywhere.

All I really knew was that pursuing a career in the limelight killed my marriage. It nearly killed Kate. I'd moved on and so had she, but did I ever want to face that kind of choice again?

Clara's voice prodded me on again. "Maybe I should leave them up, you know, to see what happens."

My jaw tensed. I jerked a look at her. "No. I want you to take them down."

She drew back slightly. "Okay. Of course. I'm sorry, Brax."

I had to get out of there. I didn't wait for confirmation of the videos coming down. She was working fast, her hands flying, her shoulders tense. I made my way to the front door. By the time she turned back around, I would be gone.

Clara

THAT MADE two days this week that Brax walked away from me abruptly. Had to be a record. Thankfully, two more days had passed by since we'd seen each other. I let my gaze linger on the note he'd written me, the one with my brother's contact information on it, then I shut the desk drawer again, the note firmly out of sight.

In these past couple of days, I had taken Sport on so many walks that she was playing possum this morning.

"Psst. Girl. Don't you want to go for a walk?"

Nothing. She laid there on her side, pretending to be asleep. Pretty much me in the morning. I wasn't fooled though. One of her eyes opened to a slit, but quickly closed when she spotted me standing over her.

"Fine. Have it your way." Since I wouldn't have to be bogged down by her leash, I grabbed a straw beach bag and flung it over my shoulder. "I'm going shopping—and I know you hear me. Food and water's in the kitchen and the doggy door is open. You're on your own, kiddo." I said this particularly loud, like she was deaf.

She continued with her facade of sleep, but gave herself away with a swish of her tail. Pretty sure that was her way of celebrating my departure.

Helen stopped me at the bottom of the stairs. She was puttering around in her front garden with a watering can. "Where you off to, Clara?"

"Just a walk. Thought maybe I'd peek in at that shell shop down the road."

"More like oddities shop! One of the owners—the guy— is a pack rat. The gal is nice enough, though. Her name is

Shelly. Maybe get yourself a puka shell necklace. Would look pretty on you."

I laughed lightly. "Maybe I will." I set out but stopped and pivoted to look back at her. "Are you and Gus doing all right? Do you need anything?"

"Us? Oh, yes, we're doing just fine." Helen bent down and looked inside her house through a screened window. "Aren't we, Gus?"

"Aren't we what?"

"Doing fine! Clara asked how we're doing!"

"We're doing fine!"

She straightened up, soothing her back with one hand, a maneuver I often did myself when my muscles were sore. "See what I said? We're fine."

I laughed outright this time. "I'm glad to hear that."

"Oh, before you go, how's that brother of Zac's? Haven't seen him too much, though we did notice he limped up those stairs over there." She pointed to the rickety wooden staircase leading to my apartment. Helen might look innocent, but something told me she didn't miss much. Like the fact that Brax had visited me a couple of days ago. Probably noticed the grim line to his mouth when he left, too.

"He's as ornery as ever," I said.

Helen cackled. "For a hunk like him, you'd think he would smile more."

"Helen!"

"Don't you 'Helen' me, young lady." She poked her side with a fist. "I'm old but not blind!"

I was still giggling a little about Helen on my walk down Ocean Avenue. She was the levity I needed. A quiet enveloped me, punctuated occasionally by the crash of waves. Thin wisps of clouds tried to camouflage the sun, but warmth poked through. The humidity still messed with my hair, but I'd stuffed it under a hat today. The breeze and occasional sun-blocking cloud helped to temper the humidity.

For a hunk like him ...

Helen's assessment of Brax didn't really surprise me—I'd noticed his photo-perfect looks, the chiseled perfection of his face, his smoldering gaze, the minute we met in person. His surly attitude that day only accentuated those looks, making me curious about him. But it was his reaction to the videos I shared that I had not been able to shake all week.

Big sigh. Being an introvert all these years had shaken my social skills, made me oblivious to how my actions affected others. Hated that about myself. What had I been thinking when I'd shared those videos without asking? That somehow, I'd be the hero he needed to jumpstart his career?

I shuddered.

Still, he didn't have to be so harsh.

If only I hadn't kissed him. What had I been thinking? If his lips were as kiss-worthy as they looked? (Yes.) If he returned the curious feelings that had overwhelmed me for days? (Maybe.) If there could possibly be more to our relationship? (Doubtful.)

Yes, um, yes. I was wondering all of that and then some. My cheeks grew hot and not in a good way. Should've put on sunscreen. They did make that for shame, right?

Speaking of shame, Joanie had called yet again to check in on my writing progress, like I was Emma Thompson and she, Queen Latifah in the movie *Stranger Than Fiction*. A tiny laugh escaped me, though the laughter was decidedly nervous. Emma, too, had writer's block so her publisher sent someone to, uh, *shepherd* her along. I'd never been in this predicament before.

The truth was, a lot had been on my mind in the past couple of days, but sadly, the only thing I had thought little about was my next book. The story had been coming along in fits and starts for weeks, but I was beginning to wonder if my writing career was more than stalled—maybe it was over.

Writing wasn't the only reason for her call, however.

She began with, "About that hottie singer you posted on Facebook ..."

"You mean the video I took down."

"Thankfully, it was captured by our admin before you did that!"

"Wait, what? Captured?"

"You know, downloaded. Why in heaven's name did you take that down?" She tsked a few times. "That video drew thousands of eyeballs back to your page, Viv—I mean, Clara. The marketing team was over the moon about it."

"Glad I could help. But—"

"But nothing. You probably thought posting it was off brand, but thankfully the team realized what a boon they were to you, and they are back up."

Horror continued to overcome me and what my actions had wrought. Was I being too dramatic? Maybe. But still. Brax would be so ... mad.

I wandered into Curios and Seashells, hoping to take my mind off how I would break it to Brax that his videos had apparently grown legs, thanks to my meddling. Of course, I had no plans to see or talk to him anytime soon, so maybe I could avoid the whole thing altogether.

The shop was clearly divided in two, with bins and bins of shells in every shape, size, hue imaginable on one side.

Some were strung together, too, and hanging from the ceilings next to kitschy beach signs the color of sea glass, pinks or deep blue.

The other side of the shop was less definable. Statues, random bric-a-brac like an old drinking fountain, archaic frames, and ornamental figurines that very well might have lived former lives on the walls of historic buildings.

"Good morning. May I help you find something?" The woman peered at me from behind round glasses, her smile easy. I got the feeling she was younger than she appeared, mid-forties, maybe?

"I'm really just browsing. You have an eclectic mix in here, but I'm sure you hear that all the time."

"Oh, I do. It's a long story, but suffice it to say, my husband and I have very different tastes."

"So that's why there's an invisible line down the middle of the store."

She laughed. "You are very observant."

I smiled back. Observant. She had no idea. I glanced around, looking more deeply at the offerings—the painted crabs, delicate wind chimes, and beach-themed charm bracelets—knowing that some of it would surely show up in a novel. If I ever wrote one again.

"Well, you go ahead and browse. I'll let you be. I'm Shelly. Just let me know if you need me."

"Thank you. I will."

I took a shopping basket from a stack and wandered the aisles for a good ten minutes before the bell on the front door rang. A handsome man, early fifties probably, wandered in. He wore chino shorts, a polo shirt, and sneakers, and carried a massive battered frame. I slid a glance at the picture in it. Was that a dog in a soldier's uniform?

"What do you expect you're going to do with that?" Shelly was giving the man a what-for look over the top of her wire frames, her expression a mix of annoyance and mirth.

"What do you think I'm going to do? Gonna put it up on the wall as our mascot."

"Mascot! No, no, no. Absolutely not. It's soooo ugly. Terrible!"

The man stood back and looked at the picture in the frame, shock on his face. "How can you say that? He's beautiful. And he's at the beach, which makes him all the more worthy of being hung in a place of honor in this shop."

Shelly shook her head. "I'll hang it alright—over the dumpster outside!"

The man chuckled. He leaned over the counter and kissed Shelly on the cheek—the husband, apparently. She sighed and rolled her eyes. "Fine, Rick. But hang it over there"—she gestured in my direction—"where I can't see it from the counter."

Rick shrank back. "If you can't see it, then it might get stolen!"

A wicked grin formed on Shelly's face. She caught eyes with me and winked. "Precisely."

I looked away, but my own smile lingered. Judging by this shop, those two were very different people, and yet their gentle ribbing showed their ability to mesh. Like peanut butter and jelly. Helen and Gus were that way, too. A pang of something caught me in the windpipe again. Not the first time this week. This was what longtime love looked like. I only wrote about young heroines finding their prince. Who really knew what happened to them after their eyes—and other parts of them—began to sag?

Rick walked over to me, dragging that oversized picture.

"Let me get this lady's opinion."

Shelly piped up. "Oh no you don't! She's my first customer all day. Leave her alone."

I laughed. "You two are hilarious. I take it you're married."

Rick smiled and cast a glance at his wife. "Until she kicks me out."

"Could happen!" Shelly's laugh spilled over into the room.

I jumped in. "Something tells me you've been having this conversation for years."

Shelly and Rick went silent. They looked at each other and I was about to apologize profusely for being the one to kill the conversation—a pattern for me lately—when they both burst with laughter.

"She thinks we're an old married couple," Rick said.

"Well, she's got the old part right," Shelly said.

Rick smiled at me. "We're newlyweds—"

"Not true." Shelly shook her head, her smile lightly etched into her face. "Been married two years tomorrow."

"And she still makes my heart flutter."

Shelly slapped him gently. "You're so sweet. Now go. Get out of here with that thing. Put it in the back and we'll hang it together later."

"Yes, my love."

I stole a couple of glances at Shelly after he left. "I hope we didn't embarrass you. He likes to come in every once in a while to stir the pot."

"You two are an inspiration.

"Oh." She giggled at this, reminding me of a teenager. "My grown children think we're silly." A brief bit of soberness crossed her features.

"I don't think so at all." I looked around. "If you've only been married a couple of years, how long have you had this shop?"

"Well, that's a story. But I'll give you the fast version. I worked in an insurance company for twenty years when one day, I had a mild heart attack."

I sucked in a breath.

"I made a decision then that it was time to live my dream."

I tilted my head. "I take it selling insurance wasn't your dream?"

She pointed jokingly at me. "Bingo. No, I always wanted a shell shop by the beach and I got one. Had a few problems in the beginning"—she shook her head—"starting with a rascal of a landlord. But what can I say? The problems led to me finding Rick, or the other way around."

"Like it was meant to be."

"Exactly. Every morning I pray and ask God for his direction and then I try to follow his lead. I've been doing that for more than forty years and he's never led me astray."

Rick popped back into the main room, cutting into the conversation. "Unlike the lady over there has led me astray."

Shelly clucked a laugh. "Ha ha ha."

They were both ridiculous. In the finest way possible, though. After I bought more shells than I could possibly pack in my suitcase for the plane ride home, I wandered back to Mermaid Manor, my mind tumbling with new hope. Shelly had shared a tiny piece of her life with me, infusing me with the courage I needed to seek answers to the question of my absent father.

I determined that when I got back to the house, I would pull Brax's note out of the drawer and contact my brother.

CHAPTER NINE

Brax

Clara's bike remained the same way I left it, which meant she hadn't touched it since we rode together the other afternoon. A twist of guilt drilled through me. Served me right. I'd been a jerk the other day. Couldn't even stand looking at myself this morning, hence the baseball cap.

I needed fresh air. Zac's house was stifling. Dull. I had begun to feel trapped, the need to get out overshadowing all else. Not much swelling in my ankle anymore, so why not?

The cruiser shushed and groaned beneath my weight, and I made a mental note to pop into a hardware store and buy some oil. Otherwise, all that rust on rust might turn this beast into powder. I hadn't given this one quite the shine job that I'd done on Clara's.

The gloomy beach weather reminded me of my childhood in the Valley, when the sun would hide but still leave behind air both thick and heavy. At least here, a breeze cooled the air enough to make it tolerable. Evenings were even better.

I rode past miles of beach houses, some old with front doors that needed ducking in to enter, and others massive, like they'd been built for egos. The harbor mouth stopped my progress, but I couldn't bring myself to look at the two sea lions who sat stoic and empty. Instead, I pedaled around to the other side and found a lookout where I could stop for a while. I sat on the bike, arms folded at my chest, watching half-heartedly as fishing boats came in and sailboats went out.

What was I doing here? As if to answer, my ankle twinged, and I scowled at its timing. Still, when had I ever allowed a bum ankle to slow me down this much? Another scowl overtook my face and I was tiring of it.

A van pulled up—and what I assume was a husband, wife, and two aggressively joyful boys spilled out. The woman began laying a tablecloth out on a picnic table inches from me, you know, since I was wearing a cloak of invisibility. The kids all scrambled down the rocks, their dad following closely behind, and for one hot minute I didn't know if my heart could take the memories. Those parents could have been mine, those boys, me and Zac.

We played like kids on the rocks ...

Our thoughts untethered ...

To when it would all end ...

I shook off the tear-jerking lyrics that forced their way into my head with alarming regularity lately, like I was a country music singer in hiding. *She ain't gonna love me no more ...*

The clichéd words brought out a smile, and despite my best efforts, the warm wind and undulating ripple of water out there had smoothed out my edges. The woman with the picnic fussed about until those little boys had a feast waiting for them. Seeing it all there, hot dogs in buns, chunks of melon and chips, made me realize how little I'd eaten.

Guess I'd been relying on Clara to feed me more than I realized.

"Boys, c'mon! Lunchtime!"

I backed away from the scene as the boys came running, diving for a spot at the table. They all bowed their heads, giving thanks for their dogs and chips, and that pricked my memory bank too. Rain or shine, Mom and Dad always made sure we thanked the Lord for whatever he put on the table. Reminded me that food was a good place to start, though I had much more to be praying about.

Back on the bike, I followed the roadway toward a long harbor channel, letting my brain bob around like boats tied loosely to their docks.

I shouldn't have sold my business. If I hadn't, I would have somewhere to be, somewhere to land with both feet on the ground. Zac assumed I was some sort of drifter. "Hey, man," he'd said in his doctor voice, "maybe it's time to settle down."

If only you knew, brother …

I'd tried that. After Kate left for good, settling down was all I ever tried. My work spoke for itself, but—I'd hated it. Every living minute of it. I blinked, trying to keep my eyes on the path in front of me. Not sure why my mind tended to bounce around rather than stay on task, as my middle school teachers would lament. High school teachers were worse. I barely passed. Not that I cared all that much. I'd had my guitar and my dreams and that's all I needed.

Until those dreams disintegrated like a sand castle at high tide.

I exhaled. I left the peninsula now and continued to ride north along the busy corridor, past fountains, palm trees, and high-end homes. A sign up ahead caught my eyes and I slowed. Open mic night every Friday. *Must be the place Zac mentioned.*

The door was open, though the sign said closed. I rolled up to take a look. Guys were moving tables and chairs around while a band set up. My fingers clenched the handle-bars, a pang of something old moving me.

"You like live music?" The guy was burly with a full head of hair and a bass-deep voice. He held out a flyer to me. "Come back tonight. It's gonna be a great show."

I took it from him. "Thanks."

The guy's eyes narrowed, like he was scrutinizing me. I got it. Lots of expensive equipment being moved in and out. "Have I seen you somewhere? Have we met?"

I gave him a small smile, hoping to quell any worries that I was casing the place. "No, man. I'm just visiting family."

This seemed to satisfy him, though his gaze lingered for a beat longer. "Well, then, stop by before you leave town. Open at six."

I sat on the bike for a few minutes longer, taking in the familiar cacophony of band noise, of guys bantering, of furniture scraping and dishes clanking in the distance. Made me want to step back into it all again, even for just a night or two. My eyes scanned the window decor, a jumble of postings, including the one the bar owner had handed me. Open mic night, a private event, a competition...

There was another reason, too, for my interest—my phone had been ringing nonstop lately. It's the reason I'd turned it off today. Needed a break from it. Clara was responsible for this sudden interest in my old life.

The anger I'd felt the first time I saw the ancient videos up on her page had faded some. She said she had removed them, and I believed her, but ... still I was getting phone calls.

"Dude, you sound good!" one message said.

"Are you back?" from another.

And from the agent who took weeks to answer calls: "Did you find a new agent or something?"

All of it had piqued my interest. Not to mention, my desire to write again, though the words that followed me around poked at the protective layer around my heart. Geez, even that sounded soft. *Get a grip, Braxton.*

I rode off, winding my way through a different beach community, this one laid out like a tic-tac-toe board, giving my mind more time to think and wonder and ... create. After a while, I realized I couldn't avoid the process, even if I tried. My parents may have wanted me to live a life of stability and plans—and I had tried for a very long time—but as I pedaled through the State Beach park path, and then on to Hollywood Beach, I finally came to the realization that my brain did not think in black and white or in cells of a spreadsheet. Not unless it was forced to.

Change had a way of finding me, whether I wanted it to or not. My gut told me to move on, but I was thinking with my heart right now. Couldn't stop myself. Clara was everything Kate was not—imaginative, curious, introverted yet inquisitive. Kate had been beautiful, but Clara's beauty had sucked me in the minute we met. Like a boy with a crush, I'd tried to hide my instant reaction to her by treating her rudely. It hadn't helped that before we'd met, my big brother had delivered a warning to stay away from her.

I scoffed. He'd do that kind of thing when we were kids— give me fatherly advice in high school. Why did he think he still needed to?

Maybe because I shut him out of my life after the divorce ...

I let go of a groan. I'd been lying to myself, lying since the first day I saw Clara, acting like she hadn't moved me. Those saucer eyes and big questions had needled their way into my psyche. Though I'd treated her brusquely, she cared for me anyway. She treated everyone she met with care— Gus and Helen, the landlord, that mutt ... I didn't deserve her.

I rode faster, my mind on a bender. I would go to Clara, tell her I appreciated all she'd done for me, then I'd leave this tiny enclave with whatever self-respect I had left in me. My ankle had held up well on my journey along the beaches around here, so there was no reason to stay.

Zac's house was in my line of sight, and I picked up the pace. A couple was crossing the street, a dog in tow. I squinted to make them out, yet didn't need to. Clara's curves, her lush hair, the way she walked with her arm bent at an angle, as if carrying a high-end purse when it was really just a beach bag, was unmistakable to me. That fact alone—that I could recognize her by the way she moved— both scared and intrigued me.

I slowed, neither noticing me. Clara stepped out of her sandals, hooked them onto her fingers, then stepped gingerly across the sand. I fought the urge to ride over there, pick her up, and carry her over my shoulder. We'd ride off into the sunset. Me Tarzan and she my Jane—on a beach cruiser.

I was losing my mind.

Just as Clara stepped out of view, Carter looked up and caught my eye. A dumb grin oozed across his mug. He sent me a salute then he, too, moved out of view.

Like I thought, there was no reason to stay here. No reason at all.

Clara

I HUNG UP THE PHONE. With every pore, I wanted to call Brax, to tell him all the details of what had just transpired. He was the reason I was in this position. I lifted my cell-phone again and scrolled through my contacts until I found his number. My finger hovered over the call button.

A knock on the front door startled me. I set my phone down on the couch and answered the door to find Carter standing there in board shorts and flip-flops, a blue-and-white-striped beach towel slung over his shoulder, dark shades on his nose.

"Come to the beach with me," he said.

I glanced over his shoulder. The wispy clouds from earlier had drifted away to reveal bright sunshine and an azure sky. "It *is* gorgeous outside."

Carter's gaze brushed over me. I can't say I didn't like the attention (because that would be lying). "So you want to go lay on the beach?" He lifted a small ice chest. "I've got provisions."

My mind buzzed with details, things I wanted to blurt

out to ... somebody. If only Greta were home. Or Brax wasn't upset with me.

Carter butted into my ragtag thoughts, the ones flapping about with nowhere to land. "Unless you've got other plans ...?"

I didn't. Not today, at least (unless you counted the synopsis deadline I was ignoring). I really should take advantage of the beach for the short time I had left. Justin and I had made tentative plans, though I wasn't ready to disclose them. I glanced at Carter and his beach garb and playful smile. Laying on the beach was so west coast. No one had ever invited me to do that in Indiana. "Sure," I said, attempting to meet Carter's gaze in his shades. "I'll change and grab a towel."

"Excellent," he said. "I'll wait on the deck."

I rushed around, first changing into a swimsuit and cover-up, then sliding into flip-flops. I plunked a hat on my head, grabbed Sport's leash, and headed to the door. She clipped along behind me, her tail wagging, finally willing to go outside again.

Carter smiled at us, a chunk of blond hair falling over one eye. He reminded me of the quintessential '60s surfer and I began hearing the song "Wipe Out" in my head.

"Ready?"

I nodded and all three of us walked across the street to the beach. I slipped out of my flip-flops, hung them on my fingertips and went barefoot in the sand, each step a massage to the bottoms of my feet. This was a welcome diversion. Maybe not rushing out and telling anyone about my conversation with Justin was the better choice. I could lay on the sand, listening to the ebb and flow of the surf, and relive the call on my own. It was totally okay to celebrate on my own. Why not start now?

"What's got you smiling over there?"

"Huh?"

"You're grinning like you just heard a cool joke."

"Oh. Well, there *are* voices in my head."

"Yeah. I have those too."

I laughed. "Somehow I'm not surprised."

"Some of the best conversations I have are with the voices in there."

"Is that right? What do they tell you?"

He was sitting up, one knee pointed toward the sky, his arm leaning across it, extended toward the ocean. "They tell me that I'm the very best and that I should accept nothing less from anyone."

I peered at him. "Very best what?"

He shrugged. "Realtor. Landlord. Fill in the blank—I'm the best."

"Pretentious much?"

Carter splayed a hand on his chest, turning to me. "I beg your pardon, Clara. I'd prefer to call it confidence." He looked out to sea again. "No one's going to sing your praises if you don't start them off in the right key."

Maybe this was the reason my publisher had always advised me to avoid my book reviews. Not like I complied completely, though lately, I had. All kinds of readers singing off-key on the review pages. Could that be the reason for my writer's block? Maybe. Or maybe everything had come so easy for me in the past, revealing my inherent laziness, my unwillingness to push through this tough spot. I must have been frowning because Carter said, "Wow. The voices you're hearing must have a case of schizophrenia. Seconds ago, you were smiling. What are they saying now?"

"Nothing. Just a lot on my mind."

"Well, put it aside. It's not worth it."

I wrinkled my nose. How did he know?

He continued. "I have something to ask you."

I pushed myself to switch gears. "Okay."

"The West Coasters Realty Association is having its annual costume party, and I'd like you to come with me."

I bit the inside of my cheek and stole a look at him beneath my hat. *Stay cool, girl. Stay calm.* I cleared my throat. "Are non-Realtors allowed?"

"Sure, if they're a plus-one. Will you come? I was thinking we could go with a twenties theme, you know, since that's what got the Barnes sisters here in the first place.

There was no hesitancy on Carter's face or in his voice. I'm sure he was asking because, clearly, we'd hit it off and become friends in a short time. He also knows I won't be here all that much longer, so I'm sure he doesn't have anything long term planned where I'm concerned.

I considered his request. The thought of making small talk with strangers made my stomach drop. Then again, I had the perfect costume. Something I'd found in our grandmother's attic. I'd brought it with me to show Greta, but oops, with all the wedding planning, totally forgot. So I guess I could go and use it to pretend I was someone else. What harm could there be in that?

"Sure, Carter. I'll go with you."

"I knew you would."

"Careful. Your confidence is showing."

He grinned and flipped that blond hair out of his eyes. "That's my goal."

We lounged on the sand for at least another hour, watching surfers come and go, and letting Sport dig furiously after renegade smells. I had to reposition her a couple of times because whenever she got on a roll in her quest to clear the beach of sand, damp clumps of it would land on me.

When the snacks were gone and our water bottles empty, Carter and I packed up and wandered back home. We made plans for the costume party and then retreated, each to our own unit of the house.

After showering and making sure Sport had been watered and fed, I logged onto the computer. An email from Justin awaited me. I had been bursting to tell someone that my long-lost older brother wanted to meet me, but in the end, I'd kept the news to myself. I wish Greta was here. I had been moved to second in line when it came to my sister, and when she had children, I would drop even lower on the list.

I exhaled. When I talked to Justin, he only said that he would be interested to meet soon. That had given me enough to float around on for the past few days. But we hadn't formally chosen a date or time, so maybe this email in my inbox would have some details of his thoughts. He lived somewhere in Arizona, so it could be awhile before I could get there.

Dear Clara,
I have decided that I would like to come to California to meet you. I am due a vacation, so I have booked a room at Royalty Suites for this Saturday evening. Perhaps we can meet at the hotel for coffee and conversation.
Sincerely,
Justin

HE'S COMING HERE? My mind swam with the details I couldn't yet fathom as my heartbeat thudded in my ears. A brother I never knew I had, son of the father I also never knew I had, would be traveling to California. To meet me.

I picked up the phone and punched in a number.

CHAPTER TEN

Brax

"Dude," Zac said over the phone, "thanks for helping Clara find her, uh, brother, but Greta's concerned."

"Why's that?" I punched a throw pillow and tossed it across the room. It landed on the couch.

"Because the guy's coming to Hollywood Beach to see her. I assume you set that up."

"No, man." *I didn't even know about it.* Confirmation hit me in the windpipe. Clara had news, really big news, and she hadn't chosen to tell me about it. Probably told Carter instead. I glanced at my bags packed and sitting by the front door, more sure of my decision to leave than ever.

"Oh. Well, since you're the one who located him, I guess I thought you knew of their plans to meet." Zac blew a sigh into the phone, and I could tell he was revving up to say something serious. "Clara called Greta all excited."

"I'm sure the situation still seems strange to her."

"No, that's not it. Greta is thrilled for Clara, but like I told you, her sister's sweet, but she can be a little naive sometimes."

I cracked a smile. "She writes romances. Doesn't sound all that naive to me." She had to be part psychologist for that. Then again, she did have the ending to *La La Land* all wrong.

Zac laughed back. "Well ..."

I shifted my weight off my tender ankle. "So what is it you want me to do?"

"Watch out for her. What if this guy's a—"

"An axe murderer?"

"Do murderers carry axes? Does anyone these days?"

"Probably lumberjacks."

"Well, then, spy on them and see if the guy's wearing plaid."

I scoffed. "Marriage hasn't changed your dorky sense of humor."

"Yep. She's stuck with me now." Zac laughed a little. He sounded happy, content. Made it difficult to be annoyed with him.

"I'd help but I'm out of here today, as a matter of fact."

"Wait. You're leaving? Already?"

I frowned. I had been here long enough, hadn't I?

Zac lowered his voice. "I meant to say, I thought you'd be enjoying it there—like a vacation."

"It's fine, but I've got to see a guy in Texas about a bar ..."

"What about Gus and Helen? I'm sure they've been knocking on your door every night."

"Not once. Those two seem perfectly capable, if a little eccentric, to take care of themselves."

Zac dropped a sound like a long, low sigh into the phone.

"I'll be blunt: Greta's worried about her sister. Frankly, I am too. We don't understand all that transpired to get Clara to this point of meeting up with her supposed brother face-to-face and why it needs to happen so soon. We're concerned. Both of us. If you could—"

"Babysit her?"

"Come on, Brax."

He was right. This was on me, and I couldn't leave—why did I ever think I could? Guilt crept into my gut. Kate's final words to me were that I'd never protected her. "You always think of yourself first!" she'd charged before walking out the door forever.

I glanced again at my hastily gathered things—my bag, my guitar. Was that what I'd been doing? I shoved away the memories of Kate's departure, and the guilt that poured in afterward, and focused on my brother's request. If I didn't stay, I'm sure he and Greta would rush right home. Do I really want to be responsible for cutting my brother's honeymoon short?

Not a chance.

And the bigger question: was Clara's safety in question? She had probably already told Carter her news, but let's be real, that guy couldn't wrestle a For Sale sign out of dry dirt.

"Sure, man. I'll stay. I'm not sure what I'll be able to find out about it"—I didn't mention that Clara was currently annoyed with me—"but I'll be here for her."

"Keep her safe?"

"Absolutely."

After we hung up, I contemplated my next step. If I hadn't been such a jerk the other day, Clara might have called me with her news before picking up her phone to call Greta. She might have even showed up on my doorstep and launched herself into my arms with her good news, plopping another soft kiss on my lips ...

Stop that. I was not going there again. Ever.

I groaned into the quiet room. Did I really blame Clara for not telling me she'd not only contacted her brother but had plans to meet him too? This really was spectacular news, and a twinge of regret coiled my insides. I had been short with her, when all she had been doing was trying to help. I didn't want her help, of course. But ... she'd been breathless the other night, her face flushed, telling me how much she loved hearing me sing. I hadn't been able to shake that ever since.

I had planned to go to her after my impromptu cycle around the beach town. Up until the moment when I saw her with ... Carter.

My mouth involuntarily turned upside down at the thought of her with that guy. Not that I had any reason to dislike him. But she seemed to like him. Wasn't that reason enough?

A rap came on the front door. I stirred. Before I could answer it, the knock came again. I swung open the door. A leggy blond with oversized sunglasses on her mane of styled hair stared back at me. I'd seen her somewhere before ...

She reached a manicured hand to me, metal bangles dancing on her arm. "I'm Lisa. You must be Braxton."

I shook her hand, my mind still searching for details about where and when we might have met. Was she at the wedding?

"May I come in?" She was bold and pretty, though not my type.

"That depends. Are you selling Amway?"

"I have no idea what my housekeeper uses to do my laundry, but it better be organic and sustainable."

I grinned. She had a sense of humor and I couldn't say it wasn't attractive.

She lifted her chin. "You might recall me as the woman who was once engaged to your brother. We spoke on the phone once briefly."

Recognition ran through me. Lisa? Wasn't she the fiancée Zac bought this house for originally? The one with lofty plans and high-end taste?

"Hello again." I opened the door wide enough for her to enter. My curiosity beat out the warning flags in my head.

Lisa sashayed into the house and down the hall, stopping at the living room. She tilted her head forward, letting the sunglasses slip down her nose. "Not the decor I would have chosen, but to each their own." She spun around on her heels, her very tall, narrow heels. "I saw your video, Brax, and you are brilliant."

"Would you like to sit?" I gestured toward the comfortable couch. She took the chair across the room instead, so I made myself comfortable.

"I know we haven't seen each other in person before, but we were almost family, so I hope you won't think me too forward." She smiled at me, and I noticed her airbrushed looks. The woman could be a model, no doubt the reason Zac was attracted to her initially.

"I would like to invite you to accompany me to an event this weekend for the West Coast Realty Association."

A beautiful woman asking him out? He chuckled and rubbed the back of his neck.

"You're surprised?" She looked unbothered by my reticence.

"Is it that obvious?"

She stood up and walked closer to me. "I'd like you to meet the owner of the venue where the event will be held. Chuck is a good friend of mine, owns the bar, and I think you'd be a great addition to the talent over there."

I spat a laugh.

"Something funny?"

"Yeah, I haven't been called the talent in years."

She didn't flinch. "That's a shame. Listen, you'd be doing me a favor, too. It's a costume party and I need a date. If you really want to know, I asked your neighbor, Carter Blue, but he is already going with someone."

I froze.

She continued. "I will pay you back by introducing you to Chuck. I thought since we practically know each other, you would consider going with me. It'll make it a win-win."

"So you know Carter?"

She smiled, though there was a slight hesitancy to it. "Yes. For years."

"And he has a date already," I stated, thinking.

She bunched up her forehead. "With someone who's staying in his guest apartment." Her eyes popped open. "You would know her, of course. The bride's sister? Vivian?"

I kept my gaze steady, my eyes giving away nothing. "Her name is Clara."

Lisa waved her hand in the air in an offhanded way. "Right. Clara. She probably prefers Vivian, though. I mean, wouldn't you?" She laughed a little too loud.

The last thing I wanted to do was attend a party with this woman whose beauty had dimmed in the five minutes she had been in my presence. But she'd presented me with a perfect opportunity to follow Clara around. I'd be doing this for Zac and Greta, and to keep Clara safe and in view, not for any other reason.

"Sure," I said. "I'll take you."

Lisa gasped. "Wonderful! I'll pick you up at seven on Saturday night."

"You're picking me up?"

"We'll take my Mercedes. I'm assuming that's your ... Jeep out there?" She asked it as if she hoped it wasn't.

"I'll meet you there," I said instead. "I'll see you at seven."

Lisa leapt forward and impulsively kissed me on the cheek. "You're wonderful. It'll be a grand night. You'll see."

I walked toward the door and held it open for her. She had almost left the outside landing when she stopped and called out to me. "Oh, and it's a costume party, Braxton. Wear something dashing."

I watched her step quickly down the stairs, my mouth hanging open. What had I just agreed to?

Clara

Sport was watching me with curious marble eyes. Her furry little face tilted to one side. "What?" I asked while examining the back of my dress in the mirror. Hmm. Quite the booty there. I tossed Sport a fake withering glance. "Thanks for pointing that out."

My grandmother had a smaller derrière than mine and it appeared as if I had done more than my fair share to fill mine out. I bit my lip. If it weren't so warm, I could wear a wrap, but as it was, the humidity level had reached the level of a twenty-minute shower. Not that I'd ever taken one ...

I coiled my curly hair on top of my head, using another trick I'd learned online, then added a black veil. There. All I needed was a red rose and my costume would be complete.

Carter gave his signature theatrical tap to the front door. When I opened it, I gasped. He wore a short-waisted tuxedo, a black vest beneath his coat, and under all that, a white-collared shirt and silky white tie. His hair looked dipped in oil, his locks slicked back, and fake sideburns ran to the middle of his cheek. The eye shadow and liner, though, blew the entire outfit over the top.

"Rudy Valentino, at your service, m'lady."

He bowed and I laughed. "I think m'lady is the wrong era, but I get you. Good job, Carter."

"How about this: *How do you do, Signorina?*" He took my hand and bowed again.

"Perfetto!"

"Ah, bellissimo!"

I laughed. "I think we've covered all the Italian we know for now. Wow, Carter, you outdid yourself. I love the five-button sleeves on that coat—such detail. We should take a picture sometime tonight. Greta will love this."

"Your sister had quite the obsession with Valentino when she arrived on these shores last year."

Carter cracked me up with his colloquiums. "Well, she had good reason, what with finding that old postcard in our mailbox."

"I was surprised when you told me about the costume you found in your grandmother's attic." His eyes lingered on the fine lace of the dress. "And you're absolutely sure this is a copy?"

"You mean, do I think one of my ancestors was the real woman in black? The one who showed up at Valentino's grave year after year?" I tittered. "Please."

Carter lifted his hands in surrender. "All right, all right. But your great-grandmother did have ties to Hollywood by the Sea, and, well, the woman in black's identity has never been proven."

"That's what I love about you, Carter. You've got a million stories in that head of yours."

"Just like you."

"Ha." I hoped my quick laugh would mask the truth that I was still struggling to map out my next book. I changed the subject. "Some say they know exactly who she was. She never married and died in a house full of memorabilia."

"Adds to the mystique."

I smoothed my hands down the sides of my gown once more and Sport took this as her cue to trot over to her bed and get comfortable.

Carter offered me his arm. "Shall we?"

A mere five minutes later, we arrived at the dinner venue. I peered through the front window of Carter's car. The place looked like a bar. Shew. Okay.

Inside, however, my preconceived ideas were transformed with bright lighting and color everywhere. On stage, a band played crooner-style music low enough for conversation.

"Well, look who the cat dragged in." I turned to see who had just uttered that overused phrase. The skinny blonde wore a short, tight nurse's uniform with boobs nearly spilling out of them. A walking cliché, for sure ...

Carter nodded. "Clara, this is Lisa, a friend and sometimes business partner."

"Fabulous to meet you, Clara." Lisa offered me a hand that looked as if it had never washed a dish. She then leaned toward Carter to kiss his cheeks, those boobs leading the way. She lingered. Was her chest keeping her from standing upright?

Carter glanced around. "What? No ball and chain tonight?"

"Au contraire, I caught myself a doctor."

"Another one?" Carter said.

Lisa's laugh sounded put on. "Touché, Mr. Blue." She turned toward a server and took a flute of Champagne from his tray. Another server appeared with appetizers that looked like tiny squirrels with mayonnaise on top. Lisa turned up her nose at those and I had to agree.

Carter turned to me and said in a low voice, "You might not be aware of this, but Lisa once dated Zachary."

"Zachary?" The dots didn't connect right away, but then Lisa turned back around and gave me an appraising grin and I realized, she was *that* Lisa. Greta had mentioned Zac's ex, but in her characteristic way, hadn't gotten overly dramatic about it. Kinda wish she had—might have had a new antagonist in mind to write.

"So anyway, darling," Lisa said to Carter, while sweeping her spare hand around, "you look divine. This whole place looks scrumptious."

"Ah, with thanks to you for your design skills, I'm quite sure," Carter said.

I stood next to them lamely listening to their banter, not part of it, but nowhere to run to either. I didn't know anyone here except Carter and wasn't the type to go over and flirt with the band—though, let's be real, I could write a fantastic flirt scene when I wanted to. Just don't ask me to deliver those lines in person!

All this was flowing through my head while I stood by, thankful that my veil mostly covered my bored expression.

Suddenly, Lisa pivoted and announced, too loudly in my opinion, "Here's Dr. Holt now."

Dr. Holt? As in Zac Holt? So confused ...

Instead, Brax approached us wearing a lab coat pinned with a handmade badge that read: Dr. Holt.

Lisa took his arm and yanked him toward Carter like an IV pole. "Carter, have you met Zac's brother?"

Carter chuckled. "Brax and I met at the wedding of the century."

Lisa scowled as Brax took Carter's hand and shook it. "Hello, Carter." Brax turned to me and nodded slowly, his eyes lingering, that telltale smirk quirking the edges of his smile. "Clara."

Lisa leaned into Brax and he was gentleman enough not to spare a glance at the boobs attached to his elbow.

Carter cut in. "She writes romance novels."

"Yes, of course—bodice rippers, right, Vivian?"

I coughed a laugh. First, because I hadn't heard that term in years. Second, because my books didn't have enough heat in them to rip a bodice, and third, because of, well, *the obvious*. (Keeping my eyes averted here ... don't mind me.)

"Clara is my ...." Brax continued to stare after me, a variety of thoughts appearing to cross his face. He smiled. "She's my sister-in-law's sister." He glanced at Lisa. "But, of course, you knew that."

Lisa offered up some stage laughter. "Yes, of course. Right. You're the sister of"—she snapped her fingers and made a big show of looking off into the distance—"Greta. Right. The one named after some kind of two-bit actor."

"She's named for Greta Garbo," I said.

Brax smiled. "And you are named for Clara Bow then. Is that right?"

How could I stay angry at this stud? He remembered the names of famous actresses of the silver screen, for crying out loud.

Lisa swiped a hand in front of her face. "Whatever. Anyway, it's you we should all be talking about." That same hand landed on Brax's chest, and I don't know why, but I felt a kind of protectiveness come over me. "You are a marvelous singer-songwriter!"

"Really?" Carter said. "How did you know that?"

"I saw him on Vivian Blackstone's Facebook page, just singing his beautiful heart out." She shook her head, that little white and red cap holding onto her mane of hair for dear life. "If it weren't for the internet, we wouldn't have met."

Excuse me while I go and unplug my modem ...

Carter looked at Brax. "I'm impressed. Had no idea you sang. Good for you." He said that as if Lisa had declared that Brax had just learned to tie the shoestrings of his leather wing tips. *Good for you, old boy.*

Lisa cut in. "Mm, yes, Brax is *so* talented."

I excused myself to go to the restroom, when really, I only wanted to get away. Mainly because I could feel Brax's heated gaze on me every time Lisa gushed about his talent. He was still mad at me—I could feel it, but there wasn't much more I could do about that now, though I'd tried. I texted him yesterday, you know, to ask about his ankle and all I got back was a gruff, *Yeah.* Well, I looked across the room now, an hors d'oeuvre table calling to me. I responded enthu-siastically.

"You're the woman in black, aren't you?" a female voice said as I surveyed the charcuterie.

The woman was piling her plate high with goat cheese. A mask covered her eyes but she sounded so familiar. She smiled. "I'm Shelly, from the shell shop."

"Yes, of course. Nice to see you here—my name is Clara, by the way. And you're right—I'm the woman in black." I tossed a quick look over my shoulder. "My friend Carter is dressed as Valentino."

"As well he should be," she said.

"Are you a Realtor as well as a shop owner?"

She smiled. "My husband worked in title. He retired from that career, mostly, but still enjoys coming to these things." She wrinkled her nose. "He's the extrovert in the family."

"I can relate—my sister's an extrovert who actually plans events like these." I took in her costume. The long thick dark hair reminded me of a cross between Yoko Ono and Cher.

"I'm Eve, in case you're wondering," she said. "I refused to wear a fig leaf, so this huge wig was our compromise."

"You mean ...?"

She wrinkled her forehead, then laughed. "No, ha ha, no. You won't find Rick running around in a fig leaf, if that's what you're worried about."

"A little."

She laughed harder at this. "I talked him into a leafy Hawaiian shirt and cargo shorts to go with his own big wig. He's also wearing a name tag that reads: Adam."

I smiled. "You two are so funny. I really can't believe you're still newlyweds."

"Because we act like an old married couple?"

I shrugged. "You act the way I assume two long-time married people would act. Finish each other's sentences, chide each other without malice, etcetera, etcetera."

Shelly spooned a couple of cheese chunks off her plate and added them to mine. "I took too many and you're a wisp, so you could use these."

I laughed.

She continued. "Rick and I tease each other a lot, but never to extreme. Even when we met—I'll have to tell you about that sometime—we each wanted what was best for the other."

"That's love for you."

"Yes, it is."

"May I ask ... how did you know?"

She smiled. "Know that he was the one?"

I nodded.

"Oh, honey, how much time do you have?"

I glanced over at Carter who was gesturing wildly with his hands, making a big show to a small group that had surrounded him. "All night," I said.

Shelly followed my gaze and laughed. "Okay, then, honestly, there were dozens of indicators, but the bottom line is each of us sensed God's presence in the other. And we just knew he had brought us together—though I will tell you I fought it at first."

"Fought God?"

"Crazy, isn't it?"

"No, well, yes." I paused, thinking about the faith that I had all but left behind in Indiana. "Sounds like a beautiful thing."

She pressed her lips together into a smile. "Oh, it is,

Clara." She paused. "Don't look now, but there's a hottie coming this way and he's looking right at you."

I glanced over to see Brax approaching the table.

"That's ... Brax. I'm sure he's just hungry."

Shelly's smile grew wider. "Sure, honey. Whatever you say."

I flinched at the touch on my shoulder, but the look of contrition on Brax's face all but broke me.

"We need to talk."

I swung a look back to the table saying, "I'd like you to meet ..." but Shelly was gone. Vanished. *Traitor.* A sigh left me, and I popped a look at him. "Let's just get through this evening, shall we, Brax?"

"I know you're mad at me. You should be."

I rolled a look up to the ceiling. "Stop trying to make me feel guilty. I'm over it."

He quirked a grin, the lines at the corner of his mouth drawing me like a pulley. "I'm sorry I was a jerk the other day."

"Again." My hand flew to my mouth. Had I said that out loud?

"You're right. Things got out of my control and, well, it's my downfall." His gaze washed over me in a way that made me feel like I was the one wearing that flimsy nurse's uniform. "I wouldn't blame you if you said you were sick of me, but I hope and pray that you're not."

"Pray?"

"That surprise you?"

Yes, yes it does. Thought he was going to call it a figure of speech or something. Well, whether he prays or not, doesn't mean he has to be as rough as sandpaper all the time.

"Clara?" Brax's head leaned to one side as he stared at me.

"Sorry. Lost in thought a moment." I snapped another hard look at him, moving away from the table so others could pass. "Aren't you worried your boobs, I mean, your date is going to miss you?"

A tiny smile danced on his face. "Forgive me?"

My mind flipped through the many scenes I'd written like this. The coy tête-à-tête, the palpable tension, the eventual happily ever after. But I was beginning to wonder if I'd missed some things, like the way the hero of the book smelled so good—intoxicatingly so. My physical awareness of Brax's closeness shocked me, as did my desire to know, not just more about him—but *everything*. What did he eat for breakfast? What did he pray about? And why did bringing up music cause such a painful expression? When falling for a guy, I expected to feel a certain familiarity, perhaps a coziness, but this! I nearly couldn't breathe from all the questions jostling for answers.

I lifted my chin, making my gaze meet his. "Of course, I forgive you."

An expression of relief and vulnerability crossed his face. "Thank you. There's more I'd like to talk to you about. Do I dare?"

"Well, I don't know. Are you going to continue to insist that *La La Land* had the wrong ending?"

He scoffed. "Yes, and I'll defend my position to the end."

I tilted my head to the side. "I want to know why."

"I've already told you, that ending should have been the dream sequence."

"A cautionary tale, then?"

"Exactly."

"But that's not what I was asking. I'm really curious, Brax. Why does that ending mean so much to you?"

He opened his mouth, but then closed it as if in slow motion. I had the feeling that he had more to tell me but couldn't. Or wouldn't. In a way, the same held true for me. In two days, I would be meeting my brother and Brax was responsible for that. I wanted to tell him. I *should* tell him. I'd told Greta, but something held me back from telling Brax. I felt ... protective almost.

Brax lurched forward suddenly.

I yelped.

Lisa laughed wildly, her arms around Brax's middle now, practically knocking the poor guy off his boots. "What are you two talking about over here?"

He eyed me. "Family matters."

"Oh, that's right, you two are related now, aren't you? That's so sweet."

Not exactly true, but whatever ... I nodded to them both and began to make my way over to where Carter was surrounded. I drew close enough to hear him use the word *preposterous* in a sentence, when a towering man in a Frankenstein costume stopped me. "Vivian Blackstone?"

"Yeah?" I was in no mood ...

"Lovely to meet you."

I gave him the side eye. Really? He had a bolt coming out of his neck. Did he really read romance novels?

He thrust a flyer at me. "I met Braxton Holt the other day but didn't realize it. He rode up on his bike and I knew he looked familiar."

"I see." Brax rode his bike without me?

"I'm Chuck, owner of this place."

"Hello, Chuck."

"Anyway, I was hoping you'd put in a word with Braxton for me. We'd love to have him enter a competition we're holding here next week. I've invited some bigwig producers up from LA to do the judging."

When I didn't answer right away, he continued. "I mentioned it to his date, Lisa, but she told me to bug off." He chuckled and it looked so creepy with that blood dripping down his face. "She said he's not interested, but I thought, well ..."

"That I could talk him into it?"

"Yes. Could you?"

I hated to disappoint a monster, but there was no way I would be bringing up Brax's music to him again. Though he had apologized, so much remained unsaid between us. When we met, I hadn't missed Brax's swoon-worthy appeal, of course, but what scared me more was my heady reaction to his presence. *Breathe, Clara, breathe.* I nearly ached standing so close to him back there yet knowing that all touching was off limits.

No. That's a solid no. I already clung to tenterhooks where Brax was concerned. If big-bosomed Lisa wasn't even willing to talk him into it, why would I?

"Sorry," I said, "guess you'll have to ask him yourself."

Then I hurried away before "Frank" could ask me again.

CHAPTER ELEVEN

Brax

THE WAY LISA was hanging all over me and talking to anyone who happened to pass by, I knew. She'd had too much Champagne. I'd vaguely noticed her take glass after glass from wandering servers. How many had there been? Three? Four?

Some date I was. I'd been distracted, though. Had noticed the bar owner, dressed as Frankenstein, talking to Clara. He had tried to hand her a flyer, but she had rebuffed him and I knew why: Clara did not want to risk upsetting me again. Inwardly, I cursed myself. I had overreacted the other night, and though I'd apologized, it was obvious she had not forgotten.

Or maybe ... she just didn't care to ever hear me sing again.

For the next hour, while the night's program progressed and speakers took their turns at the podium, I turned thoughts of Clara over in my mind. Occasionally, the band would play an interlude, bringing forth memories of being on the dance floor with Clara. She'd shocked me with her rapid-fire questions. It took me awhile to realize she was searching for a hero, but really, she'd been mine that night. After the fall, she'd whisked me away from that stifling dance floor and gotten me home. She'd scared me, though, and it was from more than her driving.

Ever since then, I'd been asking myself the same tired questions: What if ... what if I let myself fall for Clara only to have it all crash like it did with Kate? What if our relationship ended up unraveling the family?

The lights came on, and the music died. Lisa leaned toward me, her eyes lolling. "Take me home with you." Her words slurred.

"Thank you for an entertaining evening, but I think it would be best if I took you home."

A slow smile pulled like taffy across her face. "Perfect. You can stay with me tonight."

I rose, slid my chair back in, then offered her my hand. She leaned on it heavily, and I realized it was going to be a slow walk to the car. Even Frankenstein offered me a look of condolence as I helped Lisa into the Jeep, which included scooping up her legs and safely tucking them inside before shutting the door.

She cooed and hiccuped on the ride home, but perked when I pulled into her driveway.

I walked her to the front door, used her keys to unlock it, then waited back while she stepped inside. "Stay with me?" she asked in a kitten voice.

"Thanks again, Lisa. But not tonight."

"Awww, come on, Brass-ton. Pretty please."

I removed her hand from my arm. "You need to sleep it off. Doctor's orders. Goodnight, Lisa."

I had already reached my ride when I heard her shout, "You're just like your brother!"

Minutes later, I pulled into the driveway of Zac's house. Light shone from a small window in Clara's apartment. I grabbed my keys, refusing to overthink things, and took the stairs to her place two at a time, only wincing on one landing.

She answered the door wearing a long pink T-shirt and white fur slippers. "You making a house call?" she asked.

I dropped my gaze to the stethoscope still swinging around my neck. With a quick laugh, I pulled it off and stuck it into the pocket of Zac's lab coat. "May I come in?"

"Well, I'm not sure that's appropriate."

"If it would help, I could run home and get my Sponge Bob slippers."

"Only if you wear them with Squidward jammies."

I grinned. She rolled her eyes.

"Fine," she said, "come in."

I followed her inside. She disappeared into her bedroom and returned seconds later wrapped in a thin robe covered with colorful books. "It was a gift from my publisher," she explained.

"Naturally."

She padded into the kitchen, as if walking around in her pajamas in front of me was an everyday thing. I swallowed. *Wouldn't mind that at all ...*

"Want some tea?" She didn't wait, but put the kettle on to boil.

I hadn't had tea since I was a kid with a sore throat. Some in the music industry drank the stuff that coated their throats, but I'd never gotten into that. Mom always made Zac and me drink some with honey and lemon when we were sick. That should have made me hate the stuff, but this moment made me crave all that again.

She pulled a mug down from the cabinet and looked at me with an expectant raise of an eyebrow.

I nodded. "I would love some." I dumped the lab coat on a chair, glad I had worn a tee underneath it, and slid onto a stool to watch her work. She had to stand on her tiptoes to grab a sugar bowl and part of me wanted to rush over and gently lift her by the waist so she could reach it better. The other part of me decided I should stay out of the way.

I cleared my throat. "Thought I'd come by and check on you. I, uh, wanted to make sure Carter had been a gentleman."

"Ha." Her back was to me. Not sure what that meant.

"Is that a ha, of course he was, or ha, I need to go over and put him in a headlock?"

She turned back around and put sugar, honey, milk onto the island. Her expression wasn't downcast. Wasn't full of smiles and butterflies either. "It means I can take care of myself."

Fair enough. "There's another reason I'm here."

"Oh?" That eyebrow shot up again.

I shifted. "Yes. I've decided to enter a competition."

A smile appeared on her face. "What kind? Costume? Muscleman? Best hair?"

"You like my hair?"

Her gaze flipped to my hair. A blush formed on her cheeks, and she looked away. "Are you saying you're going to enter that contest Chuck's holding at the bar?"

"Sounds seedy when you say it that way."

She laughed fully now. Something in my chest flipped at the sound of it.

"But yes. I've been writing music again—"

"Oh, I hope it was that melody I heard in the garden that day."

I caught eyes with her. "It is."

She smiled again and turned away to fix our teas. Gotta say that elation in her buoyed my confidence. Pity parties aren't cool, but I couldn't shake the truth that not a lot of people in my past had much to say about my career path. Other than those set to profit from it, that is.

She served up a hot mug of tea and came around to sit beside me. We drank in silence for a minute, and for once, neither seemed to feel the need to fill the quiet with words.

Clara reached over and put her warm hand over mine. Reflexively, I captured it with my thumb. She looked at me and I at her. "I'm really proud of you," she said.

Her words broke me. She was ... proud?

"I really am, Brax."

My brain told me to pull away, to shut down her swelling of pride. I didn't want her to end up disappointed. I hated to admit this to myself, but I had only told Clara my news in hopes that it would encourage her to tell me hers. How devious was that?

She still had not mentioned anything about her call with Justin. She'd just told me she could take care of herself. How would she feel if she knew Zac had called asking me to keep an eye on her?

Clara turned. She now took my hand in both of hers. The look in her eyes—the colors of waves in the morning light— about melted me on the spot. "We didn't get to finish our conversation earlier tonight, you know. I was asking you why a silly movie's ending meant so much to you. If it weren't for Lisa's boobs—"

I coughed a laugh, remembering how my date crashed into our conversation.

"Well, anyway," Clara continued, "we were interrupted, and I don't know, I really thought you were about to say something."

I clamped my mouth shut. She didn't look away. Instead, Clara continued to implore me with those saucer-sized kaleidoscope eyes.

The subject of her brother was fading, and suddenly, I felt very, very small. I'd casually mentioned in our conversation that I prayed and she'd reacted to that in a way I hadn't expected. Like it meant something.

Truth was, it did. I had been praying more than usual lately, those kinds of conversations that wake you up in the morning and remind you of your ongoing conversation with God at night. I'd realized some things, but, until now, hadn't found reason to share them outside of my personal head space.

Maybe that's why I wrote songs, to share the things I never could find a way to say out loud.

I raised my eyes to meet hers. "Earlier ... when Lisa interrupted us"—I sighed, then pulled in a strengthening breath —"I was almost relieved."

"Why?"

"Because that wasn't the time."

"I see."

"But now is." Gently I pulled my hand from her grasp and ran it through my hair. Hadn't realized how much I did this when I was anxious, but given the way her eyes followed my actions, I guessed she knew. And, by the way she watched me so intently, it appeared that she dug it.

At least I could take solace in that.

"Here's the thing. I was married once, a long time ago. To Kate. She, uh, wasn't too crazy about all the time I spent with my guitar."

"I'm sorry."

I shrugged. "Wasn't her fault. She thought it was a hobby when we got married. My parents did too. I hadn't been honest with myself, let alone with them. They all wanted me to find something more stable to do long-term."

"Like the machine repair business you ran?"

"Yes, like that, although even that wasn't quite what they wanted. I tried, Clara, I really did."

"But you hated it."

"Not exactly hate—"

She reached forward and squeezed my hand.

"Okay. Yes. I hated it." I gave her a sad smile. "So after a while, I started playing again. And writing. Took up a lot of my nights."

"I'm sure. Because you were working days on your business."

I searched her face for judgment and found none.

"Is that why Kate left you?" she probed.

"How do you know that she left me?"

Her smile was kind. "Because you're a brooder."

I frowned. "Let me guess—you've written brooding heroes before, guys nursing their egos after a brutal walk out."

"It's not just their egos that get them, but their hearts, Brax."

I let that sink in. "Well, that's one analysis, but all I felt was shame. Shame that I let Kate down. She used to lob verbal grenades at me. One of her favorites was to tell me that I was always looking for stardust."

"Aren't we all?"

I leveled a gaze at Clara. To that question, I'd have to say no. Many people aren't looking for that at all. Then again, she was a writer hunting for a story. Another one. Clara and I were similar in that way. Not sure why I hadn't realized that before.

She was staring back at me, so I exhaled, telling her more of my secrets. "Kate hadn't wanted me to play that night. I was to make a big pitch to a mammoth corporation the next morning, and she felt I should stay rested, so I'd be on my game. But I'd gone ahead with it."

"Because it meant something to you."

"Yeah. Supposedly a well-known producer would be there. Plus, I'd written a new song—the one that went viral on your Facebook page."

"I loved that song."

I quirked a small grin. "Thanks, but it was my downfall. The guy never showed up, but Kate did."

"Oh … didn't she love it? Or did you have a fight or something?"

"She never heard it. Actually, Kate left after one set."

Clara's shoulders drooped. "I'm sorry, Brax."

"There's more. She, uh, had an accident on the way home. Hydroplaned."

"Oh no."

"She broke her wrist. Had all kinds of bruises on her face, arms. The recovery was long and brutal." I groaned, reliving the severity of it. "The car was totaled."

"And so was your marriage."

"Now there's a tagline for you."

Clara shook her head. "Brax. I'm taking this seriously."

"I know."

"I've probably seemed a little desperate lately to come up with a new story, but rest assured, I wouldn't plagiarize your life." Clara leaned forward. "I'm very sorry to hear about your heartache, and your wife's accident. It must've been awful."

"It was life changing."

She wore a thoughtful, sober expression. "It's why you don't sing anymore. Isn't it?"

"I tried to give my business another big push, but my heart never really was in it and it was beginning to show. I sold the whole thing before I could drag the whole crew down with me."

"Really? That's great. So that's why you're able to take some down time here? Because you're independently wealthy and don't need to work?"

I laughed. "I wouldn't say that, exactly, but I did okay with the sale. As for working, I've never stopped doing whatever came my way. Not until my ankle grounded me, that is."

"Sounds maybe like you're running."

"I like to think of it as keeping busy."

I watched Clara move about the kitchen, her robe clinging to her body in the best possible way and wished this could be the life I came home to every night. And woke up to every morning. I pushed the impossible thoughts from my head.

Clara stopped fussing about. She turned, holding a wadded-up rag in one hand, and peppering me with questions as if she'd suddenly become inspired. "Can I ask you something? Is your past the reason why you hate *La La Land* so much? Because you wish your life could have had an alternate ending?"

When I didn't react right away, she said, "That's it, isn't it?"

I considered that. If that were the case, I wouldn't be here with Clara right now. That thought alone brought with it a deep emptiness.

"In some ways, you're right about that stupid movie. Maybe I do want an alternate ending, but not to my life, Clara." I cupped her cheek with my hand. She didn't move. "What I wish is that I hadn't made so many mistakes in the first place."

"We all wish that, Brax."

I let my hand drop. It wasn't right to move something along that shouldn't be. "Truth was, I didn't love Kate the way I should have. We should have never gotten married. I carry tremendous guilt over those broken vows." I exhaled. "My mother was so disappointed. It shook her faith. Worse than a broken marriage was disappointing my mother. I'm not sure I've ever forgiven myself for that."

Clara's eyes fluttered as she reached up this time and stroked my face. "Maybe it's time you did."

Clara

I ALMOST TOLD Brax my news last night. Almost.

But he had just unpacked a lot of his past with me. I knew when I met him, underneath all that gruff blustering, that he had a soft heart. Even when I couldn't hear it in his voice, I saw it in his eyes. The way they crinkled slightly at the edges when he said nothing, as if he was really listening. Frankly, with four women in my house growing up—God love them all—there wasn't all that much listening going on.

In the end, I didn't mention that I would be meeting Justin today. Besides, I was beginning to think I was all on my own with this one anyway. Oh, I'd told Greta—how could I not? But ... she hadn't sounded as excited as I felt. I understood. This was my story to unearth, my past to bring to the surface. It broke my heart to say this, but Greta would probably never understand why I've pursued my father's side of the family because she never pursued hers, which up until recently, I thought was mine too.

Maybe I didn't quite understand it all myself.

I checked my sundress in the mirror. Before this trip to the West coast, I'd never been much for wearing dresses, but I don't know, something changed along the way. Maybe it was simply me following the when-in-Rome adage. *Or maybe it's the fact that later this afternoon you'll be seeing your flesh-and-blood brother for the very first time!*

Possibly. My thoughts rewound to last night, when Brax told me his secrets. I couldn't get his handsome face out of my mind, but more than that, I wanted to comfort him. To assure him that he didn't have to live a life of drudgery because of mistakes he believed he made in the past.

"It's time to let go, Brax," I whispered.

Maybe you need to let go too.

I frowned, not knowing where a thought like that would come from. To my knowledge, I hadn't been holding onto anything destructive, no past sins to forgive myself for—well, other than the usual ones of sleeping in late (laziness) and eating ice cream at midnight (gluttony).

Sport whined. I dug my hand into my side and gave her a sideways look. "Okay, I'll take you for another walk. Something tells me Greta's going to get home and tell me I've been had, though. I bet she never had to walk you this much."

She whined again, and this time it sounded like a question. I laughed while clipping her leash to her collar.

My flip-flops slapped against the pavement as we walked along, the sea air like a summer wrap about my shoulders. In the distance, a familiar figure walked toward us.

Brax. My heart did a little flip, that kind that squeezes your lungs in a good way. It happened so fast that it surprised me with its impact. Just as quickly, my sudden lift plummeted. Brax had shared deep cares with me last night, and for a little while, I thought he felt the same stirrings for me that I had for him. Okay, let's be honest here. These weren't stirrings, but an all-out party going on in my heart.

But showing him that, after he'd slit open an old wound, would have been taking advantage of his vulnerability. So maybe my reading-o-meter was off, that the vibe last night was simple, straightforward: Brax sharing the burdens of his past.

Sport spotted Brax up ahead and tugged me forward. And no wonder. We were mere body lengths apart now, and Brax was noshing on a burrito?

"Hey," he said between bites. He handed me a bag. "Brought you brunch."

"Really now. Brunch?"

He shrugged. "A breakfast burrito with the works."

"I can't believe you brought me food."

He took a bite and chewed it slowly, his eyes dropping to my dress, then trailing up to my eyes. "I kept you up late last night and figured you'd be sleeping in. Didn't expect to find you out here looking ... like that."

"And how do I look?"

He gave me an amused smile. "Like you were on your way to meet me."

My lungs squeezed, then released with a laugh. I almost thought Brax had figured out my secret. Although I had considered telling him about meeting Justin today, I had decided against it. Greta implied that, even though I write about lives, I don't have a whole lot of real-life experience myself. Maybe she was right, at least a little bit. I needed to handle this first meeting with Justin on my own.

"You're a flirt," I said.

He wiggled his brows. "Guilty."

The heat of a blush warmed through me. Maybe my search for a hero had ignored obvious heroic moments that happen every day ... like bringing someone a breakfast burrito without being asked. I clamped back a sigh. Rogue kiss or not, sometimes I had the palpable sense that Brax felt the same about me that I, well, that I felt about him.

But then he'd make a teasing joke or look away about the time I was ready to make a somersault dive toward him and the moment was lost. Brax cleared his throat, his eyes looking awfully amused. "You look lost in thought there."

"You know me." I laughed, diverting my gaze to the bag. I handed Brax Sport's leash and reached inside. The burrito was still warm, and I imagined that Brax's touch had kept it that way. Oh, shiver, shiver, I needed to stop it with the romantic notions.

After a few bites, I rewrapped my breakfast, retrieved Sport's leash, and wished Brax a lovely day. Before he headed home to give his ankle a break, he looked like he had something on his mind, an indecisive cast to his mouth. No doubt he was rethinking last night. I hated to think he had any regrets about sharing his past with me.

Sigh. Maybe the burrito was a mea culpa gift, one that said, *I divulged too much. Sorry! And, by the way, could you keep all you heard to yourself? Thanks, bye.*

Hmm. I looked over my shoulder briefly, but Brax was nowhere in sight. I hope he knew his stories were safe with me.

"Well, hullo there." Rick from the shell shop waved at me from the front doorway.

"Hi to you too." Sport snuffled around Rick's feet, and when I tried to pull her away, the shop owner squatted down and began to pet her.

"Aw, she's a good girl. Yes, she is, yes, she is." All that baby talk coming out of a grown man's mouth cracked me up.

Shelly appeared by his side. "It's good to see you, Clara. Such a pretty dress you're wearing."

"The weather's perfect for it, so I figured, why not?" I didn't need to add any more than that, say, that I'd be meeting my older brother for the very first time in my life later today.

Shelly chided Rick. "You're blocking the door, dear heart. Move aside so Clara can come inside and see what's new around here."

Rick scooped up Sport, baby talking to her the entire time. "Do you hear that? My old lady's trying to get rid of us. But we won't allow that. No, no, no, we won't." He backed into the store, still carrying the dog. "We'll just go on over to the water station and make ourselves at home, now, won't we ..."

Shelly rolled her eyes at me, her laughter tinkling. "He can't help himself. The man is who he is."

"Well, that's refreshing." I followed her inside, immediately taken with the way the morning light streamed in through the shop's front windows, illuminating Shelly's gorgeous array of sea glass in every combination. A new mermaid sculpture graced one corner of the showroom, and I slid a look at Shelly.

"Rick found that one. Said her eyes reminded him of mine."

"Oh, he's good."

"Then he pinched my butt. Again, the man can't hide his true self."

"Wouldn't that be great if it was true of everyone?"

"The part about butt pinching or hiding one's self?"

I laughed. "Um, the keeping it real part. Sometimes I'm not even sure if I know myself anymore, let alone who other people are."

"Oh, dear. Hard day?"

"No, not at all." I wasn't sure why I'd said anything. "Actually, it's a good day all around. I was just thinking out loud. When this trip is over, I'm going to have to make some decisions about my career. This has nothing to do at all with Rick over there"—I smiled in his direction—"it's just, well, I've been sensing that change is on the horizon."

"Good for you," Shelly said. "It's important to know yourself."

Rick piped up. "Yeah, so you don't end up a cursed fig tree."

I frowned.

Shelly's laugh was incredulous. "Don't mind him. We

were just talking about our pastor's sermon from last weekend. I'm sure it doesn't apply here."

"May I ask what it means?"

"Well, sure, honey. Let me think a minute ..."

Rick cut in. "Pretty sure Shelly was catching a few winks during that part. Allow me to explain."

Shelly shook her head.

"Anyway," Rick said, "in the Bible, Jesus curses a fig tree when it doesn't produce any fruit. See, some people think the Lord was just being mean because he was hungry."

I knitted my brows together. "Doesn't sound like Jesus to me."

Rick's eyes widened like he'd just seen a hunk of dark chocolate for the very first time. "You know him?"

"I've believed since I was a child. My Grandma Violet made sure of it." I smiled to hide the tweak of my heart. How long had it been since I'd reached out to the Jesus I once knew?

"That's good to hear." Rick clapped once, like a teacher trying to get the attention of his students. I began to wonder if I'd ever get out of here ... "Back to the tree. The way our pastor tells it, Jesus was using the fig tree as a parable—not to get even with a barren plant. That tree was full of leaves when it was out of season. In other words, it was pretending to be something it clearly was not."

I raised my brows, not quite understanding.

"Don't you see? It looked like a lush tree full of figs, but on closer inspection, it was all leaves and no fruit!"

"Ah." Like people. Maybe like me at times.

"The disciples were all standing around watching this, so Jesus cursed the tree as an example—not to be petty."

I smiled. Though I hadn't been in church in a long while,

I knew that the words petty and Jesus didn't belong in the same sentence.

Rick continued. "He wanted them to know that without fruit—and that could mean all kinds of things, like right-eousness, holiness, etcetera—a tree might as well wither and die away. So he made it happen."

"Wow, that's ... heavy stuff."

Rick swiveled a look at his wife. "How'd I do?"

She gave him a little shove. "Not bad, Pastor Rick. Now go and sweep the front entry. Go. Shoo."

After he'd returned Sport to me and dutifully gone on a hunt for a broom, I stayed awhile to admire the pretty seashells. I'd never had lofty plans. I just wanted to make a living writing stories, and after that? I'd had no plans. That niggled at me, especially being here in the simplicity of this shop and seeing how its kind-hearted owners interacted.

I was still thinking about Rick, Shelly, and withered fig trees as Sport and I climbed the stairs to my apartment. I know Rick hadn't meant this, but I was starting to wonder: Was I pretending to be something I was not? I stopped at the base of the stairs and looked out across the street. I didn't have the answer to that, but one thing was for certain, this trip had cracked open a door I hadn't realized was shut.

CHAPTER TWELVE

CLARA

WHEN I WOKE up this morning to the realization that I would be meeting Justin, four o'clock seemed like such a long way off. But now that I approached the hotel, cool sweat pushing through my skin, the day seemed to have disappeared faster than a cat at bath time.

I smoothed down my dress for the tenth time, noting the start of an afternoon breeze. Pants might have been a better choice, linen not denim—we're not on a farm here! I licked my lips, wondering if I should duck into the restroom to check my makeup. Granted, it was only a short walk here from Mermaid Manor, but I hardly ever wore lipstick. Had I stayed in the lines when applying it?

Stop it already.

The bellmen at the front of the hotel greeted me with smiles and nods, and even some eye contact. I took that to mean all clothing parts and dribbles of makeup were in the right spots. Might not have meant that at all, but a girl had to hang onto something when she sensed she was about to have a breakdown

Again—stop it with the dramatics.

One more deep breath and I stepped into the cafe at the back of the lobby that overlooked the pool. Not many tables occupied, which made sense, given the time. Four o'clock had seemed an odd time to meet at first—too late for lunch, too early for dinner—but after I thought about it, the time made perfect sense. We would have our privacy to meet and talk and, well, cry a little. Maybe just me on the last one.

I swished a look around, spotting two men by a window, but that was it.

"Table for one?" The hostess smiled and proceeded to pick up a menu.

"Actually, I'm meeting someone. Justin Smyth?"

"Yes. He's here. Right this way."

Confused, I followed the hostess around the bar and toward the back of the restaurant. One of the two men at the table by the window stood up. I slowed. Was this Justin or was the seated man my brother?

"Clara?"

And I knew. So much about the forty-something guy standing in front of me seemed familiar. Dark hair that curled at the collar, large eyes like mine, and a sense of confidence, as if he was not a bit nervous (like me). I grasped his outstretched hand in both of mine. "Hello, Justin."

The hostess left the extra menu on the table. "I'll leave this here for you and send your waiter over for your order."

"Clara." Justin gestured to the other man. "I'd like you to meet my friend, Andrew."

Andrew stood. He was on the short side, dressed in quintessential tennis wear, and his spike-cropped black hair contained sprinkles of grey throughout. "Pleased to meet you," he said.

I said hello and took a seat next to Andrew. I hadn't expected anyone else to join us. Not sure why. Maybe it's because Justin hadn't mentioned bringing anyone. *Or maybe it's because we have a lot to talk about that's, you know, private.*

Both men had cups of coffee in front of them, so I ordered the same but added a bowl of strawberry shortcake. This part of the state was known for their strawberries, and, no joke, I could use some sugar and comfort food right now.

"Thank you for meeting me," I said.

Justin nodded. He wore a slight smile, but his eyes looked hard somehow. I supposed he too was looking for some resemblance.

"My wife bought one of your books," Justin said, breaking the stark quiet. "She wanted me to have you autograph it, but I didn't want to bother."

"Oh ..."

Justin looked across the table to Andrew, then quickly added, "What I meant to say was, I didn't want to bother you."

I smiled, happy for broken ice. "I would have loved to have signed it for her. If you can find out which one she has, I'll send her the next one in the series."

He nodded. "Thank you. I will do that."

I put my hands in my lap. They were starting to sweat, which was uncharacteristic for me. That's something that usually happened to Greta when she was nervous. Maybe I adopted the habit. "Tell me about you," I finally said. "What kind of work do you do?"

"I'm an insurance broker. Have been since soon out of college."

"Important work."

I wanted to ask about our father, but thought I should get to know Justin better first. He wasn't all that forthcoming about his life over the next several minutes of questioning. He didn't ask anything about me, but then, there are interviews with Vivian on the internet, not to mention the Facebook page I don't run. He probably thought he knew all there was to know.

Our waiter appeared with my coffee and an over-the-top strawberry dessert. So many huge berries on it. I laughed, maybe a bit too loud, but it felt good to let loose a little.

"This is so gorgeous." I spooned up a couple of fat strawberries. "Please, share these with me." I looked at Justin and then to Andrew, who sat tapping his coffee cup with his forefinger.

But Justin waved his hands in front of me. "I don't care for any. But thank you for the offer."

I pulled the spoon back and took a tentative bite, a sudden feeling of claustrophobia. If I looked at Justin, I could sense Andrew's eyes on me. Same was true if I were to sneak a glance at the tennis-garb clad friend—I'd sense Justin looking me over.

This wasn't the way it was supposed to go. At least, not in my mind. I should have prepared a list of questions beforehand, you know, other than the ones swimming around in my head, looking for the drain. Same could be said for my next novel. If only I could outline it, I would be able to give Joanie what she wanted. Until now, I'd relied on my gut instinct, and so far, my insides had failed me.

Maybe that's because you haven't lived a lot of life outside of your head ...

Greta's words jabbed me hard, like those times she would reach over and poke me while we played Monopoly as kids and I took too long to make my next move.

I must have grimaced because Justin said, "You were lost in thought there." He was watching me with a sort of scrutinizing look, his eyes narrowed.

"I was just thinking that this is all very strange. Isn't it?"

"It is."

"I mean, did ... did you know about me?"

"Honestly, Clara, no. My father never mentioned that he, uh, had another child." Justin sat back, still doing that scrutinizing thing. "Frankly, it would kill my mother to know about you."

His mother? "I ... didn't realize your mother was living."

He gave me a rueful look. "Disappointed?"

I frowned. "Why, of course not. It's just ... I lost my mother when I was a teenager"—I mustered a smile, though his words stung—"so I'm happy to hear that you have not gone through that."

He nodded, began to say something, then stopped. Silence awkwardly sank among us. Andrew didn't say a thing, and I was really beginning to wonder why he didn't run off and play some tennis or something. I straightened, finding steam. "Justin, it was nice of you to come all this way to meet me. I'm, uh"—I bit my bottom lip, willing myself not to lose it—"I'm just really touched that you came."

A server came by with a coffee pot, but when she attempted to refill Justin's cup, he put his hand out to stop her. "No more for me. I'll be leaving soon."

Leaving? Questions filled my head, but my voice

wouldn't work. Had I said something to bother him? Was I not who he thought I would be?

Andrew cleared his throat, startling me out of my misery. "Justin."

Slowly, Justin pulled something, an envelope, out of his back pocket. "Here." He slid the envelope across the table to me, thrusting his head forward like he was herding a dog. "Go ahead and open it."

I stared at it for a few seconds. Then I pulled a folded sheet of paper out of the envelope. A check fell out, made out to me, in the amount of ten thousand dollars.

I raised my eyes to meet his. "I don't understand."

Justin looked again at Andrew, who put a pen on the table and began to speak.

I turned toward him. "If you don't mind, this is between Justin and me." I turned back to my brother. "I want to know what this is."

"Just read it."

"I would rather you tell me."

Justin's eyes widened to their familial potential, appearing more emboldened now. "I don't want any trouble. If you sign the document that Andrew drew up—he's our family's lawyer—then you can keep the check. Just sign that you won't be suing my father's estate for more and the money is yours."

"You-you think I want your money?"

Andrew cleared his throat. Justin darted a look at him.

"For heaven's sake, Justin, stop looking at the tennis coach sitting next to me. Put on your big boy pants and speak for yourself!"

He lowered his head and smashed his palms together until parts of his skin turned white. He raised his chin again.

"I've already told you that my father never said anything about having another kid. It's obvious he wanted nothing to do with ..."

"With me."

He nodded once, like we were at a business meeting. "He would have said something."

I sat there, dumbfounded. Justin was right. Why hadn't I thought more about this? The reality that my father never came after me felt like old news in a way. It was as if I had known about it for years, but only now allowed myself to hold this broken shard of my past up to the light, where its scars could be illuminated.

The light blinded right now, making those scars deeper.

Justin continued to sit back, wielding his words. He looked far more relaxed now than when I first arrived. "My mother is not to know about this. You are also signing to never tell her."

I didn't want Justin's money. I wanted ... what did I want? For my long-lost brother to take me into his arms and invite me to Thanksgiving dinner? To spend the evening sharing old stories and laughing about the times that never were?

No, no, no—NO.

Coming here was a huge mistake, biggest one I'd made in a long time. And I'd made plenty. I should have flown out here for Greta's wedding, then gone right back home. If I had, I would probably be curled up in my favorite recliner chair, finishing my next novel with a hot cup of tea. Life would be good, if not exciting. Expected. NORMAL.

I slid the document—and the check—back to his side of the table. "I'm not signing anything. And I don't want your money."

Justin, who seconds ago looked like some feral cat with a bird in his jowls, darted a look at Andrew that said *what now?*

I stood and looped my bag over my shoulder. Justin followed suit, standing across from me. I forced my chin up, leveling my gaze at the man-child in front of me. Suddenly, we looked nothing alike. Nothing familiar about him at all. We were ... strangers.

Andrew stepped between Justin and me, gesturing for me to sit down. His voice was calm, like a beloved grandfather's, yet the manipulating words were jarring. "You are being offered a very generous settlement, Clara. Take a moment to consider what you would be losing should you walk away."

Justin cut in, his jaw set. "There won't be future offers from my family, Clara."

"Right now, I'm grateful for the mother who raised me, a sister I adore, and a grandmother who loved us all." I looked Justin up and down, slowly. "Quite obviously, I won't be losing a thing."

I walked out of there, willing my chin to stay level and my trembling to stop, and knowing that the minute I reached one of the beach's towering dunes, I'd let myself cry it out.

Brax

CLARA HURRIED out of the cafe, breaking my heart with every step. She didn't notice me stalking her, but kept walking, head down, a hand covering her mouth, and ... were those tears? Another knife-like twist in my chest. I followed behind her, walking quickly, yet leaving her some space. Whatever happened in that restaurant was not according to plan. Well, not according to *her* plan anyway.

I had expected to follow Clara home, from a healthy distance, so she could tell me all that transpired while in the privacy of her apartment. But instead of heading south toward Carter's place, Clara turned toward the beach. She slipped out of her sandals, stepped onto the sand, then began to trudge up an imposing sand dune.

She still hadn't noticed me following her. I made a mental note to tell her later that she needed to stay better aware of her surroundings, i.e. not allowing strange guys to follow her up a sand dune. Probably should save that lecture for another time.

At the base of the dune, the wind carried the soft sound of her tears. A pulsating desire to kill someone quickened my blood pressure. At the very least, I could go back into that hotel and break a limb or two. But my act of chivalry in the form of violence would have to wait. For now.

I found her at the top, sitting cross-legged in the sand, in need of a tissue. I pulled my burrito wrapper out of my back pocket, still there from this morning, and handed it down to her.

She gasped and darted a look up at me. "What are ... what are you doing here? Did you follow me?"

"I promised my brother I'd look out for you." I continued to hold the wrapper down to her. "It's all I have. Take it."

She took the wrapper and smashed it against her wet eyes and cheeks. "So that's a yes," she said. "You're here to spy. Go ahead then. Report back to my sister and brother-in-law. I'll wait."

Her tears flowed now, and it shook me. I squatted down beside her. "What happened, Clara?"

More tears. "The better question is what didn't happen." She did not sound angry or bitter, but deeply sad. "I can answer that question: my big brother didn't want me."

"I'm sorry."

She sniffled. "Not a big deal."

Instinctively, I took her hand and rubbed the soft skin on the back of it with my thumb. "It's a very big deal."

A salty breeze took hold of several tendrils of her curls. I wanted to brush them back and let her wrap herself around me. But that wasn't why I was here.

She turned sharply. "Can I ask you something? Why do people assume the worst in others? Is it because there are no good people left in the world?"

"You're good people."

"That's bad grammar."

"It's poetic."

She shut her eyes, but the tears found an escape route anyway. Man, I wanted to hurt someone. I attached my gaze to hers, willing her to give me answers. "The guy was a jerk, I take it?"

"He wasn't who I thought he'd be."

"And who was that?"

She gave me a tiny shrug, apparently noticed my thumb caressing her hand, and quickly pulled it away. "I don't know really. Maybe I thought he'd want to know about me as much as I wanted to know about him."

"And your father too."

"I *am* curious about my father. I mean, he's gone, but his son has a lifetime of memories he could have shared with me." She swallowed, her voice turning lifeless. "Instead, he offered me money to go away."

I hung my head. The guy didn't deserve her. "Clara."

"Stop. No pity. I should have known, should have anticipated that he'd reject me."

"Why would you?"

"Because everyone else has." She wiped her eyes with the back of her hand and I really wished I'd done the napkin grab at the burrito place this morning. She sounded dejected and a little helpless. And for the first time, I detected a hint of bitterness lining her voice. "I've never even had a boyfriend, Brax. I'm a romance writer who hasn't been on a date in … in years!"

"You're discriminating. That's admirable."

"No, it's not. It's dumb."

"Hold on. You write men into your stories, guys with jobs like construction foremen, lawyers, hunky doctors, whatever that means, but you've never, to my knowledge, had any of those jobs. Nor are you a guy."

She gave me a small smile, a doubtful one, but still a smile. "Your point?"

"You are creative. You have an imagination. You don't have to be a serial dater to write amazing stories."

"Ha. You're sweet."

"I'm honest."

She smirked. "Greta was right. I don't have enough life experience to be a writer."

"Did she really say that?"

"It's what she meant."

The pain in her voice ate at me. "Clara, who has rejected you?"

"My father, my stepfather … you."

"I've never rejected you."

She looked me full in the face now, those expressive eyes of hers controlling me like a laser. "I kissed you, you know. You've said nothing about it." She swung a look out to sea, her voice calmer now, resigned. "Obviously, I felt something you didn't reciprocate, but I'm not looking for you to deny that. All I'm saying is—"

"I remember the kiss."

"Please. Your pity is, well, it's gross. I get it—you're here because you were assigned to me, because Zac told you to come or else he'd put you in a headlock or something. That's what guys do."

I reached for her hand. She tried to pull it away, but I entwined my fingers with hers. She implored me with a look that begged me to disagree with her. "Zac had to tell me about your meeting with Justin because you never did. I wish you had, Clara."

"Why?"

"Because it mattered to you, so it mattered to me." I let that sink in. "Why didn't you tell me?"

"I wanted ... I wanted to do something on my own, I guess. To break out of my recliner chair bubble."

"Your what?"

"This whole trip has been me trying to break out, Brax. I've lived a simple life at home. I write books under a pen name while sitting in a recliner chair in a house that our mother left us. When that postcard showed up last year and Greta decided to come out here, I was excited at first."

"Until she decided to stay here."

"Yes. And then our grandmother died."

"I'm sorry, Clara."

She gave a little shake of her head. "All of a sudden I

started noticing the creaks in that house. I'm sure they were there all along, but"—she shrugged—"I hadn't really noticed until life changed dramatically."

I put my arm around her, and it felt as natural as the setting sun. She leaned her head on my shoulder and a force broke through my stubbornness. I've wanted to get out of here since the second my boots landed on the pavement in Hollywood Beach. But not anymore.

Clara must have been dwelling on what happened inside that hotel because she exhaled a ripple of a sigh mixed with more tears. My heart broke once again.

"Maybe I'm just not that worthy of a hero in my life."

I thought about that, though I didn't need to. "Your worth is not based on what someone else says of you, Clara."

She sighed. "You don't need to go there. I really am not looking for a pity party, I promise."

"I'm going there anyway."

Clara's expression dulled. "Okay, so what's it based on?"

I held my tongue.

"See?" she said. "You agree with me."

"Not at all. I was just trying to phrase what I want to say to you right." I swallowed. "God determines your worth, Clara, not anyone else. And he created you, so ... you are worthy in his eyes. That's all that matters."

Clara tilted her gaze up to me.

"I told you I prayed."

Slowly, she nodded. "That's beautiful, Brax. I wish I believed it."

Gently I pulled her closer and kissed the top of her head.

We sat there, she and I, listening to the unending loop of waves rolling onto shore and back out again. I'd never been that guy who heard the siren call of the ocean, but that had all changed. This moment and all the other moments leading up to it conjured up shockingly new melodies in my heart and mind. If only the same could happen for Clara.

After a while she pulled away from me and sat up stick straight in the sand. "It occurs to me now that I've been making up stories for years, but maybe this is the first time that I'm actually living in one." She filled her lungs, the remnants of her tears still evident in her uneven breath. "The truth is that Justin's rejection took me by surprise. It hurts more than I imagined it could and I'm in knots."

"Then write yourself out of them."

She stole a glance at me, her forehead tense. "I'm not sure if I can."

"I understand that, Clara. In my own life, I've been running from my problems for a very long time, but they kept catching up to me. I've finally decided to stand in place and stare them down. You helped me with that, you know."

"Me? How did I help?"

"You listened to me pour out the past. I had no idea how much that would help me overcome the hurdles that had seemed like mountains in front of me. After spending time with you last night, I went home and wrote for hours. Lyrics had been like tumbleweeds in my head for weeks, but all the whirling stopped. The words came easily, and the music followed."

"You didn't mention anything about that this morning."

I bit the inside of my cheek, my heart picking up the pace. "I had planned to."

"That's why you brought me a burrito, isn't it? So you could tell me your news."

"Partially."

"But I brushed you off."

"I wouldn't say that, no. To be honest, there was more on my mind than my song. I was hoping that if I told you my good news, then, well ..."

"Then I would tell you mine. So you wouldn't have to stalk me."

"I stalk because I care."

She smiled now, a real one. I wanted to reach out to her again, to tell her that she'd found what she was looking for. I could be her hero. I wanted to be that for her, only, maybe my brother was right. Clara needed stability, not a rolling stone, not a guy whose attention was on his music and late nights and spontaneous travel. If I'd learned nothing this trip, it's that no matter how much I've tried to deny it in the past, I am that guy. Kate figured out early on that there would be no changing me.

As Clara relaxed against me again, the sound of her exhale wrapping itself around my heart, I knew that we'd formed a special bond. Of friendship. And that would have to be enough.

CHAPTER THIRTEEN

CLARA

I PRAYED this morning for the first time since Gran was sick. I'd prayed a lot back then, but when she died, I buried my prayer life with her. But something Brax said yesterday made me recall the chat I'd had with Rick at the shell shop. The last thing I wanted was to be a withered fig tree. Ha ... why did that picture make me laugh? Maybe it wasn't the tree that had me laughing, but the pages and pages and PAGES that I'd written so far today.

After asking God to help me with this bugger of a book this morning, I'd let the dog out back for a minute, then poured some coffee and hunkered down with my laptop. No recliner chair here, so I'd made a makeshift one with pillows and bolsters on the bed and settled in.

I wrote for hours, listening to the cry of the early morning foghorn until the wispy air dissipated into blue sky and re-energizing sunlight. My eyes caught on my phone lighting up.

"Clara, you haven't answered the phone all morning." Greta had her worry voice on.

"That's because I had it set to Do Not Disturb."

"Oh, honey."

I should have called Greta last night, but I was exhausted after everything that transpired. She finally texted me after midnight:

GRETA: How'd it go meeting Justin?

ME: We didn't hit it off.

GRETA: Want to talk? (I do.)

ME: Not really. Tired. Yawn. Brax helped me through it. Talk tomorrow?

GRETA: k

MY SISTER always signed off with "k" when she was annoyed.

Guilt slithered through me. "Sorry, Sis. It's been a really good morning, though. I've been up for hours."

"Wait. That sounds like an oxymoron because you're not a morning person."

"Ha! I know! But today I am. I've accomplished so much already."

"Does that mean ...?"

"Yes. I'm writing again. Finally."

"Woohoo ... oh, but now I've interrupted you. Sorry."

I slid my laptop onto the comforter and pulled my knees up to my chest, stretching. "That's okay. I needed a break anyway."

"Well, you must be relieved. And I'm sure your publisher will be too."

"I have Brax to thank. He helped me find my voice again."

"Brax? Wait ... I want to hear about that, but first, what happened yesterday with Justin?"

"I'm sure Brax already told your husband."

Greta shushed a sigh. "No! When I couldn't get you last night, Zac called Brax, but he only said that you were fine. That's all he would say."

Brax had kept my confidence. Even more reason to fall head over heels in love with him. I closed my laptop and stood up to stretch. "I'm sorry I worried you, Greta. But don't you think I've disturbed you during your honeymoon enough? I'm horrified that I called you at all."

Greta laughed. "Sisters have priority. You know that. Now, tell me what happened."

I relayed my entire meeting with Justin, every last ugly detail, right down to the strawberries I never finished and the ultra-polished lawyer in tennis wear that he'd brought with him. This morning had been otherwise perfect, so I hated to relive the part of yesterday that had nearly shattered my heart. But Greta deserved to know. Actually, she should have been there with me. I knew that now and fully expected an I-told-you-so from her.

"I'm so sorry he was such a disappointment. If I'd been there, you know I would have given him an earful."

I smiled. "No doubt. You'd be proud of me, I think. I was caught off guard, but I did manage to get a few choice words in anyway."

"I worry too much about you, don't I?"

I glanced out the window, seeing the sky. "I think you worry just the right amount."

"What are you going to do now?"

"Well, I'm going to finish the synopsis of this book—I've actually written the entire first scene already."

"Want to tell me about it? Zac's taking a nap."

Hmm. Must've been very tired ... I cracked a smile and gave my head a shake. "Well, I think I'm done with straight-up romance novels."

"So what ... you're going to write sci-fi now?"

"Hardy-har-har. What I mean is that I'm writing women's fiction with romance. Nothing wrong with my other books, but I'm finally inspired to write something new, so I'm going with it. It's a story about a woman who travels to a historic beach town, meets the locals, and while she's chasing down a story, she finds pieces of herself that end up making her feel complete for the first time in her life."

"So you're still using me for your muse."

"Nope. I'm using me."

"But what about a man?"

I stilled. "What about a man?"

"Well ... not to be ... I mean, I'm just ..."

"Spit it out!"

"You don't have a man for this story yet."

Oh, but, I'm hoping that I do. I didn't say what I was thinking, of course. "I told you, this isn't pure romance—it's women's fiction." I sighed dramatically. "It's a much-expanded story, my dear sister. Longer than all my other books, with much more going on. But if you must know, there is a man, one who's confused. He's loved, but doesn't know it yet."

"Clara?"

"Hmm?"

"I'm proud of you and I can't wait to read the book. Change can be ... cathartic." She paused before adding, "I'm really, really sorry about the way Justin treated you."

"I know you are." I turned from the window and plopped back down on the bed. "You know what? I've been thinking about Mom lately, and all the rejection she faced. She really protected us from all that, didn't she?"

"You're absolutely right." I could hear the smile in Greta's voice. "Our mom was the best."

After we signed off, I leashed up Sport and took her for a walk outside. The sun greeted me with the gentle warmth of a kiss from a sweet aunt. Sport tugged me along, taking surreptitious glances back at me here and there. She thought she was in charge. I could tell by the way she bopped along, shooting a confident bark to animals stuck out on their decks.

When we returned, I slowly headed upstairs, listening to Brax's guitar licks. He was working through a melody, searching for the right order of the notes, just as I, too, had to go back inside and smooth out the words that I had dumped onto the page.

I hadn't seen Brax this morning, nor did I expect to, but somehow, that was okay with me. He was writing his music up there, playing with sounds and thoughts and words, and that took quiet and focus. I, too, realized the need for introspection in the creative process. Without it, my words struggled to find their pattern, their purpose.

Sport filled up on water while I put her food in her doggy dish. After she'd had her fill, she made a couple of spirals on her pillow bed and plopped down into it before falling asleep. My phone buzzed, indicating a text coming in:

BRAX: Thanks for the invite.

ME: I wasn't aware that you enjoyed kibble.

I hoped he got the joke.

BRAX: You went to the beach without me.

Okay, maybe not, since he, you know, felt the need to clarify.

ME: Didn't want to interrupt all that beautiful music making up there.

BRAX: I'm blushing.

ME: Doubt that!

BRAX: I'll shave and you'll see.

ME: I like your whiskers.

He doesn't answer right away and I'm wondering if that was too flirty.

BRAX: You doing okay today?

Okay. Change of subject. I get that, but he really does not need to worry.

ME: I'm doing great. Thanks to you. Guess what?

BRAX: What?

ME: I'm writing again! Yesterday's talk helped so much. So excited for this story.

BRAX: I'm happy to hear it, Clara.

I GLANCED AGAIN at the screen. Seeing that Brax had used my name in a text sent a happy chill right through me. Suddenly I was fourteen and the boy next door had bothered to say hi.

I began to type a response. Then stopped, erased it, and started again. My thumb hovered over the send button while I considered my words. Finally, I hit send.

ME: I'm going to write now with my window open so I can hear you play and sing. You're going to be my mood music, Brax. XO

I PULLED my computer back onto my lap and looked over where I'd left off, but stalled. Had I really texted "XO" to my sort-of brother-in-law? I shut my eyes, wishing for some way to edit that part out. Actually, for a way to edit away the entire text.

Way to bare your soul to the guy who's just trying to make you feel better, Clara.

With a sigh, I hunkered down on the bed, laptop open, and tried to focus. My phone dinged and I shut my eyes, afraid to look.

BRAX: XO to you too, kiddo.

KIDDO.

I knew I shouldn't read too much into his response. Texts were famous for masking someone's true meaning, and he probably was just being a brat. Yeah, that was probably it.

I poised my fingers over my computer keyboard and got back to work.

CHAPTER FOURTEEN

BRAX

"ARE YOU EXCITED?"

I took the ice cream cone from Clara's outstretched arm. It was Rocky Road, and though that might have excited me when I was ten, I was anything but thrilled right now. Unsure as all get-out. I wasn't ready to climb back on stage, and I wasn't sure if I ever would be.

"Go on now," Clara said, biting into her chocolate-nutty-mocha-sprinkle thing. "You know you want it."

I laughed at the silly look on her face. She managed to smear a swipe of chocolate ice cream on her nose, and it took all my willpower not to lean over and lick it off.

She pointed at my legs. "Whoops."

I glanced down to find a drip of ice cream on my board shorts. "Great." I swiped a lick of ice cream before another drip embarrassed me.

"Told you to hurry up!" Clara laughed and took another bite of her cone.

I wanted to hold onto moments like this, just sitting outside on a sunny day, eating ice cream with a beautiful woman. Before I knew it, she'd be gone back to Indiana and I'd be—well, who knew where I would be. Thinking of Clara out of state, far away from me, made my appetite for ice cream suddenly dull.

"You didn't answer my question, Brax. Are you excited about tonight? Are you ready?"

"It's not that big of a deal, Clara."

She shrank back, those expressive eyes popping open. "You're about to perform for the first time in years, and in front of a scout. Once you win—"

"*If* I win."

"Oh, you'll win. I know it!"

I shook my head and took another bite from my cone, my smile lingering. She had more confidence in my abilities than I did.

"As I was saying, once you win, you'll have a chance to perform in Los Angeles in front of some big-time music execs."

I scoffed. By then—if it even happens—Zac and Greta will be back and I'll be a third wheel around here. "What does big time really mean in these days of social media fame?"

"Oh, they'll be big. Really BIG! You'll see."

"You should be my agent."

"Well, darling, I would love that, but as you know, I've got a book to finish." She said the words as if channeling some high-brow agent, but then did a quick swipe around the base of her ice cream with her tongue.

"Speaking of that, have you heard anything?"

"From my editor?"

"Yes. I'm not sure how publishing works, but has she given you the feedback you were looking for?"

Clara shook her head tightly. "Not yet, because I haven't sent her the complete synopsis yet." I didn't want to mention that I was still mulling some parts of the story. "I'll be done soon, though, and then there'll be some wait time, because there's new management."

"Means a lot to you, doesn't it?"

She rubbed her lips together and nodded. Her eyes flashed with something that reminded me an awful lot of apprehension. "It really does. It's ... everything."

I reached out and rubbed her back, reassuring her. Had to use all my willpower not to linger there. Finally, I said, "You inspire me."

Her eyes widened, a mess of thoughts in them. She took another slow bite of ice cream before saying, "Well, then, channel all that inspiration into your performance tonight."

Winning didn't matter, but I had to admit that getting back on that stage had propelled me through the past couple of days, especially as I finished the first song I had written in, well, years. On the other side, if I won, I'd be sticking around. Might even ask to stay in Clara's place after she left.

My stomach ached at the thought. I allowed my eyes to take her in again. She was simply eating the rest of an ice cream cone while looking out over the water. A pelican dove into the marina, bringing a smile immediately to her face. I wished I could stay here all day and watch her live life.

And I knew. I didn't want her to leave. Crazy as it sounded, even to me, I never wanted to leave here either.

We walked back to our separate households, our hands sticky, and I watched Clara climb the stairs to her place.

She turned back around with her hand poised on the railing. "See you tonight?"

I nodded.

She smiled down at me. "I can't wait."

Instead of practicing, when I went back inside I called Zac. "I want to pursue Clara."

Zac didn't answer me right away and I had to resist the urge to reach through the airwaves and grab him by the stethoscope that, theoretically, hung around his neck.

"Did you hear me, Zac?"

"I heard you, man, but I'm trying to process. You are kidding, right?"

"I've never been so serious about anything in my life."

"Even your marriage?"

I scoffed. "You didn't have any trouble processing that comeback now, did you?"

Zac paused. "Look, we talked about this. This isn't the time."

My jaw clenched. "You know I can do whatever I want."

"But I hope you won't." Zac lowered his voice. "Listen, Clara's, well, I know I've said this before, but maybe you need reminding. She may write about romance, but don't be fooled. She's very creative but also inexperienced. You're not." He sighed. "Plus, she was wounded by what happened with her jerk brother. I promised Greta that her sister would be safe with you, man. You know as well as I do that if you form a bond with her, in the end, she'll likely get hurt."

I scoffed again.

"Don't let me down."

Zac's words pinned some dark part of my past. I hadn't

always wanted what he had, what our parents had, though in an effort to fit in, I'd tried. And failed. Kate's voice, husky and emotional, roared through my head: *You let me down, Brax!*

Maybe Zac wasn't far off—though it irked me to admit that. If I were to try again, and fail, this family would be forever torn apart and I would be one-hundred-percent at fault for its downfall. I blew a breath out hard and threw my cell phone onto the desk, watching it clatter.

I shoved my hand into a pocket and pulled out a quarter. Heads I tell Clara how I feel about her. I laid the coin on my thumbnail, poised to flip it. *And tails? What about tails?*

I couldn't do it.

Clara deserved better than a guy whose greatest potential would be to mess up her life. Hadn't she had enough of disappointment this week? Of being let down? I shoved the quarter back into my pocket and determined to leave well enough—alone.

THREE HOURS LATER, I arrived at the bar, the same stage still set up from last week's event. Clara would be coming in about a half hour with Carter, and though I hated her spending time with any guy other than me, it was for the best. I needed a few minutes to clear my head. My conversation with Zac still twisted in my gut. In one day, I'd both talked myself into pursuing a relationship with Clara and then watched my plans disintegrate during one defining moment during a phone call with Zac. The last thing I needed right now was to allow my mind to be dragged under, rendering me unable to get on that stage and give it my all.

Chuck approached, wearing a top hat and tails, and I almost made a quip about the costume party being last week. He slapped me on the shoulder. "Great to see you again, Braxton."

"Yes, sir. You too."

"The rest of the contestants are tuning up. Most of 'em have been here for hours."

I kept a poker face.

He cleared his throat. "So you feel free to go on up and do the same. We'll be keeping the lights up for another twenty minutes, then we'll turn 'em down and let the audience in."

I nodded and made my way to the back of the stage where two women, a guy about my age, and a girl who looked no older than a teenager waited for the night to begin. By the looks of terror on each of their faces, I knew I'd been wise to take my time getting here. Had given me time to talk my anxiety into staying at home tonight.

I rehearsed the lines of my song in my head, though I didn't need to. What I should have been doing was finding a way to share the emotion of the song without allowing my bare heart to sever as I sang the words.

Before long, Chuck was on stage, handing us each a card with our number on it. I tried to concentrate as he relayed instructions while the front doors were opened to allow the audience to file in. Clara's entrance was unmistakable. Even from here I could tell she looked ... happy. We'd managed a great friendship, she and I. Though I longed for more, I was satisfied knowing that she had come here tonight as my biggest fan.

Carter sat down beside her, bending her ear about who

knew what. He bugged me, but so would any guy who spent time with Clara who wasn't ... me.

Get used to it, Braxton.

The lights dropped low and a spotlight appeared. The first contestant drew up to the mic. Even from here, I could see her trembling. I whispered a silent prayer for her to keep it together, then sank farther into the back of the stage to wait for my turn.

When it came, I took my place on that stool, like I had done so many times before in my life. My fingers wrapped around the neck of my guitar, my fingers newly rough and ready to play. The first chord brought the melody to life. And then I sang for an audience ... of one.

I WAS STANDING OUTSIDE NOW, needing air. On my way out the door, Chuck had grabbed me by the sleeve. "Don't be gone long. We'll be announcing the winner soon."

At this moment, I didn't care who won. I meant it. All I wanted to do was get out of here. Take a drive down the coast, maybe. Or turn inland and drive by the old house I grew up in, the one with juniper bushes running up either side and a picture window in front, the one my mom often sat by when reading a novel.

"Your song ... it's beautiful, Brax."

I didn't need to turn to know who had followed me outside. Clara stood next to me, a shawl wrapped about her shoulders. *I wish it were me.*

I nodded my thanks.

She was searching my face now. "There's something about it ... a pull on me that I've never felt."

I swallowed any semblance of a reply.

"Look at me, Brax. Please?"

I blew out a breath. Why hadn't I taken up smoking like all the other ruffians I'd grown up with? At least I'd have something else to concentrate on out here, under this lonely sky.

She reached up and tipped my chin toward her. Our eyes connected. "Did you write it for me?"

The ocean rang in my ears. She let her wrap drop from her shoulders, the night's humidity overcoming us both. I hadn't looked at her once during the performance, hadn't allowed my words to land anywhere near her. But she'd reacted regardless of my best efforts.

I needed to let her down gently. I'd already let things go too far. Gently, I pulled her hand away from my cheek. I gave her the kindest smile I could muster, but shook my head. "I'm sorry, but no, Clara. I didn't write that song for you."

Her expression faltered, her long eyelashes lowering. She could not have smiled back at me if she tried—her body wouldn't allow it. I'd cut her deeply and wanted to pummel myself for that. But I couldn't tell her, couldn't admit that I had, indeed, written every note for her.

Finally, she dropped her gaze to the ground.

"You going to be okay?" I asked.

She didn't answer, but I suspected she'd be fine. Any minute, she would look up and smile at me and say, *Of course! We're good! Let's go have a glass of wine.*

Instead, she lifted her gaze, a certain refusal in her eyes. "I agree with you, Brax. I see it now. *La La Land* had it all wrong."

The bar door opened, and a bouncer leaned out. "Hey,

Dude, the boss wants you inside. Time to announce the winner."

I nodded and turned to head back inside, but Clara stopped me. She was still searching my face, clouds of determination in her eyes.

"Dude! Now."

I swallowed. "I'm sorry, Clara, but I have to go back inside."

She shook her head, still staring up at me. "I want the dream sequence, Brax."

I knew exactly what she meant, because I wanted it too. I didn't want Clara to end up with the guy who wasn't me, even if he could give her a normal life doing normal things, like a life without late night gigs and days apart, a life with all the stability money could buy.

But I couldn't be that selfish. I wouldn't. I loved her too much.

"I'm sorry, Clara," I said, walking backward toward the door. "But I'm not the guy to give it to you."

CHAPTER FIFTEEN

Clara

Two days had passed since the competition. Brax had won, of course, just as I had expected he would. I didn't have to think hard to remember that night. A shift happened at the start of his performance, a quieting of the crowd. I knew the audience was as mesmerized by his voice, his skill, and his words, as I was.

But for far different reasons.

I pressed my eyelids together, trying hard to shut out my desperation of that night. Thinking it over, it's no wonder Brax rejected me. How pathetic had I sounded trying to get him to say that he had written that song—that hypnotizing, gorgeous melody—for me?

Then again, who could blame me? Superficial as it sounded, Brax had worn my favorite jeans. And that charcoal-colored V-neck tee, the one that strained around his biceps, giving me a glimpse of what I could find underneath. He'd done that for me. Right?

Exhale. Fine. I had misunderstood. I knew that now, and more than that, I realized that I had been so moved by Brax's voice, so taken with his song, that I had somehow mistakenly thought he was performing it for me. I pressed my eyes shut again. My wounded pride had to go, but I hung onto it like a favorite line in a book that, in the end, really did not work.

A sigh fell from my lips. I guess he had achieved one goal, beyond the big win, of course. If Brax's aim was to make every woman in the room fall in love with him—he had surely accomplished that.

My phone trilled, calling me out of my gloom. Greta was on the line. I debated whether to let it slide right into voice-mail. In the end, I put on a happy face, hoping my forced contentment would seep into the conversation. "Hello, my sister," I said.

"Clara, hello. You sound better today."

My evil plan worked. Next, make up a pithy response: "That's because it's a new day!" Then, deflect: "How are you, Greta?"

"Fabulous. It's been a perfect trip in every way, but I'm looking forward to getting back home. I can't wait to give you a big hug and hear all about your stay at the Manor."

That was the term Greta used occasionally for Carter's place, and it always made me laugh. "When will you be returning again?"

"End of the week. How's the book coming along?"

"Actually, it's, well, it was going fine, but all of a sudden I've hit a bit of a block. No biggie. I'll figure it out."

"I've no doubt. You always do."

"Thanks for the cheerleading. I'm glad one of us has confidence in me."

"Always. Just write the story you were telling me about the other day. I have to say that was the most excitement I've ever heard from you regarding one of your books."

I shifted positions, pulling my knee up toward my chest. "Really?"

"It sounded more raw and—I hope you don't mind me saying this—but honest. I could tell how much you were looking forward to writing it, so I hope you can find that fire again."

"It's been a struggle," I admitted.

Greta was quiet a moment. Then, "I've learned that struggling is sometimes the best way to move forward."

She was right. Despite all my wrestling with the story, being here had opened my eyes to new sounds, smells, experiences ... people. It had nothing to do with the old things being wrong or unworthy, and everything to do with, I don't know, discovery maybe. Suddenly writing from my recliner —or even this bed—didn't seem so exciting or perfect anymore.

"You're right." I drew in a breath and cast a look outside again to the clear sky. "I'm going to keep digging and find all the pieces of the next story I'm meant to write."

"I know you will. I love you, kiddo."

I blinked hard as the phone went dead. She'd called me kiddo before, but it had hardly ever registered in my head. This time it did because Brax signed off with the same casual word the other day, a word that landed a virtual smack to the shoulder in a sisterly—or brotherly—way. This was a final reminder to me, one last sign, that whatever feelings I had developed for Brax were not returned. And if I were going to keep myself together, and pull my fledgling manuscript along, then I'd better accept it.

Sport whimpered at the foot of the bed. The cursor on my screen taunted at me. I stood and padded over to the window, sliding it open. Not a single note of music floated in on the breeze, except the melody of the sea.

Quickly, I grabbed my laptop and some pillows and went out to the deck, Sport clamoring behind me. I plopped one pillow on the deck beside a chair. I then dragged over an umbrella and set it up over the bistro table, laid two pillows on the chair, then opened my manuscript. I closed my eyes and listened for the story: the sea's outbursts, idyllic chatter, the soft whir of a sightseeing plane. My pulse quickened at the pictures the sound made in my mind, and almost on their own volition, my fingers began to type.

DAYS LATER, I stepped onto the deck in my robe and slippers to find Brax leaning his back against the railing, facing my front door. "Where've you been hiding?"

Was it too late to turn around and dive back inside? "I could say the same about you."

"I've been right here all along."

I swallowed. That simple statement sounded like a lyric in a song about a couple who finally found each other after a history of misfires. *Stop. Please.* This was what happened after days and days of back-to-back writing hours. Even after the synopsis, and outline, and several sample chapters were done and sent over to Joanie, my mind continued making up stories out of every little curious phrase—like the one he'd just said.

"So, I see." I padded across the deck, even though my curly hair was pulled up into a flouncy ponytail and my face was, sadly, in its birthday suit. Well, tough. Welcome to the real me.

"You look relaxed." Brax's brushed his gaze over me, a question in his eyes. I didn't owe him any answers, and he knew that. If he wanted to talk about the other night, he'd have to bring it up, not me.

"In answer to your question of where've I've been"—I nodded toward the bistro table—"right there. That's where I've been. I finally finished my synopsis while sitting outside under the umbrella, the roar of waves for a backdrop."

Brax turned toward me. He smiled. "No hunkering down in bed to write, surrounded by pillows and loads of tea?"

I shrugged. "A change of scenery sounded nice."

"So you're done then." Behind him, in the street below, beachgoers pulled chairs, towels, and ice chests from cars.

"I'm done. Yes. Well, with a good chunk of the novel, which is more than what the editorial board wanted. Just a formality now."

"Congratulations. That's great news, Clara. When will you hear back?"

I looked out over the street again. We were bantering as if no tension had ever existed between us. "No idea, but it hasn't stopped me from writing. I feel good about what's been completed so far. By the time I'm contracted, I'll be halfway there. That's never happened before."

He was watching me curiously so I gave him a small smile. "Slow writer."

"Thoughtful writer."

Shoot ... he was so handsome when complimenting me.

Not just hot, but straight up good looking. Caress-able. Adonis-like. I exhaled. Too far? I turned my head so he wouldn't be on to me. I'd already forgiven him for breaking my heart. Had to. We're practically related and I had to find a way to be around him at holiday dinners without becoming a moony-eyed middle schooler every time the corners of his gorgeous eyes crinkled at some benign story shared over a scoop of mashed potatoes and gravy.

That didn't mean I wasn't hurt. My face was beginning to ache from the fake smile I'd tacked on, and though I didn't want him to leave—I really couldn't keep this up much longer.

"I'll be leaving in the morning," he said, startling me.

"Leaving?"

"For LA."

"Oh, of course. The meeting with the music exec."

I averted my eyes hard right now. He didn't need to see my disappointment at not being able to share this with him more fully. Brax had earned a chance to perform for a major studio. Hopefully even sign with one. I wanted to be more than an innocent bystander to his good fortune—I wanted to wrap my body around his and congratulate him until the sun came up.

A flame of a blush heated my face. I wasn't coquettish—I'd written scenes of wanting hundreds of times—but I'd made it all up. All of it. I was *that* good. I almost laughed out loud at my brazenness, but he would think I'd lost my mind. These past few weeks had been a slow build, the kind of fire that could burn casually through the brush until it ignited, bomb-like. Hard to admit that Brax had this kind of sway over me, but there it was.

"You okay?" He was watching me with an amused

expression and I flushed at being caught. Suddenly I had found my way into a little church and begged God's forgiveness for my wayward thoughts. Yes, that's what I would do. Go to church. Confess my sins. It was good that he was leaving. I should suggest he take a few days, stay at a hotel, see the sights. *And stay far away from me.*

"Clara?"

"I just know you're going to kill it," I blurted out.

He grinned. "You lie to me."

"I would never."

"But I appreciate it, Clara. Your confidence in me is"— he stuck his tongue to the corner of his mouth, thinking —"well, it's prized. You've lit a new fire under me."

There we go with that fire again ... "Thanks, but I think you did that all by yourself."

"I also buried me by myself. You're a creative, so I suppose you've heard of imposter syndrome."

"When you think you're a phony, a fake, undeserving of the accolades?"

"So, I take it the answer is yes. You are familiar with it."

"Sure. Many writers feel this way, and those who don't probably should." I laughed, then waved my hand. "I'm kidding, of course."

"How do you write yourself out of it?"

I smiled at the way he understood me. Of course, I would attempt to write myself out of those feelings, though not everybody would face that challenge the same way. "Well," I said, "the main thing I do is write an imperfect hero, someone with a lazy eye or a limp."

"Or both."

"Even better." I smiled honestly at him, surprising even myself. "Seriously, though, I try to make him as realistic as possible, with attributes that can be overcome. The heroine too."

"Like?"

"Um, let me see. Someone who's too guarded, stubborn ... hardheaded."

"Wow."

"I could go on."

"No doubt. Have I mentioned that you inspire me?"

"Stop it."

Brax reached out and touched my shoulder, that small sensation almost too much for me. Would I look too desperate if I placed my hand on top of his and leaned my cheek against his touch? Yes, probably, I would. Not recommended.

"I want to talk about the other night," Brax said, blind-siding me and making me grateful I had resisted the urge to lean into his touch.

I wrapped my arms around my middle, breaking contact with him. It was a reflexive move that I wasn't proud of, but desperate times and all that ... I dragged my gaze to his, facing up to this talk that I really didn't want to have, a palpable shift in the mood. "It was an emotional night," I said with all the lightness I could fake. "We can both agree on that, I think. I'm fine and you're obviously fine too. I mean, look at you? Going to hobnob with the bigwigs in LA."

"There will be no hobnobbing."

"Oh, but there will."

He chuckled, but it faded away until a noticeable silence swung between us. Finally, he said, "I'm sorry I hurt you."

I lifted my chin. "You didn't."

"Clara."

"Let's not make this about me, Brax. We both know that

these past few weeks have been intense, with both of us out of our element." Look at me, sounding all understanding when all I wanted to do was run back inside. "I mean, if you think about it, we're just two strangers thrown together, expected to get along and be family, to take care of our siblings' home and pet, while also bungling through each of our own personal problems."

Brax reached for my hands, which were flailing about as I spoke. "Clara," he said, "I'm going to leave for Texas straight from Los Angeles."

"Oh. Uh-huh."

"The happy couple will be back this weekend."

"Yes, yes, that's right." I'd been so buried in writing that I had not noticed each day turn into the next. He was right. Zac and Greta would be back tomorrow, probably, sometime late. And their life as a couple would begin, which meant, I had to figure out where my own was headed next.

"So I figured I'd take off from there."

"That makes sense ..." I raised my gaze. "What about when bigwigs want to whisk you away to a studio to start your album?"

His eyes tracked mine. "Then I suppose I'll be in LA a little while longer, chopping it up." His voice was dull, as if he didn't believe my prediction would happen.

"You know this really is the big break you've been looking for, right?" I looked into his eyes for confirmation but all I saw was a storm brewing, a storm of darkness staring back at me. Brax had asked me earlier about imposter syndrome, and now I wondered if he had a case of it himself —and how he would ever be able to overcome it.

If only he would let me help.

CHAPTER SIXTEEN

BRAX

YOU KNOW this is the big break you've been looking for ...

Clara had said the words, but honestly, all I had been aiming for lately was a way to have the two lives I wanted—one with Clara, and the other with the music that had never left me. It wasn't lost on me that Kate always wanted me to change, while Clara kept pushing me toward being the guy I had been running from for so long.

Early this morning, I climbed into my Jeep with enough on my mind to keep me occupied till I rolled into LA. I was approaching my exit now but felt worse off than when I'd started. All I kept thinking over the miles was that if I couldn't have both lives, I only wanted one.

The one with Clara in it.

I rubbed a hand across my stubbled face. I had just enough time to find my hotel, shave, then get over to my meeting. Or ... I could turn around and go back to the beach house, pull Clara into my arms, and admit: *I wrote that song for you.*

My cellphone rang. Zac. Groan. I punched the answer button. "Yo."

"Hey, Brax. Heard you headed out."

"You did, huh?"

"Clara called Greta to talk and, well, she mentioned you had left. No details though."

I hadn't told him about the competition and subsequent prize, and apparently, Clara hadn't either. Served me right. I'd clearly broken her heart—though she was too stubborn to admit it. Why should she be singing my praises? A good move on her part, protecting herself like that.

The same way you should be protecting her heart, too, Dude.

I glanced at the stoplight ahead, my mind changing again. I should stick this out. This meeting could be life changing. Besides, I knew myself well enough to know that Clara would be better off without me.

I cleared my throat. "I have a meeting with some music people."

"You're kidding."

I rolled my eyes. Zac wouldn't understand, precisely the reason I hadn't thought to tell him about it. "Yeah. Listen, bro—"

"That was a joke," Zac said. "Guess I have to work on my delivery. In all seriousness, why didn't you tell me about the competition? This is huge, man!"

"How did you ...?"

"Clara's proud of you, Greta said."

Oh. So much for thinking she no longer cared. My jaw ached from clenching my teeth. "But you don't approve."

Zac sputtered. "Why would you think that? Don't you remember? I told you about that place ... at the wedding."

Oddly enough, I could picture that. At the wedding, Zac had nearly shouted over the music, *Hey, you used to sing ...* But I'd brushed him off. Why hadn't I listened to him? "Sorry, yeah, I forgot we talked about it."

"Clara says you were amazing on stage. Wish I'd been there to see you, buddy."

Zac had lapsed into the language of their childhood. He was the nerdy older brother, and I was simply *buddy*.

"Sorry, bro." I pulled into the circular driveway of the hotel where I would be bunking for the night. A valet approached but I waved him off and pulled to the side to continue this call. "I'll call you later when I'm on the road," I said. "Real quick, though, how's Clara doing?"

"You heard then," Zac said.

I frowned. "Heard what?"

Zac lowered his voice. "About her publisher. That's why you're asking about her, I presume?"

My jaw hardened against Zac's need to clarify why I would be asking about Clara. His way to confirm that my interest was nothing but brotherly, no doubt. I blew out a rough breath. "I hadn't heard anything about her publisher. What's going on?"

"Clara received a call from her editor today. They are not going to contract her next book."

I pressed my head against the seat rest. "No. Why?"

"Yeah, it was a quick turnaround, I heard. Greta says Clara is putting on a brave face for her. I don't know too much about that industry, but from what I hear, she feels abandoned after a long relationship with her publisher. Not sure what she's planning to do about it."

"Ah, man. I'm sorry to hear it." I ran my palm down my face. This wasn't good. I knew how much this story meant to her, how she'd struggled to find inspiration, then finally found the mental bandwidth to tell it. It hadn't been lost on me that she'd followed my advice to find a new place to write. A part of me even hoped I had inspired her as much as she inspired me.

"I do know that when we get back, Greta's going to encourage Clara to stay out here for a while. Hopefully she'll find new perspective in time."

I barely heard Zac. All I could picture was Clara at home alone with this news. Or worse, her turning to Carter for comfort. The guy would probably try to entice her into buying an overpriced condo.

For the second time, a valet approached me, and in a flash, I knew what I had to do.

Clara

I'M STANDING AT A CROSSROADS. Not just figuratively, as in *what in the world am I going to do now?* But a real one. I had been riding my bike for a full hour after picking up flowers for my basket, while digesting the news that Joanie delivered. I stopped in front of the little church that Greta had told me about, not sure where to go next.

"The team is heading in a new direction," Joanie had said.

I expected this to happen someday. But after Brax's video went viral on my Facebook page and my followers went up, I brazenly thought I was safe this round, that my next book would get picked up like all those before it. Not that I'd had any inkling that posting that video would have such an effect. In the end, it didn't matter anyway.

"It's too different from what you've given us before," Joanie said.

"Does the team have a specific request, then?"

"All they'll tell me is that they're building a new stable of authors. Sorry, Clara."

In other words, I was out and some shiny new authors were in.

I read the street signs, still trying to decide which way to turn.

"Clara?"

An old BMW wagon pulled up next to me with Shelly in the driver's seat. "What are you doing out here?"

"Not sure. I went for a ride and picked up these flowers ..." Did I tell her my mind was scrambled? That I had been riding around aimlessly, trying not to focus on the fact that Brax left this morning, taking my heart right with him? That soon after he drove off, my career had been delivered a death knell? That at this moment, I felt so ... lost?

"I've just finished some volunteer work at the church. Let me give you a ride back. I've got plenty of room for your bike." She must have noticed my indecisiveness because she pulled her car to the side of the road without waiting for my answer.

On our way back to the beach, Shelly chattered on about the shop and all the new finds she'd be stocking, which was a good thing because for once lately, I had nothing to add. At a stop light, she said, "Is there something on your mind?"

"Hmm. Yes. No. Too much, actually." I gave her an apologetic look. "I don't know where to start."

"The beginning is always a good place."

I cracked a small smile. Then the first tear fell. My mind rolled. I thought I'd tell her about Brax leaving town—leaving me—today. Or that my career was in question. Instead, when I opened my mouth, I started at the very beginning and told her about the father I never knew.

CHAPTER SEVENTEEN

Shelly listened to my story without casting judgment on either of my parents—or even Justin. She let me talk as long as I needed to, even pulling over at Neptune Beach so we could sit awhile longer before going home. I thought that finding my next story proved that I had conquered the things that had hemmed me in all year.

"Maybe you need to let the bitterness go," Shelly said.

"I thought I already had."

"Have you forgiven your father, though?"

"He's dead."

"Yes, yes, I know, honey. But I think it would help you. And it would definitely help Justin."

I had put all thoughts of Justin out of my mind and never planned to think of him again. Likely, though, he was in my subconscious all along, poking at the undersides of my confidence. Why in the world would I give him another thought?

Shelly smiled kindly. "We need to forgive the inexcusable because God has forgiven the inexcusable in us. I can't take credit for that, I think it was C.S. Lewis who said it, but it's oh so true. It frees us and it frees them. Do you believe me?"

I wasn't sure what I believed, but I didn't reject the words. Instead, I let them sink deep into my mind, where I knew I'd turn them over for days to come.

We left the beach park behind. As Sally approached Mermaid Manor, she slowed.

Brax's Jeep was parked in the driveway.

I leaned forward, peering through the windshield. "What's he doing here?"

"He's the cutie who won the competition, right?"

I cast a look at her. "Yes, and he's supposed to be in LA." I stepped out of the car just as Brax jumped out of his. Another car pulled up, but I ignored it and charged for the driveway. Brax rushed toward me, pulling me into his arms. He smelled amazing, and if it weren't for the bombardment of questions in my head, I would have stood there all afternoon and breathed him in.

Using all the willpower I had, I pushed myself away from Brax's embrace and peeled a look up at him. "I don't understand what happened. What are you doing here?"

He cinched his arms tighter around me. "I came back as soon as I heard."

"Heard?" I paused, realization filling me. "Oh no ... you didn't." Behind me was a vague sense of movement, but I couldn't concentrate on anything else right now.

"I talked to Zac"—Brax paused and looked over my shoulder before returning his gaze to mine—"and he told me about the call from your publisher. Clara, why didn't you call me?"

I pushed him away, shaking my head. "No, Brax. You

have to get out of here, go back to LA. Are you missing your meeting right now?"

He grabbed my hand, tugging me close again with the confidence of a swing dancer. Then he dipped his chin toward me, his gaze intense, earnest. "None of that matters right now."

"Yes, it does. It matters a lot! Get out of here!" I pulled my hand from his grasp so I could shake my finger at it. "I mean it!"

Zac's voice cut in. "Brax! What are you doing? Let her go."

I swiveled. Zac and Greta stood outside of a black car that was pulling away, their wheeled suitcases beside them. "Yo-you're back?"

Shelly waved at me and mouthed, *I'll bring your bike back later.*

I watched her slowly drive away as Zac's frowning gaze focused on his brother. "Brax, you promised."

Greta's gaze spilled from Brax to me and back again, a small smile burgeoning. Whatever Zac was yarning on about, Greta didn't seem too bothered.

I looked to Brax, narrowing my eyes. "Promised?"

He wore a sudden scowl, the same one I saw on his face the very moment I met him on the hill, right before Greta and Zac's wedding. I didn't admit this then, but that sexy scowl drew me in immediately. In it I saw future hero material—for my next book. *Of course.* "Am I missing something?"

Brax shot a look at his brother. He slid an arm around my waist, gently turning me around, and pulled me close until my back molded into him. He bent down close and nuzzled my ear. "I won't let you go ever again, Clara," he whispered.

My heart did a flip. I was yearning and stretching, waking up after a long dream. I wanted to snuggle in, to explore all my questions in this moment with Brax. But my sister had returned, unexpectedly. And by the look on Zac's face, he was oh-so mad about something. Was it possible to be happy for their safe—and apparently early—return, and yet very much want them to leave us alone?

Zac abandoned his suitcase and stepped toward us, his palms outstretched, like he was approaching dangerous animals in the wild. His eyes were pleading with Brax, while occasionally sliding guilty glances at me. "Why don't we let the girls get caught up while you and I talk. We came back early just so they could do that."

Brax wrapped his arms around me more fully now, and I wasn't unhappy about it. He still hadn't satisfied all my questions, but we were swaying now, as if listening to some silent melody. Call me crazy, but why would I want to shut that out abruptly so he and Zac could chat?

"Nothing to chat about, big brother. I'm in love with your sister, Greta. You both need to trust me on this."

I spun around, still in Brax's embrace. "Wait ... what did you say?"

He swallowed and his Adam's apple moved up and down. Maybe he was rethinking what he'd just said ... going to retract it. Brax's chin dipped toward me until his lips hovered above mine. "I love you Clara Bow ... Barnes."

"You ... do?" I searched his eyes for confirmation. My gaze traversed his face, then, the scruff that barely covered a dimple, the way the corner of his mouth tilted up when he smiled.

"There's something else, too."

Zac groaned, interrupting us. "I'm so sorry, Clara. I don't

know what's been going on, but my brother assured me he could stay here to watch over the house and not come onto you."

I quirked a smile at Brax and lowered my voice. "Is this true, Braxton?"

"Maybe."

I laid my palm on his pecs. "Well."

"Well?"

I spun back around to glare at Zac, though let's be real, I wasn't too sure if I could pull off furious. "That is the stupidest thing I've ever heard, Zac." I caught eyes with my sister, whose hopeful smile betrayed her. "Greta? Were you in on this?"

She turned up her palms. "Well, I, uh, I don't really know Braxton very well so ..."

I unwrapped Brax's arm from around my waist, turning on all three of them. "You all do know I'm thirty years old, right? Able to make my own decisions? I make a decent living, well, up until now I have. I've also lived alone—thanks to Greta abandoning me."

Greta laughed lightly.

"And I took care of this big lug and his bad ankle"—I pointed at Brax—"while you two were lying on some tropical beach drinking something the color of mauve. What in the world made you think it was okay to discuss my love life behind my back?"

Greta reached out and rubbed my shoulder. I could never really be mad at her, at least not for too long, and she knew it. But now that she's married, would I ever be able to pull her opinion out of her without Zac adding in his two cents?

Ugh. This was complicated.

254

Then again, I wasn't the same woman Greta and Zac left behind. The old me would have retreated inside for an entire month, holing up in her room to write, while ignoring that insistent sea breeze and the surf's unending call. When they left on their honeymoon, the new me was already emerging, the one who tossed aside her introverted nature to do what she had to do—find a hero. It just so happened that she had found one in an unlikely place.

A throat cleared and we all parted abruptly.

"Perhaps I'd been too hasty," Zac said.

I snorted, which made Greta laugh and snort a little too. Our eyes met and suddenly I had my sister back. Hmm. Maybe this whole marriage thing was going to be okay after all.

"I just wanted to protect Clara," Zac was saying to Brax now.

"That's all I want too," Brax said.

Zac blew out a breath, but a smile emerged. "I'm not used to seeing this side of you, Bro."

"You and I have a lot to catch up on, Zac, but all you need to know right now is that I'd never do anything to hurt Clara. Ever."

Zac nodded. He looked from Greta to me, then Brax again. "So, we're good?"

Brax nodded. "Yeah."

I stepped away from Greta, shaking my head. "Whoa. Wait a minute. You're good? That's all you have to say after Zac meddled in your life? In our lives?"

Brax swung a look at Zac and back to me. He was nodding. "Yeah."

I stood there, awestruck. "That's so ... weird."

"Welcome to my world," Greta whispered.

Zac stepped back and reached for his wife. "I heard that, beautiful."

Greta's smile at me felt like my most comfortable blanket back home—warm, soft, and thoroughly well-worn. She turned and took Zac's hand. "Maybe we ought to let these two finish their conversation."

They took their suitcases and climbed the stairs together. At the top, Zac made a big show of carrying Greta over the threshold. It was thoroughly cheesy, silly, and traditional.

I loved it.

When they were out of sight, I reached for Brax's hand and pulled him toward me. I was that brazen. I tilted my chin up until our eyes met. "I still have questions for you, mister."

"No doubt."

"But I have something I need to clarify first."

"Hmm. All right."

"Did you say you love me?"

His eyes clouded over, creases forming at the corners, and I wondered for half a second if maybe I had heard him wrong. My face heated and I had a sudden urge to jog down to Shelly's shop, grab my bike, and take it for another spin.

"Yes, I did, but I have something else important to say, too: I lied to you."

"What?" I searched his face. "What did you lie about?"

"About the song ... the one I sang at the competition. I lied." He exhaled. His eyes, heavily hooded, watched me. "I wrote it for you."

"Kind of thought so." I rolled my eyes and smacked him on the pecs again.

He gave me a slanted look now. "But I told you I didn't."

"Yeah, and I believed you, but I didn't really want to. I'm glad you lied."

A smile turned up the corner of his mouth. "Everything I wrote in that song was true. It's the reason I'm here right now, Clara. I couldn't handle the thought of you here alone, dealing with that bad news from your publisher."

I swallowed the tears at the base of my throat. Did he know how sweet that was? How kind and thoughtful? Still, he could've stayed in LA—he *should* have stayed. "I know I've already said this once today, but I really am a big girl, you know."

Brax pulled me toward him again, and this time, I relented. "Rejection of your work hurts. I know it does."

I sniffled into his shirt. "It does. But ... you need to be in LA, following your dream. I want you to go after what you want."

"I want you."

I shook my head so hard I thought some of my curls would straighten. "Please don't make me the reason you gave up. I'm not Kate."

"I know that. And you're not making me do anything." He ran his hands down my sides until they came to rest on my hips. I couldn't look away if I tried. "I just ... I want to be your hero, Clara."

My eyes were glistening now. "You already are, you idiot."

A small divot formed between his brows, his eyes unwavering. "How can you say that?"

I unfurled my fingers one at a time, talking through weeks of pent-up tears. "You searched for my father. You fixed a bike for me when your ankle was still healing. You dried my tears when my brother smashed my heart. You, apparently, abided by my brother-in-law's stupid rules!"

He cracked a smile.

"And now you've skipped out on your big break when you knew I'd be crushed by my own bad news." I swallowed, hard, trying to tell him how much he meant to me, how his true character had shone through the gruff exterior. "You, Braxton Holt, are incomparable."

Brax released a whoosh of a sigh, then dipped his head until our foreheads met.

Our eyes were inches apart, my voice a whisper. "You are my hero—over and over again."

The air crackled between us, like lightning in a storm. His mouth was on mine so fast, I felt sure thunder would follow. He kissed me like a man who'd been lost at sea in a rowboat and had just found the shore. And without any reservation, all I wanted to do was welcome him home.

EPILOGUE

Clara

Five months later, almost to the day, Brax and I were married at the little church where Shelly had found me lost and not knowing where to turn. Since that day, Brax and I had both grown spiritually, which brought us that much closer together. It thrilled me to think back, knowing that the seeds of our fledgling faith had found soil and water in a place we'd never imagined.

I also finished my book in record time—making significant changes along the way— hired editors myself, and sent it out into the great unknown of readers under my new name: Clara Holt. Turned out my writing career wasn't dead after all.

Our small reception was winding down now, with guests —mostly neighbors and old friends—offering goodbye hugs and well-wishes on their way out.

Justin and his wife, Maria, and their young sons, lingered

until the end. My brother's large eyes, mirrors of my own, stared back at me. He reached out and took both of my hands. "Thank you for inviting us, Clara. It was a beautiful wedding."

I nodded, thankful for the change in his heart. Maria lunged forward and wrapped her arms around my neck. "Te quiero, hermana." She smacked a kiss on my cheek. "Gorgeous!"

After my book released two months ago, Maria picked up a copy, and as she told it: "swallowed it whole in one day!" So what if it took several heart-wrenching months to see that story to fruition? I knew I should be grateful she read it at all—and I was. Justin read it too.

In my latest novel, my heroine, Cara—so it's a little autobiographical?—forgives the older brother who had rejected her. She then falls for her brother-in-law's, um, cousin, Brent. Hey! The hero had blond hair—nothing like my Brax.

And yet everything like him, too. I mean, how could I not write the hero who had captured my heart with his first scowl?

After Justin's older son, Carlos, asked if it were true that he had an auntie somewhere, Justin called me, deeply apologetic. He asked for my forgiveness, and I told him in the next breath that I'd already given it to him. I'd learned a lot about forgiveness in the past year, and I wasn't about to hold back something that could set another person free.

Helen was beaming. I bent down to let her give me the tightest squeeze ever. "The cupcakes were amazing," I told her.

"I made extra and I'll give them to Greta for you!" She was rocking me side to side, still hugging. I was thankful that stretching and regular exercise had strengthened my back enough to withstand her, uh, enthusiasm.

"Hey now, save some hugs for this old guy." Gus, sitting in his wheelchair, wagged his head and wore a put-on frown on his mug, though I could see the twinkle in his eyes.

I gave him a kiss on the cheek and watched the two of them mosey down the path toward Zac's car. Next to me, Brax rubbed my lower back with his warm hand. I couldn't wait to sink into his touch every day for the rest of my life.

I turned to find Shelly and Rick lingering. Shelly reached for me, hugging me tightly, while Rick slapped Brax on the back. "Don't be strangers," Rick called out as they made their way toward the parking lot.

Carter and his date, Millie, were the last in line. They'd coordinated their outfits, and with their navy-and-white stripes and hats, they reminded me of a couple of cute sailors. Something told me my ex-landlord had finally found his dream girl.

"Congrats, again, you two," Carter said.

"You're both gorgeous," Millie added. "Picture perfect. You should be on a book cover!" We all laughed and waved as they said their goodbyes.

For the first time all day, we were alone. Brax pulled me tightly against him, and I wrapped my hands around his waist. He pressed his mouth against my temple, groaning softly, and I knew he was relieved. We'd done it—we were married!

"That was fun and all, my love, but ..."

"You're glad it's over."

He peeled a look at me beneath hooded eyelids. "Only because I'm ready to get this party started."

I laughed lightly, sensing he was ready to head to our

new home. Soon he'd be finishing his album, then head out on tour—we had a dizzying amount of travel ahead of us. I couldn't wait. Still ...

"Not so fast," I said.

He dipped his brows, as if to say, *what did I forget?*

I grinned, tightening my arms around him, certain I would never grow tired of this. "One more dance."

An easy smile grew on his face before he dipped his head again, nuzzling my neck. Slowly, we began to sway and I whispered, "Sing the last lines for me, please? One more time before we go?"

He didn't hesitate, but began to sing, the warmth of his voice filling my heart to overflowing:

"Girl of my heart,
were you waiting just for me?
I want to be
the hero from your dreams.
'Cause you know,
that when it's meant to be, it's like our dreams
are on their way to ... finding stardust."

ACKNOWLEDGMENTS

I would like to acknowledge my precious aunt, Cecilia Hart-feld, who passed away during the writing of this book. Such a champion of the arts, and reading in particular, she was! And always one of my most faithful and loving fans. I will be donating a set of Hollywood by the Sea novels to the library in her honor.

––––––

Thank you, Readers, for spending your leisure time with *Finding Stardust*. You may not realize how much you motivate me to keep writing! So, thank you again. If you enjoyed the story, I'd be honored if you would leave a review.

I'd also like to thank:

My sweet husband, Dan—the final reader of all of my books, my rock, and *my* hero!

Our kids:

Matt—my social media guru

Angie—my graphics guru (she created the map of Hollywood by the Sea!)

Emma—my ever-patient hairstylist and listening ear

Thank you, Mom and Dad, for always cheering me on (and buying extra copies, too!!).

Denise Harmer, I'm so grateful for your editing expertise and the extra time you gave this one. Diana Lesire Brandmeyer, aka speed reader, your comments, as always, were invaluable to me.

And to the members of my Street Team, thanks for your faithfulness—I treasure you all.

ALSO BY JULIE CAROBINI

Sign up for Julie's newsletter to learn of new releases and you'll receive a free e-novella too:

www.juliecarobini.com/free-book

Hollywood by the Sea Novels

Chasing Valentino (book 1)

Finding Stardust (book 2)

Sea Glass Inn Novels

Walking on Sea Glass (book 1)

Runaway Tide (book 2)

Windswept (book 3)

Beneath a Billion Stars (book 4)

Otter Bay Novels

Sweet Waters (book 1)

A Shore Thing (book 2)

Fade to Blue (book 3)

The Otter Bay Novel Collection (books 1-3)

The Chocolate Series

Chocolate Beach (book 1)

Truffles by the Sea (book 2)

Mocha Sunrise (book 3)

The Chocolate Beach Collection (books 1-3)

Cottage Grove Cozy Mysteries

The Christmas Thief (book 1)

The Christmas Killer (book 2)

The Christmas Heist (book 3)

Cottage Grove Mysteries (books 1-3)

ABOUT THE AUTHOR

JULIE CAROBINI writes inspirational beach romances. Her father is the author of *Navarro's Silent Film Guide* and shared his love of the silver screen with Julie and her brothers when they were kids. *Chasing Valentino* and *Finding Stardust* are nods to those years. Julie is the author of 20+ novels across two names, and has won awards from both ACFW and NLAPW. She lives near the beach in California with her husband, Dan, and loves spending time with their three grown kids.

Pick up a free story for your e-reader here:
www.juliecarobini.com/free-book

CPSIA information can be obtained
at www.ICGtesting.com
Printed in the USA
LVHW030112171221
706396LV00006B/1002